John Watson was born and raised in Glasgow. He was eighteen when he joined the Royal Air Force on the outbreak of war in 1939. He flew for Bomber and Transport Commands during World War II in the European and Far East theatres of operations and was decorated extensively. He worked in publishing after the war and also wrote many books, mostly under pseudonyms. His most famous novel – and the best British novel about World War II bomber crews – was, however, published under his real name: *Johnny Kinsman* is also available from Grafton Books.

By the same author

Johnny Kinsman

JOHN WATSON

The Man Who Loved War

GRAFTON BOOKS
A Division of the Collins Publishing Group

LONDON GLASGOW
TORONTO SYDNEY AUCKLAND

Grafton Books
A Division of the Collins Publishing Group
8 Grafton Street, London W1X 3LA

A Grafton Paperback Original 1988

ISBN 0-586-07070-2

Printed and bound in Great Britain by
Collins, Glasgow

Set in Times

1

With luck Jordaan thought he would be in time for tea as he edged the tired old Hurricane up to something like three twenty by the time he levelled out around fifty feet over Kenley. At that height he was eating distance in great gulps, and he smiled beneath his mask before switching on his RT and yanking his stick to port at the far end of the field before tearing around the airfield's perimeter at full throttle, low, low down.

'Permission to land.'

Back came the girl's voice; smooth, controlled. 'Your call-sign please . . .'

'It's me, darling . . . It is I . . .'

'Permission to land.' The voice contained a suggestion of amusement.

Level out, sharply back on the stick, and he was at a thousand feet. Throttle back, cockpit canopy open. He lowered the goggles over his eyes, and when his speed had dropped to around a hundred and forty, he lowered the wheels. God, she was such a sweet old thing. He could see the smart new 5b Spits dispersed beneath him like Dinky toys on a carpet. But the Hurricane was such a comfortable old thing. With fifteen degrees of flap he was on the approach turn now. Full flap; fully fine pitch.

Away to the west a cold golden sun was sinking behind some scattered cirrus. Fleetingly, for nothing was moving below, he had the strange sensation of being the only man alive. Over the fence; throttle back . . . easy. She touched, surely, on that good broad beam of an undercarriage. He was down.

In control they knew who it was, almost before he had undone his mask, for there on the nose of the Hurricane was the red white and blue roundel and the Swastikas like miniature headstones in three rows of five just ahead of the cockpit. Someone remembered that he liked to joke about not counting Italians, and the girls giggled quietly as they saw him throw back the straps of his parachute before raising himself neatly from the cockpit. He half ran towards them to book in.

Jordaan's whole body, like those of all men of his kind at that time, exuded an energy which was always close to aggression. There was an eagerness in the way he swung his limbs which drew people's eyes towards him. There was an intensity in him which seemed to grow from a deep concentration that all of them who were really experienced seemed to share.

In the Mess the youngsters stood without knowing why. Flash's arrival seemed to inspire jostle. The quietness of the tea time hour had been broken. Hah, you old bastard! Delight at his arrival eddied around him until Dobbie moved through them with a hand outstretched. 'Good to see you, Flash. Come down to play?'

'Hopefully, Dobbie.'

Dobson was Squadron Commander, a large man for a fighter pilot, altogether looser than Jordaan, but good. The black moustache straddling across his upper lip looked as though he had forgotten it was there. 'Flash, you're supposed to be up there resting, staying away from all the noise . . .'

Jordaan in his dry accent. '. . . and the irritation.'

'That's right.'

'What is it? Day off tomorrow?'

'Mmm.'

'What the hell are we going to do about you?'

'Dobbie, just give me one of those lovely little 5bs you've got out there – if you're working that is . . . Even if you're not working. It's the adrenaline. It needs shaking – like a cocktail.'

In the evening they laughed. Tiny Carew was there. He had been Jordaan's opposite number as a Flight Commander under Dobson. It was he who told Jordaan that there was something on for the following day, and after dinner, Dobson, good chap that he was, agreed that he would stand down a Sergeant Pilot and allow Jordaan to take his place. 'You realize,' Dobson had said, 'that I'm strictly out of order.'

'I know, Dobbie . . . I know, but old man Park promised I'd only be off for six months. I've done four at that bloody awful OTU, trying to teach those little buggers to be fighter pilots. You can't. They either are, or they aren't.'

Dobson had wondered at Jordaan. He himself was a quiet man. Before the war he had been a test driver for Riley cars. In the beginning he'd been a VR Sergeant. Married to Betty his life was on the kind of rails he liked. The Air Force had been good to him, and he knew the quiet satisfaction of feeling that he in his way had been good for it. He knew nothing of the restlessness which seemed to live in this man, his friend, Jordaan, and that night at their table, quietly, he had expressed something of his concern.

Jordaan had laughed, but Dobson persisted. Wasn't he pushing himself? Was he sure he was fit? There was a little silence around the table into which Jordaan broke hurriedly to say, 'You think I've gone twitchy?'

'No . . . no. But you could be pushing yourself.'

'I'm not, Dobbie, I'm not. It's just that . . . that I love it. I really do.'

Dobson said, 'I'm sure,' and they moved into the ante-room where they could relax into drinking.

Macarthur was on leave, and it was in his room that Jordaan thought of what Dobson had said at the dinner table when he was lying there in the dark. Pushing himself . . . Was he? The thought didn't bring sleep any closer, so he got up, switched on the light and took the bottle of Red Hackle from Macarthur's wardrobe. Gah! Bloody awful stuff, and there was no water in the room. No matter.

Jordaan looked at himself in the mirror which was on top of Macarthur's chest of drawers. What he saw was good. The hell with the face. He'd never been much of a one for those; but the stomach muscles were still showing, and the shoulders tapered to his hips. Suddenly, aware of his height, he raised himself on his toes, flexing himself. Bending with a hand just above each knee he felt the hardness of himself. He was all right. Balls. He had another Red Hackle. Gurugh!

When the man came in he had been awake for fifteen minutes.

'Mornin', sir. Nice to have you back.' The man reached on his toes to pull back the curtains. He was a little man, with his hair sleekly parted in the middle after the fashion of some years before. The eyes were set narrowly, but the voice was rich and Cockney.

'Good to see you, Jonesy.'

'Are you back with us now, sir.' His voice cracked. 'Maybe they'll learn, sir. I'll get your water.'

'No, Jonesy. I'm back for the day. That's all.'

'Ah . . . Sorry about that, sir. It's not the same . . . Not the same crowd. They're different now, sir . . .

Maybe they'll learn . . . I'll get your water.'

Take-off would take place at ten. They would fly at zero feet in two sections of two. Jordaan would fly wide on Tiny Carew's wing, well to starboard. They would cross the coast North of Boulogne, near Wimereux where Jordaan remembered he'd known a good fish restaurant before the war, and then on due west between Arras and Lens, south of Mons, until they hit the Charleroi – Namur railway. There should be their train.

Outside the Ops Room Jordaan smelt with relish the dampness of the early morning. He looked up at a sky which was almost flickering in that late Spring light. 'Good morning,' he said to Carew.

There was a slight, freshening breeze from the south east, and as Jordaan spoke to him Carew turned into it. He was a tall, slender young man of impeccable military lineage. Now his nostrils moved visibly as he smelt the breeze. 'Just right for us,' he said.

At Marlborough it had been decided by his father and his Housemaster that Carew had been useless, so at seventeen he had enlisted in the Household Cavalry as a trooper. But after eighteen months he had transferred to the Royal Air Force in which he had been awarded, as Jordaan had, a Short Service Commission. Tim liked to say that the trouble with a bloody horse was that it had no throttle.

Together they walked towards their parked aircraft and the men fussing around them. Carew, taller than Jordaan, walked in silence with one shoulder slightly drooping under the weight of the parachute he was carrying. They moved in silence. Jordaan remembered this pre-airborne mood of Carew's. He had always been like this, tense around the jaw as though he was trying to focus everything of himself towards the action to which he was committed. Eventually he said, 'What do you think of the 5b, Flash?'

'Never flown one. You had Mark 11s when I was last here.'

'Jesus, Flash . . .'

'What's the difference? It's got clipped wings and two cannon plus four 303s . . . That's all.'

'I suppose you're right.'

Jordaan smoked steadily as he listened to the chatter of the ground-crew through the next fifteen minutes without paying any attention to what they were saying. He had an itch to be gone, for this was different from the hurried scrambling of the old days; not as acceptable to Jordaan. He threw away a half unfinished cigarette and climbed aboard to settle himself on the parachute the Corporal had placed in the bucket seat. He fastened the harness, adjusted the straps. He felt his feet firm on the upper bars of the rudder control. Jordaan liked to fly with his knees slightly bent so that his stomach muscles were tensed. It gave him a greater feeling of control. His helmet was adjusted; his RT plugged in. Without realizing what he was doing he pulled repeatedly at the neat leather gloves he wore instead of gauntlets.

When he heard Carew's aircraft become alive with that peculiar near-scream of the Merlin, he signalled to the man at his starter motor with his left thumb. The four-bladed prop laboured around until with a flick of the throttle it caught. Then there was the beautiful surging of power beneath his hand. Over to his right he saw the cascading green Verey. Carew was off, zig-zagging towards take-off. Jordaan followed. They would take off in loose formation.

The slight cross-wind joggled him until his tail was up. His eyes were on Carew, thirty yards in front and to his port. At a hundred and twenty-five they left the ground, but with his wheels up Carew was holding her down, so Jordaan did likewise until at the far edge of the airfield they were touching two hundred before pulling back to reach something like a couple of hundred feet.

They made one circuit of the field to allow the other two aircraft to take off, and then, with Jordaan well on his starboard beam, Carew lost height gradually, building up speed all the time, until at about fifty feet they had reached their intended cruising speed of two sixty. In just under forty-five minutes they would see their train.

Beneath, Sussex, which for Jordaan was woman's country, spreading its rich green rolling earth; responsive, lush, proud. Carew changed course a few degrees to starboard, and as he did so Jordaan throttled back before turning to allow his leader to stay slightly ahead on the port quarter. Instinctively he swung his neck every so often, side to side and above. Over on the port the other two aircraft were skipping at the same height. Jordaan smiled to himself with the awareness of his good fortune. He was knowing the feeling of being truly alive. God, he was lucky, but he would have preferred to be in front, for Carew was sticking to the briefing. Out there in front Jordaan would have opened up: they could save fuel on the way home.

The sea was there now, with good old Brighton on the starboard. Jordaan checked for the sun. Pale in that morning light, it was up there hiding behind the high wisps as though not wishing to interfere.

At that height and at that speed they batted hard across the Channel. The suggestion of a gentle swell added to the exhilaration of their dash. Jordaan moved his ailerons gently, just for the fun of feeling her respond. Then in minutes the other coast was there. Carew had hit his landfall. Up and over, and it was France. Carew turned to starboard, and now he was increasing their speed. As Jordaan opened up to follow he could see that they were approaching two eighty-five.

All of France was there, reaching out to be hit. But now Jordaan's eyes, narrowing, were on Carew's aircraft. The leader had to break RT silence at that height. He did.

'Flash . . . Don't test your guns yet . . . I'm in front.'

Jordaan flicked his switch. 'Check!'

Carew was gaining some height now, for minutes before he had seen the smoke of Lille on his port. Approaching Mons, he realized he was too close, so he turned north again, and then again to starboard. Higher yet, and they followed. Charleroi was dead ahead. Steeply to port they turned, and then around again. Carew had started his dive with Jordaan now well behind, and he was firing before Jordaan actually saw the train. But there it was. Jordaan could feel the quick stirring of his senses.

The recoil of those four cannon juddered through the aircraft so that Jordaan had to fight to steady it after his first trial burst. Then with a second burst he was whooshing into the moving goods train. One of them, Carew or himself, must have hit something potent, for the train was burning now as he went down to skip over it and on. The two behind followed with hits, but by the time Jordaan had followed Carew on and into his steep turn to port something on the train was firing back. As Carew was emptying his guns on the second run the whole train seemed to straggle to a stop and then buckle. There was a relief at being out as he tore through that burning screen. Then he saw Carew rising just above the horizon. Jordaan swung his neck for the others, but he could see no-one.

The formation for Jordaan was pointless. This wasn't

air to air fighting. There was no need now to act as Carew's wing man. In a half turn to port he turned towards Charleroi, and as he beat over the little town it occurred to him that his cannon could still be functioning. He fired, and they thumped into life. There was Lille to the north west: it would be worthwhile stirring that lot up. He turned again and went on winding his way alone across the rise and fall of the country beneath.

Lille was startling. As he approached its southern suburbs he held his fire. Then in seconds he was leaping over the town centre, giving it the last of his ammunition. This was something he had never done before. One man against a city. Nothing could retaliate before he was over and away.

Now down again and north west towards the coast. There was no sign of the others. Come on coast, for this was a scuttle and run job. Jordaan wiped with his gloved hand at the sweat which had gathered around his neck, and was at the coast before he realized he was over. Seconds more had passed until he realized that what he had seen as he swung over the beach was a party of men in the water. They'd been bathing. The bloody fools were bathing.

In a long arc to port with his wing almost skimming the swell Jordaan concentrated on his turn. He climbed a little and then in a straight and level descent with his throttle wide open he went at them. There was nothing he could do. His guns were empty, but he laughed at their panic as they struggled to get themselves out of the water. He'd do it again, and he did. This time towards the south from a turn at the top of his climb which was awfully close to the stall. He was screaming down at almost four hundred miles an hour as the poor devils in the water, who couldn't have known he was harmless, were gasping in panic to get themselves to the beach.

Up again. Maybe he'd do it once more, but no. It was then, as he was almost touching a thousand feet, that there was the shattering carrump, and with a sudden sadness, he knew that he was hit.

There was a fierce rushing of cold air as part of his canopy disappeared. His body twisted in panic, and as he forced his head over his left shoulder he at first couldn't see it; but then it came up, and in the corner of his eye there was a yellow nosed Messerschmidt 109. It had to be one of Galland's, perhaps the man himself.

Jordaan's engine kicked before a quick gushing flame shot out of its starboard side. At that height he was too low to jump, even if his canopy, shattered as it was, would have moved; so he threw over his stick and thrust heavily on his starboard rudder, forcing her into a side-slip to port and the gathering flame away from his cockpit. A stream of tracer caught the leading edge of his starboard wing. He had to get down. There was no thought in the decision as he checked the slipping Spitfire before swinging it to the opposite side. She was dropping fast, and instinctively Jordaan held his head forward as though expecting at any second to have it blown off from behind.

Wheels would be useless, so he left them retracted as, straightening up with the engine still turning, he steered towards the water's edge of the beach. His height he could only gauge by looking out at an angle of forty-five degrees, for in a Spitfire with that great Merlin in front the cockpit was away back on the fuselage. She was dropping fast without power, too fast. If she hit too hard she would blow up and it was then through the jungle of his thoughts and vision that the Messerschmidt which had hit him swept over his head in triumph. He hit and bounced, twice. He was down. Switch off! And he cursed.

What was left of the canopy did open, and for one moment of stupefied surprise Jordaan sat there. But he had to get out. He pulled on the split-pin of his harness before twisting and smashing at his parachute release. Getting out, he half fell over the side. And as he emerged from the smoke which was now tumbling from the shattered engine to labour through the shallow water, as his enemies had done minutes before, he could see half a hundred naked men running towards him. He could only stand there in total disbelief, his breathing held still against the horror of it all. Only gradually, with the noise as they approached, was he filled with the knowledge that he was their prisoner.

2

There had at first been a confusion in his captors which more than matched that of his own. Jordaan wasn't really hurt, but there was an uncertainty in him which he did his best to hide. The sight of those men, though, with their balls shrunken by the sea and dangling uselessly as they jabbered on at him until some kind of NCO with commanding voice and unselfconscious enough to ignore his appearance managed to exert some kind of authority. That was very funny. Jordaan smiled.

They without weapons, but then, so was he. There was nothing to be done.

Encircled by a kind of crazy gaggle of bodies he was more coerced than marched back along the sand to the place where they had left their clothes. At points where the sand was so soft, Jordaan looked back again and again at the broken Spit which was still smouldering. In his head, when he had become accustomed to the nonsense of all those naked Germans surrounding him, there hammered away the thought of his friend Dobbie back at the Squadron, and the trouble he would be in because of his, Jordaan's, bloody stupidity.

The Germans dressed while two of them, big enough, if not what might have been called match-fit, held him by each arm. There didn't appear to be an officer with them – which was no doubt why they had been in the water in the first place – so Jordaan, with the gradual re-mustering of his strength, decided to utilize his rank against them. His German was non-existent, but he did try when the

NCO who seemed to be in charge approached in uniform. 'Ich Bein ein Major,' he said as he pointed at the two and a half rings on his sleeve.

The man looked at him quizzically, his eyes searching Flash's face. Then he scanned the uniform until eventually he said, 'Major?'

'Ja . . .'

At that the NCO turned to the men behind him. 'Horst!' he called.

A little man – they were a motley lot, not exactly the flower of the Wehrmacht – pushed his way through the encircling soldiers. There was a kind of pride on his face as he started to speak in English. 'I have worked in London and New York,' he said. 'What is your rank, sir?'

Flash decided to remain expressionless. 'I am an officer of the Royal Air Force. Take me to one of your officers.' And as he spoke he felt a kind of regret at using the tone of voice he had done, for the little man looked disappointed, almost crushed. It was apparent that he had wanted to display his command of English before his comrades.

There was a hurried exchange in German between the man, Horst, and his NCO. The latter appeared to Flash to be considering his best course of action. Then he decided. The men were formed into an untidy column as they slithered on the sand. Then the NCO, with one other man, took Flash to the head of the column before calling out the command to move. They scrunched across the sand until they came to a break in the long waving grass atop the beach which led towards the coastal road. There they were halted and formed into decent order.

At an easy marching pace they moved north for perhaps a mile and were at the turning which would take them to the main road which Flash imagined would take them towards Wissant when Flash, as they turned right, saw the neat little BMW sports car approaching. The NCO marching alongside seemed to guess who it might be, for he stiffened himself into smartness before the car screeched to a halt. The driver leapt from the front seat, leaving a man with a rifle in the back.

A Luftwaffe pilot, Flash recognized immediately. The man was young, dark, with a strong moustache which seemed to give him an air of being untypical. He approached with an attitude of exhilaration. It was all there as the man acknowledged the NCO's without taking his eyes from Jordaan. 'Lieutenant . . . Congratulations . . . I shot you down.'

Flash, somewhat bewildered by the fact that so many of these people could speak a reasonable brand of English, responded accordingly. There were some hurried words in German between the pilot and the NCO who had first taken control of the situation, and then the man said, 'Here . . .' and he pointed to the car.

Jordaan smiled at the NCO and then turned to follow the pilot to the smart little car where he sat next to the man who had shot him down. With a great flurry of revs they swept past the bewildered looking bunch who had been bathing, and back along the road on which minutes before Flash had been marching at the head of his captors.

The smoke from the now burning Spit led them towards its grave, and as they halted the German pilot leapt from the car, and at that there was in Flash the fleeting thought of running in the other direction – until he remembered the chap sitting in the back with a rifle. He followed the German until he was standing alongside him, high above the beach.

'Very good the Spitfire.'

The 5b was now ablaze, but the German made a move to run towards it.

'Don't!' Flash caught the man by the arm. 'It could blow up.' And almost as he used the words, the Spit in fact did, as though in protest.

Geisler, good man that he was, turned to Flash. 'You understand,' he said. 'Me, I would be the same . . . Come.'

They went back to the BMW which, when he had revved it, responded nimbly to the considerable dash which Geisler applied to his driving. 'You will have lunch with me, yah . . . My friends will love to see you.'

Lunch?

The German's mess occupied a small chateau – altogether more grand than Jordaan had ever seen at operational level in the RAF. But then, of course, it wasn't theirs: they had occupied it.

White-coated waiters seemed to be everywhere, and as the Luftwaffe man with his prisoner climbed the few elegant steps and walked through the open French windows into what Jordaan took to be their ante-room, there was a great bustle of talk as those present stood to their feet, more out of curiosity, Flash felt, than respect. They seemed to be a cheerful lot, not all that different from the men with whom he had been drinking on the previous evening. Something of a cheer went up – for Geisler, who was laughing, and, with justification, mightily pleased with himself. There was nothing, nothing at all sinister in the atmosphere.

Waiters flurried around with trays of drinks; there was suddenly a uniform cry of, 'Geisler!', as they toasted their man, and then to Jordaan's astonishment, someone called out, 'The Royal Air Force!' It was unbelievable, but most of them were raising their glasses.

The lunch which followed was more splendid than Flash had eaten for a very long time. The wine flowed across the long table at the head of which sat the Squadron Commander with Geisler and Jordaan. It was as though the presence of Jordaan, their prize, had raised their spirits to a heightened level.

When they stood from the table someone had gone to a piano. There was lots of scattered singing, and Flash, wondering why a Squadron of Messerschmidts should be able to behave as they were in the middle of the day suddenly realized when he looked out of a window facing north that low cloud was scudding in from the sea and a heavy rain was beating down: they were 'standing down'.

All of this went on for maybe three hours. Flash switched from champagne to schnapps; but if they expected to get their guest drunk, they were wrong. Their spirits and their laughter seemed only to deepen his awareness of being their prisoner, try as he might to respond to the hospitality they were offering him.

It was around four thirty when the proceedings seemed to become out of step at first and then falter into a silence which was total in its embarrassment. Jordaan was probably more aware of the situation than his hosts. The Wehrmacht had arrived.

At first it was only the Squadron Commander who spoke to the little man with the thick-lensed glasses as they stood in the doorway of the ante-room. The Wehrmacht man from where Flash was standing appeared to be adamant: he had to have his prisoner *then*.

And so it was over. A gradual silence enveloped the room, as though growing from an innate sense of politeness in the men gathered there. They weren't in any way sorry for Jordaan. On that occasion he was their prisoner

– perhaps they were merely annoyed at the interruption this soldier had brought to their festivities.

Flash left the group which had been surrounding him with their curiosity and walked towards the doorway where the Squadron Commander, looking perhaps a little concerned, was talking to the man who had come to collect the prisoner. As Flash approached in steps which were as measured as he could make them, the German CO turned to face him. His lips were turned down at the corners. He gestured towards the man with the spectacles, and then, spontaneously, his right arm was outstretched and Flash took his hand. Nothing was said.

'Hey, Jordaan . . . Jordaan!' It was Geisler, the man who had shot him down, now drunk. 'Jordaan' – the man was laughing – 'Better you than me . . .'

Flash smiled dryly. 'Thanks for the lunch.' Then he moved on with the Wehrmacht man at his heels.

For what seemed like hours Jordaan slept in the back of the truck into which they had more or less thrown him. Two men sat there with rifles between himself and the back of the truck. Finally he was awake; the effects of the drink had almost gone. What the hell was their word for water? His mouth felt like the bottom of a birdcage. He tried 'Wasser'.

The larger of the two men who was chewing on a cold sausage seemed to understand. He offered Jordaan his water bottle, and Flash drank deeply. 'Danke'. Was that it? But the man seemed to understand. He shrugged and took his bottle. They trundled on, through many villages, until they seemed to be in the suburbs of a largish town. To the man sitting there Flash said, 'Lille?' But there was no response. It had to be Lille.

Now Jordaan's brain was filled with thoughts of escape.

Good God, this war could go on for years. There was a sudden despair in him which was awfully close to fear with the thought of spending years behind barbed wire. No, no, no. The thought blackened before him.

The place was in fact Lille. This was confirmed when Jordaan saw the address on the side of a van which was parked in the station yard where they unloaded him. Somehow he would make a break for it between this place and wherever his ultimate destination was.

On the platform to which they had marched him, they emptied the waiting-room in a rather surly, stupid fashion which denied protest. Jordaan was told to sit when there was no-one else there, to consider his fate with a growing sense of misery for perhaps two hours. A train had come into the station which he had rightly considered to be heading east, and he was up at their command 'Kommen sie!' Now there was no question who was in charge.

The evening was dying as they entered the train, and again his guards used their authority to empty a compartment before entering it with Jordaan. It seemed like a very long time before the train jolted into movement.

Rumbling into the night, it looked at one point as though these two, the guards, might fall asleep, so he moved one leg by way of exploration. But no, they were not asleep, nor did it look from the suddenly alert expressions on their faces as though they would be.

The man who had been in the truck on their way to the train was again chewing on a sausage, but this time he offered some to Flash, who took it, for it was a long time now since he had eaten. He thanked the man and considered the possibilities of jumping from the train. Then they were travelling fast, but there had been times already when the train had slowed. There had to be again. If he were lucky enough it might be possible to get out by way of a window in the lavatory, but he had heard so much of that means of escape that he almost smiled to himself.

Flash waited as the guards sat there, one on either side of the compartment. They appeared to be slumped in a dumb apathy. They never spoke to each other, except monosyllabically as though voicing some kind of complaint. But he had seen squaddies in England who were exactly like these two; men who seemed to be forever content to accept whatever fate was theirs.

It was good for a little time to stretch his mind across the endless armies of the world and the reluctant hordes who peopled them. The proportion who, like himself, actually enjoyed the business must have been in a very small minority. Maybe his kind were the freaks, and these two sitting there with him in that compartment more representative of the norm.

When enough time had passed Flash signalled to the larger of the two men, and went through the motions of patting his stomach and getting into a crouching position, indicating his need for the lavatory. He did this at that time because of the slight jolting which seemed to indicate a degree of braking.

The larger man said something to his colleague, then, raising his rifle and pointing to it, he stood up while indicating to Flash that he should do likewise.

In the lavatory, Flash examined the window. That part at the top was too small for a man to get through. He would have to slide through feet first, and then the chances of ripping himself to pieces on the way out of a moving train would have been considerable. First he decided to stick his head out and take a look. But as he did so, first one way and then the other, there, grinning at him from the compartment he had just left and holding a rifle through the open window was the face of the man who had given him the sausage.

Flash decided to use the lavatory.

Eventually they chugged to a halt, and as they stepped down from the train there was another room emptied for them on the platform. Sitting there, waiting, he was filled with a resignation which seemed to be utter. Then they were in another truck, moving slowly through that city which is Frankfurt where the people he could see seemed to be moving about their business as though the thing that was happening to him had nothing whatever to do with the normalcies of living.

In time they left the city and were joggling down a dirt road of such unevenness that it was difficult to sit there in the back of the truck in an upright position. They halted.

The camp at which they had arrived sat there heavily in the darkness, swept by reaching searchlights. Guards at what Flash took to be the main gate allowed Flash and the soldiers through without protest. He was in.

The room in which they had placed him at a table could have been a dining room. The guards stood at the door for perhaps ten minutes, during which he could only stare thoughtlessly at the whitewashed walls until there was some movement at the door, and there, entering, was a stout little man with an uneven haircut who wore the uniform of a Feldwebel.

The man approached to sit opposite Jordaan.

'Good evening.' The English had something of an American accent.

'Good evening.'

'Squadron Leader Jordaan . . . you are not English.'

Flash cleared his throat. Then he looked at the man with his face slightly averted before saying, 'You have my name and you have my rank. I will give you my serial number, and that is all.'

At that the Feldwebel produced a paper from an inner pocket. But Flash chose to ignore it. He gave the man his number, and then he said slowly, 'I will say nothing, and I will sign nothing . . . and in future I will only speak to someone of my own rank.'

For some long moments there was silence, until the German said, 'Squadron Leader, there is much to learn in a place like this.'

'I'm sure.'

'Shall we go?'

As they stood, Flash could see the two men who had brought him there shuffling off with something like relief in their attitudes. The Feldwebel led him towards another exit and then across an empty, darkened yard towards a wooden hut which when they entered, Flash could see was separated by a long corridor with doors on either side. Outside each door there were boots, shoes, flying-boots, left there as they might have been in an old-fashioned hotel.

Flash looked at his own boots, well-polished in black leather, and as he did so his escort said in his American-accented English which had the sound of being somewhat forced, 'They are not for cleaning . . . Everyone leaves their boots outside at night.'

When they came to the cell which had been assigned to him and were inside, the man said, 'If you will undress, Squadron Leader . . .'

'Undress?'

'Everyone must for a body inspection . . . I'm afraid the officers are not here at this time, and in any case they don't like doing it. Usually our customers' underwear is so filthy . . .' There was an attempt at a laugh.

'I am not dirty.'

'This I can understand, because of the nature of your capture, Squadron Leader.'

Jordaan stripped himself until he was naked. The German spread his hands around his body, and, finding nothing in the anus, appeared to be satisfied. In fact the only escape aid which Flash had was the compass in the top button of his tunic, which was fundamentally why fighter pilots never used the thing.

When he had dressed, and the man had gone with his rather beautiful flying-boots, there was the clank of the lock, and Flash, for the first time in his life, was totally alone and could look at his surroundings. He saw the meaning of nothing.

It was that way for days. He lay there, occasionally angry when there was the need for a toilet and his battering on the door could raise no response; until in the end he understood the nature of their game and could find solace in imagining himself back where he had begun, with all that space and the feeling in his lungs of that air. A smile could gather on his lips as he remembered the old man, his grandfather.

Gus Jordaan had been known throughout the Northern Transvaal as 'the helluva hunter'. He was a man who offered praise to no one, least of all to himself. His son, the father of Flash, had fought on the Western Front until taken prisoner in nineteen seventeen, and that, apart from his own memories of fighting them, had reinforced his hatred of the British.

And yet, remembering him, Flash knew there was no hatred in the old man – except for that which was lifeless. Gus, apart from his grandson, his old servant, Mawli, and the black woman with whom he occasionally slept, had been a man alone. My God, and Flash lying on that bed of straw, could smile remembering the smell of the old man: those had been such days.

None of these people surrounding him could know that you can never be a prisoner if ever you have lived to the extent of your capacity.

And so it was for days. Jordaan lay there living on the fat of his memories. The place was stark, but as he thought it out he realized the purpose of their holding him. He was to be another blob in the overall picture of their intelligence.

Odd people came and went, but after some days, in spite of the fact that he ignored their questionings, he gradually became pleased to see them. The moods of the men who were trying to break him were never predictable. Sometimes they were taciturn, sometimes truculent. But they wore at him as though trying to reduce his existence to that of an alimentary canal. Old Gus had taught him how to hold off what might appear to be inevitable: it would all get better.

The old man had taken over when his only son, Flash's father, had shot himself when the boy was fifteen. The business of remembering the old man and his wisdom; of remembering the vast skies over that country of his, and of his running with Bobby, hunting like two untamed young animals amidst all the breathing life of other kinds, only partially worked. Perhaps it didn't show, but he was beginning to break when at last they told him he was being moved.

3

As senior British officer at Leinefelde, Wing Commander Glaisop's quarters were more than adequate in the circumstances. The faint smell of the decent tobacco his wife sent regularly draped the room with a pleasant familiarity. The small, fading, badly framed picture of himself and Dorothy and the children which someone must have taken in their garden was for Glaisop the focal centre of the room. It was a long time since it had saddened him.

The very starkness of his surroundings had come to suit Glaisop, for from life, if he had ever asked himself the question, he had never asked for much. Even in this awfulness, it was enough that he was alive. A tall thoughtful man, Glaisop's expression, reinforced by the rigours he had endured through the previous eighteen months, created the impression of his being someone who could be unbending.

Outside, a thin slanting rain drifted across the camp, and it occurred to him as he stood at the window waiting for the others that he preferred the weather to be like this. Sunlight, with its suggestion of other times and other places, could pierce the armour with which he had encased his mind.

Mathers, in a khaki greatcoat thrown over his dark blue Fleet Air Arm uniform, was bending against the heavy drizzle as he made his way across the compound towards the window at which Glaisop was standing. There was no sign of the other two.

In spite of his year at Leinefelde, Mathers still retained

something of a naval breeze in his attitude. 'Whew . . . bloody awful . . .' He saluted casually. 'What's up, skipper?'

Glaisop motioned to the Naval man that he should sit, and as Mathers removed his coat and began lighting a cigarette before doing so, there was a knock at the door. Squadron Leader Carpenter entered. 'Morning . . . morning,' he muttered.

'Morning, Jeffrey.' Glaisop knew how much the new arrival hated being called 'Chippy'.

'Something wrong?' Carpenter asked.

'Could be. Don't know yet. Where the hell's Jordaan?'

Neither of Glaisop's two subordinates said anything. They both liked Flash, with all his fighter-type swagger, but they knew the irritation he could produce in the old man. Carpenter moved to the dripping window. 'He's coming now,' he announced with a suggestion of relief in his voice.

Jordaan didn't knock. 'Morning . . . morning, sir.' His salute was executed with a smartness which verged on mockery. 'Something wrong?'

Glaisop was a decent man. He found it difficult to be blatantly unpleasant, so, before saying anything, he breathed deeply to cover a trickle of irritation, inserted his pipe and then removed it. 'I . . . I have news for you . . . Something which may affect all of us to our considerable disadvantage . . . Only got it from Muller.' But he couldn't yet go on. He had to strike. 'Before we get to that, Jordaan, I would like to ask you why you and that Italian friend of yours were so drunk last night.'

'Drunk?'

'Yes. I want to know how you got so drunk last night.'

Jordaan smiled, leaving his eyes on the Wing Commander. 'How?'

'Yes, how.'

'On Del Renzio's gin. That's how.'

'How the hell does Del Renzio get gin, Jordaan?' Glaisop's training was telling him that he should control himself. He was conscious of a certain discomfiture, annoyed with himself that it should always be so in the presence of this swaggering South African fighter-type. Mathers, the Naval man knew, so to ease the atmosphere he said, 'If the gin's decent, Flash, I wouldn't mind some.'

But it was no good. Glaisop was not the man to provide someone like Jordaan with a temporary satisfaction. Everyone knew of Jordaan's record. But his kind and their behaviour had caused the fundamentally decent Germans to tighten their grip. Even the garden Glaisop had tended so carefully was now at risk. 'Where,' the Wing Commander insisted, 'did Del Renzio get gin?'

'He made it.' Jordaan appeared to stiffen. 'Sir, I should remind you that he does help out in a purely voluntary capacity in sick quarters.'

'So that he can make gin . . .'

'Exactly.'

Mathers and Carpenter laughed, but Glaisop was pressing on. 'The point is . . . the point is, Jordaan, that you wear the rank of a field officer, temporary though it may be, and I don't think that the spectacle of you and that Italian Communist behaving as you did last night in any way helps those whom I represent as senior British Officer in this camp.'

Flash, slighter of build, boyish even with that silken sweep of a blonde moustache reaching across his upper lip, simply stared at Glaisop as the latter went through the motions of re-lighting his pipe. He had done so when Jordaan spoke. 'I'm sorry you should feel this way, sir;

but Del Renzio is not a Communist – any more than I am.'

'How do you know? He fought against Franco, didn't he?'

'Perhaps we should have fought against Franco.'

Little Carpenter, who was by now much embarrassed, tried to do what he could. He said, 'Easy, Flash . . .'

But Jordaan was going on. Without moving his eyes from the Wing Commander, and knowing that Del Renzio would have laughed at this defence of his reputation, he said slowly, with the remnants of a South African accent, 'Del Renzio is a friend of mine. I happen to know a good deal about him . . .'

'How can you know a good deal about a man you meet in this place?'

'I know he was in the Italian Air Force.'

'The Italian Air Force . . . the *bloody* Italian Air Force . . .'

'Yeah . . . He deserted.'

'He can't have been.' Glaisop's voice was very firm now. 'I heard he'd fought against Franco.'

'He did . . . Deserted from the Italians when they tried to send him to Abyssinia to bomb wogs . . . Didn't believe in it . . . The Spanish Republicans picked him up in Casablanca when he was hiding out. He joined them as a flying instructor . . . became a fighter pilot.'

'Look, Jordaan . . . Do you really believe all this?'

'Of course I do.'

'I can't . . . It can't have been easy for a chap like that to get into the French Air Force.'

'Sir . . .' The tightness in Jordaan's voice told of his impatience. 'All I know is what the man has told me over the months. He's an Italian Count, and with the help of a cousin or someone who's something in the Papal Nuncio's office in Paris he got himself into the French Air Force when he escaped from Spain. He joined the Free French when he escaped to us.'

'Do the Germans know all this?'

'No idea.' Flash looked at the other two, Mathers and Carpenter. 'But I do know that as a Free Frenchman, he's more at risk in here than any one of us is. He hasn't even changed his name.'

Mathers spoke. 'Must say I've always found him a pretty decent fellow.'

Little Carpenter nodded eagerly. 'I do. Don't know the chap well, but I think he's rather amusing.'

Into this respite, the Wing Commander, in a lowered, thoughtful voice, passed his judgement. 'Be that as it may, but last night was a bloody bad show – especially on your part, Jordaan. You should be showing a better example . . . Now the reason . . . By the way, Jordaan when you leave here tell your friend Del Renzio that I want to see him in my quarters immediately.'

'I'll do that.'

By now, Mathers, the Fleet Air Arm man, was becoming restless. 'Why did you send for us, sir? Carpenter and I weren't drunk last night . . . unfortunately.'

Glaisop sensed their mood. He swung on the Naval man. 'This morning I learned that we are to have a new Commandant. Old Chumly, as I believe you called him, has gone. The new man arrives today.'

Carpenter got up from his chair. 'Chippy' had come into the Air Force from the uncertainties of civil flying before the war. He was a little man with a tendency to roundness which was a physical characteristic that so many of his generation of flyers seemed to share. Personal conflict disturbed him, but behind his readiness to laugh in that dry throaty voice of his there was a resolution which was distinct. He had been a Flight Commander in a Squadron of Hampdens when they had shot him down. To Glaisop he said then, 'Does it really matter, skipper? He'll be a dug-out like all the rest who could as easily be in their fire service as in the Wehrmacht.'

'Not this one . . .' Glaisop lit his pipe again. 'According to Muller who I can tell you was distinctly apprehensive when he spoke to me this morning, we've got a different animal on our hands this time . . . Which is why I've called you together. I want you to do what you can to keep the chaps in order. It could be that this man has been sent to turn the screw even tighter . . . as a result, no doubt, of your last ill-fated attempt at escape, Jordaan.'

Jordaan shrugged his shoulders with his hands deep in the pockets of his battle-dress trousers. 'I was led to believe that it's an officer's duty to attempt to escape,' he said, as though tired of the whole confrontation.

'All right, Flash . . .' Mathers raised his eyes to the Wing Commander. 'What's so special about this one?'

'Apparently he's a much decorated Major, badly wounded on the Russian Front. Muller didn't say a great deal – he's thick that man – but his behaviour did suggest that he was worried. We could have a tartar on our hands. You chaps are in much closer touch with our people than I am. I simply want you to spread it around that they should go easy – at least until we see how things work out. If the gentleman's embittered it could mean that we'd lose the few last privileges we've got.'

Immediately Jordaan said, 'I think we should make it as unpleasant for the bastard as possible.'

'Shut up, Flash!' Mathers and Carpenter seemed to speak with one voice.

'So there it is.' Glaisop turned towards the rain-sodden window. 'Do what you can. That's all . . . Don't forget,

Jordaan, I want to see your friend Del Renzio immediately.'

The consequences of the previous evening were rumbling around in his gut as Von Mansdorff sat in the rear of the Mercedes. He felt awful. Perhaps Leipzig had not been such a good idea after all. To the driver in front he said with a slight raising of his voice, 'If you see a place, stop. We need some champagne. How do you feel, Karl?'

'Not good, Herr Major.'

In the beginning it had been a good idea, for he hadn't felt all that brisk when they had started out from Berlin. It had seemed reasonable to break his journey in a city which he remembered as being civilized, and when, after examination of the little black book he always carried, he had discovered the address and telephone number of a girl he had once met on holiday who lived near the Gewendaus, the notion was sealed.

But no one had heard of the lady when he called her from his hotel. So it had been the bar and the pleasure or, more accurately, the satisfaction he felt when he walked in there and saw the hurried changes of expression on their faces.

In minutes there had been someone there whom he had known from Vienna. Hans Ploch, a Lieutenant, had been a good chap, but in spite of the fact that they had known each other rather well he approached Von Mansdorff with diffidence. Von Mansdorff understood. It was not so much the presence of the Knight's Cross or the Iron Cross, first and second class which disturbed his friend: it was the black patch covering the empty socket and the attendant scar running down the left side of his face: the empty sleeve tucked into the left pocket of his tunic.

Ploch held himself erectly as he drew his heels together.

There was a slight bow . . . 'Herr Major . . .'

'Shut up, my friend, Hans . . .'

'Rudi . . .' Ploch took Von Mansdorff's extended hand. 'It's good to see you . . . You're alive!'

'I think so . . . a little.' There was always just beneath Von Mansdorff's words the suggestion of latent laughter. It erupted then as he ordered champagne. On that morning he could almost hear the clink of their glasses as he sat in the back of the car which was heading fast along the empty road which led towards Halle. 'Did you find yourself a woman last night, Karl?'

'Just a little one, sir.'

Himself, he thought of the women Ploch had eventually found for them on the previous night. With the thought of that girl of the night before, he winced. The pity she had shown for him had been unbearable.

The driver announced that there was an inn ahead. He drove on into a courtyard. Some wine would make a difference. That couldn't have changed. With his driver, to the obvious confusion of the man who served them, Von Mansdorff shared a bottle of champagne. He smiled to himself with the thought that there had been a virtue in conquering France. 'Better, Karl?'

'Sir . . .' The man smiled.

Beyond Halle, through which they would pass in less than half an hour, there would be this place, Leinefelde, to which he had been consigned. That, too, was a pity. God, that he should have been reduced to becoming a prison governor. He was grateful for the intercession of his brother who had made possible this alternative to leaving the Army. But, still, it was awful. Somehow he would get back. He would. In spite of these damned stupid wounds.

Was there something in him which wanted to die? Yes,

there was. He looked into his glass, revealing nothing of his thinking to the man who stood with him. But, then wasn't there in all men? Men, that is, with the possibility of options; even poor men with only their imagination. He had had so many options. But it had only been in the Army that everything had been made clear for him. The way ahead had been defined. Before, there had been Oxford and the fun of it all; his disgrace and the confusion of his family: the years of dodging around Europe. Never in his life had he thought of himself as being soldierly material. But in the Army he had discovered that he was, and he had been grateful. He had to get back. He would not rot in this prison camp.

In the car again, he thought of sleep, but so much was stirring in his memory that it was impossible. With the weariness that lies in the aftermath of much drink, he thought of his mother and his father and wished despairingly that they could have been alive long enough to know that he had not been entirely worthless. There was a sudden smile at the thought of his brother sitting there like a stuffed gherkin at Luftwaffe headquarters. Paul had won all the approval, but he, Rudi had done the fighting. It had always been that way, but only he had known it.

On they drove through Halle towards Nordhausen, where they would turn off towards Leinefelde. There it would end: the fates had withdrawn their favours. Von Mansdorff smiled. 'Karl,' he said to the man in front, 'why don't you steal a couple of days at home on your way back to Berlin?'

'That would be good, sir.'

'I'll arrange it.'

Having said that he searched for a reverie that would be pleasant for himself. But only the road slipped by. He looked at the watch on his right wrist. They would arrive within the hour.

He should have gone to Ilse. Amidst the disarray of his mind, she was suddenly there; clear, alive, vital as she had always been, smiling on him. He could remember the fun of their growing years. Brave Ilse, she had been more of a brother than Paul had ever been. He laughed suddenly to himself so that the man in front, said, 'Yes, sir . . .'

'It's nothing . . . it's nothing.'

But it had never been nothing. Never, not even beyond their ultimate knowing of each other, and her disappearance into marriage with her Italian Duke, who wasn't, really, such a bad chap. It had never been nothing. But what could he as a man have taken to her? Slowly, and still with some difficulty, he extracted a cigarette from the right hand pocket of his tunic. He smiled at his lack of an expertise that he was determined to gain. Perhaps his failure to equal the measured quality of Ilse's womanhood had been the reason for all his running. Perhaps.

'There it is, sir.'

He saw. The camp lay on a slight rise ahead of them; grey, thick, as though someone in a hurry had left it there.

4

Tony Del Renzio was sitting on his bed with his chin buried in his hands as Van Reine leant against the wall. The Dutchman, with that peculiar clacking intonation which they seem to impart to their English, was regaling him with a rumour he had heard about a new Commandant arriving, and Del Renzio had just said, 'Dutch, for God's sake, I don't give a damn – and in any case I don't believe your stupid rumour. There are more rumours in this place than fleas,' as Jordaan arrived.

Del Renzio looked up at the sound of his voice. 'It's true, Tony,' Jordaan assured him. '. . . And the Housemaster wants to see you now.'

'Me?'

'It's about last night. It'll be a rocket. He's already seen me.'

'Oh, Christ . . .'

'Really, he does. Now.'

Del Renzio stood with a look of tiredness on his face. Jordaan laughed.

There was leisurely elegance in the way the Italian took his tunic and slipped it on. Everything in Tony's movements had a quality of unhurried assurance.

'Good luck,' Van Reine said.

'What for? What for? . . . What can the bastard do to me? Shoot me for getting drunk? Fuck him.'

Jordaan laughed. 'That's the spirit, lad.'

Gently Del Renzio pushed his friend away by the

shoulder before turning to be off. Then he halted. 'Can I borrow that thing?' he asked. 'It's raining.'

Jordaan threw him the battered Army raincoat which someone had found and he had won in a poker game.

There was no inner resentment of authority in Tony Del Renzio, but Wing Commander Glaisop did try his patience. Now as he skipped to avoid the puddles of rain which had gathered on the compound throughout the morning he was conscious of a heaviness in his feelings as he approached the Wing Commander's quarters.

Del Renzio knocked briskly on the senior officer's door.

'Come in.'

Glaisop, with his face slanting upwards, had the usual unlit pipe between his teeth. 'Del Renzio . . .'

'Sir.'

The Wing Commander gestured towards a chair. 'Sit down.'

Del Renzio did, more heavily than was necessary.

'. . . It's about last night; you and Jordaan. I've had the most awful reports about your behaviour.'

'You mean we were drunk, sir.'

'I do.'

'It is necessary to be drunk, sir, occasionally in this place. That is if you know how to get drunk.'

'I don't agree . . . I don't agree at all, Del Renzio.'

My God, Del Renzio was thinking of how at home this man would have been a functionary of his father, a doctor, or a lawyer maybe. But now, here he was, the Senior British Officer. He had probably joined the Royal Air Force to find security.

'I view . . . I view with the greatest misgivings . . .' Glaisop was becoming aware of how shallow was his impact on this man – for he was not a fool – '. . . your influence on the younger inmates of this camp. You do realize that many of the chaps here are mere boys?'

'There are no boys here, sir. They are all men, good and bad. That is why they are here.'

Glaisop, who had been sitting, shuffled around in his chair. 'I don't agree . . . I don't agree at all.'

'I'm sorry.' There was something which suggested that Del Renzio was in charge of the confrontation.

'Damn it, man. Don't you realize how easily this whole situation could slide into chaos?' Glaisop slammed the table. 'I know what you think of me. I know. I know that you think I'm some kind of damned old fuddy duddy . . . But the Royal Air Force is not the Spanish Republican Army, Del Renzio – nor is it the Italian Air Force! We have our own ways. Your . . . your background is so entirely different from anything my chaps have known, especially the younger ones . . . You were with that rabble in Spain.'

'Rabble?'

Glaisop, poor man, stumbled at that. 'Well, as far as I hear, it wasn't exactly a highly disciplined force.'

Del Renzio spoke slowly. 'Very highly disciplined,' he said. 'If you got out of line, they shot you.'

'Hrmm . . . Exactly . . . Del Renzio, my job here is to act as a sort of referee. I'm responsible for my lads, and that, I'm afraid, includes you. I'm also responsible to my lads insofar as it is my concern to ensure that the enemy treats us as prisoners of war according to the terms of the Geneva Convention. Anything . . . anything – and your behaviour last night is the kind of thing I'm talking about – which disturbs the even tenor of the running of this camp – from my point of view that is – will be stamped out. Do you hear?'

'How? How, Wing Commander, do you intend to stamp out anything? How?' At that Del Renzio was on his feet, at which he in his turn banged his fist on the desk. 'We are in the middle of a crumbling world, and you talk to me as though you were some kind of Scoutmaster in the suburbs of London. It is ridiculous . . .'

There was a knock on the door, which, in a way was a blessing. 'Come in,' Glaisop said.

It was Lieutenant Muller.

'Yes, Muller.'

'Wing Commander, the new Commandant, Major Von Mansdorff, wishes to have all British personnel on parade in thirty minutes' time.' Poor Muller, he didn't look at all happy.

'In half an hour . . .'

'Yes . . . Wing Commander.'

'Thank you, Muller.'

Glaisop swung around towards the window, looked at nothing, and then turned to Del Renzio. 'Right, my friend – you heard what I had to say. Now, be off. Tell Mathers and Carpenter and Jordaan to have everyone on parade in twenty minutes. Right?'

Del Renzio, involuntarily, held himself to attention. 'Sir.'

On parade their attitude was casual, but orderly. They were lined up in four ranks. Wing Commander Glaisop was standing edgily a couple of paces from a group which comprised Jordaan, Mathers and Carpenter as they awaited the appearance of the new Commandant when it happened.

There had been a certain amount of larking about, as there always was on such occasions. The rain had almost finished with itself, but there was a cold dampness in the air to which they had to respond. Young Temple, in the front rank, was getting the laughs. He was a good lad.

Once an apprenticed accountant, he had become a navigator in Bomber Command. Somehow, for whatever reason, he had decided that his role was that of the joker; and he could be funny. On that occasion the substance of his humour concerned itself with Lieutenant Muller's sex life – which wasn't really fair.

Muller, who had never really understood the nature of being an officer, and who was too conditioned by his origins ever to learn, knew just enough English to know that he was the target for Temple's remarks. The group around Temple was sniggering enthusiastically, but Muller, solid man that he was, could not take their banter. Vaguely they reminded him of his daughters: silly girls whom he had loved when they were young and so dependant, unaware of all that he had done on his and their behalf.

God, he had come out of the first war as a senior NCO, totally bemused. He could remember his wedding, and how little anyone, all those people of hers in Augsburg, had really understood the bleakness that confronted him. Their laughter, their toasts, their faces had all been false. There had been the attempt to re-establish himself as a carpenter which his father had been, proudly. But nothing.

The Nazis had offered some kind of release for his confusion. First he had become a Brownshirt, and then in recompense for his dedication in Munich in the early twenties, a good man called Hochner who had learned to have influence, had secured his re-entrance into the Wehrmacht. Eventually a commission which would never really mean anything had followed. It was security. And now, when he was too old to be really active, he was secure unless he made some dreadful mistake. Herda, still in Augsburg, and obsessed with her influence on her grandchildren, would always be all right.

And this little English puppy was mocking him!

Lieutenant Muller struck the Englishman, Temple, which was unfortunate, for at that precise moment, Major Von Mansdorff was walking across the parade ground to address the Englishmen for the first time.

Mansdorff was suddenly behind him. With his one gloved hand he struck Muller across the back of the neck. It was an awful moment, something which should never have happened. The English were stunned.

'*Warten Sie auf mich in Meinem quartier! . . . In Meinem quartier!*' Major Von Mansdorff's voice had the resonance of authority. But there was no hysteria. Muller was absolutely still. He knew with whom he was dealing. For a moment he looked into Von Mansdorff's face, drew his own tightly and said nothing. He saluted and was gone.

'Now, Wing Commander . . .' Von Mansdorff had turned to Glaisop. 'Will you forgive my glove?' Von Mansdorff extended his right hand. Glaisop took it with an expression on his face which was almost bemused.

'How do you do, Herr Major.' For a moment he hesitated. Then he said almost gratefully, 'May I introduce Squadron Leader Jordaan, Squadron Leader Carpenter, Lieutenant Commander Mathers . . .'

'How do you do . . .'

Each of them – and each of them was concentrating on Von Mansdorff – was looking at the man as though transfixed. There was his appearance; the missing left eye covered by the black eye patch; the missing left arm, the scar which travelled down his cheek almost from his left eye's socket to the side of his mouth. And there was the accent: he spoke in almost perfect English.

Von Mansdorff was not tall, but yet – and perhaps it was his uniform and the focal point of the Knight's Cross he wore which created the impression – he appeared to those facing him as someone taller than they. Each of them, Jordaan, Carpenter and Mathers, saluted.

'I would like to say a few words to your men, Wing Commander.'

'Certainly . . .' This was the most unusual German Glaisop had met so far. He turned to the men assembled behind him. 'Gentlemen, this is Major Von Mansdorff. He is the new Commandant of the camp.'

For a moment Von Mansdorff looked at them in appraisal. There was no restlessness in the ranks, for by now everyone was intensely curious. When he spoke they even seemed to draw their breath to attention. 'I know,' he said, 'chaps, why you're here – and I know why I'm here . . . And I don't like it any more than you do.' There was silence and then the suggestion of laughter. '. . . But this is a military situation. It is my duty to run things that way, and it is your obligation to be aware of my duty. Let us live as amicably as we can in this very unfortunate situation.' With that he turned quickly to Glaisop and said, 'Wing Commander, may I see you in my quarters in half an hour?'

Glaisop nodded.

The morning was drifting away as were the clouds which had swept the place for hours, when Wing Commander Glaisop met Lieutenant Muller coming out of Mansdorff's office. Old Muller said nothing. But Glaisop, with a rare appreciation of a situation which was in his favour, wasn't missing the opportunity of taking advantage of the German. He said, 'We meet again, Lieutenant Muller.'

On entering, Glaisop saluted Von Mansdorff's office.

'Wing Commander . . .'

'Major . . .'

'Sit down, Wing Commander, sit down.' Von Mansdorff gestured towards a leather armchair. Glaisop noticed again that it was in a particularly attractive shade of green, but he didn't sit. Somewhat hesitantly he said, 'Thank you, no. I think I'd prefer to stand in order to hear what you have to say.'

'As you wish . . . Have a cigar.'

'No thank you. I only use this.' Glaisop fingered the pipe he pulled from his battle-dress pocket.

'Use it then, by all means.' Von Mansdorff stood from behind the desk. '. . . Wing Commander, I have seen from the records left by my predecessor that he had a difficult time here. I've *had* a difficult time. How can I avoid having one in this dreadful place? Shall I try being kind?'

Glaisop hesitated, holding his pipe as though it was a necessary prop. At his age, his face was beginning to take on the grizzled look of a countryman. The eyes were strong, mistrusting. He could, standing there before Von Mansdorff, have been a farm manager appearing before a new employer for the first time. Eventually he said, 'That must be your decision.'

'Right. For a start I will restore the privilege of a bar. In a few days it will open in your canteen. Beer only will be available. Your officers can sign my chits, which one day, when we have won the war, will be redeemable. How does that strike you?'

'I'm sure the men will be pleased.'

'Good. Shall we have a drink now?'

'Er . . . No thank you.'

Von Mansdorff shrugged carelessly. There was the suggestion of a laugh. Then, when he had produced a brandy bottle, he hesitated before saying, 'Would you mind opening this thing?'

Glaisop was embarrassed. He took the bottle, removed the cork, and poured some into the glass the Major held. 'I will have a drink with you,' he said, 'but I would remind you that you are my enemy.'

Von Mansdorff flicked his face at Glaisop. 'I know who my enemies are. They are everywhere. And most of them are not soldiers. In Russia, Wing Commander, I was for a time a prisoner when I was wounded. There was a Russian sister. For three weeks I was with her. It was she who arranged my escape. Was she my enemy?'

This kind of talk embarrassed Glaisop, whose life had been comparatively straightforward – in spite of the uniqueness of his present situation. He said, 'I shouldn't think so.' And then he consumed in one gulp the brandy he had poured himself.

Wing Commander Glaisop was confused. Was this man intentionally playing some kind of role? Rightly, Glaisop had always behaved with the utmost correctness. He was trying to do so now while feeling that there was some kind of humanity in this German which was totally unexpected. Perhaps Von Mansdorff was simply playing the role he had always played. Perhaps, as was suggested by his name, he didn't have to play the role of anyone but himself.

Von Mansdorff held out his glass for more brandy, which he drank quickly. Then, himself, with his good arm, he refilled it. Over his glass he said, 'Did you think I was wrong when I struck my man this morning?'

'Yes.'

'I was angered because that man Muller is not a front-line soldier. Your men, in my opinion, are. I am recently removed from that front line. The front line, Wing

Commander, tends to embody a certain kinship between them and you. I know as you say that you are my enemy. Do you realize, Wing Commander . . . Do you realize? . . . Of course you don't . . . Of course you don't! Do you realize that in my country we are still running a fully staffed Casino at Baden Baden? That is not for front line soldiers, Wing Commander! Von Mansdorff threw his glass in the direction of the fireplace.

Glaisop – it was all he could do – went to a sideboard and took up another glass. He poured some brandy, and without saying a word passed it to the German.

'Wing Commander, an hour ago a telegram arrived at my office . . . I think you have met Muller, the man I struck, as you were entering this office.'

Glaisop nodded.

'The telegram announced that his wife had been killed by your Bomber Command in Augsburg – along with two of her grandchildren. I couldn't tell him when he was here, because he was here for a different reason. I have *yet* to tell him. One of the things about war, Wing Commander, is that it's irony. If you'll excuse me.'

Von Mansdorff turned his back on the Englishman, and Glaisop, with a steadied certainty, left the office. Or was about to when Von Mansdorff halted him. 'These two men who were drunk last night, the Italian and the South African – tell them to be here at seven this evening. I want to speak to them.'

When they arrived at seven, Von Mansdorff could have been described as being drunk. But then there are men who can hold their drink, and he was one. Muller had been told of his wife's death, and had gone with his grief frozen on that rather flaccid face.

There was one extra visitor, Van Reine, but at first Von

Mansdorff didn't seem to realize this. His eyes focussed on Jordaan as he sat there behind his desk with a half empty bottle before him. 'You are Jordaan?'

'I am, Herr Commandant.'

'You are Del Renzio?'

The Italian nodded.

'Who's this?'

It was Del Renzio who said, 'Van Reine, Flight Lieutenant Van Reine . . . He . . . He also drinks.'

'Ha . . . Good.'

It had been Van Reine's suggestion that he be present on this occasion. 'He's going to strop you two,' he had said. 'Why don't I go along with you? We'll overwhelm the bastard with numbers.' The other two had laughed. Why not?

As though to himself Von Mansdorff spoke downwards to his desk. 'Your people killed my man Muller's wife and two grandchildren in Augsburg last night.'

The three prisoners stiffened. But then he looked up at them. 'But that I suppose is what war has become . . . Would you like some champagne, gentlemen?'

Relieved, it was Del Renzio who said quickly, 'Yes, please.'

'Jordaan – open a bottle. My days of opening bottles are over. In emergency, I have to smash them.'

Flash Jordaan took a bottle and gave it to Del Renzio. 'You're better at this than I am.' So, with something of a flourish he couldn't suppress, Del Renzio opened the bottle, and as he did, Van Reine, huge, with the look of a man who would eventually become obese, reached out to take it. It had been a long time since he had tasted champagne.

'Easy . . .' Del Renzio laughed, and when he saw that

Von Mansdorff had suddenly stiffened, he placed his hand on the bottle's top. 'Please,' he said, '. . . my friend.' His left eyelid flickered and Van Reine released the bottle. 'Herr Major.' Del Renzio filled the glass the German was extending.

Von Mansdorff, with that capacity for lucidity in drink which some men have, stood. He raised his glass. 'To victory,' he said, 'yours and mine – and may the best men win.' Then he turned away from them. 'Already,' he announced in that peculiarly detached accent he used in English, 'you have a minor victory . . . Nothing to be compared with those we have already achieved. But it is still there. We are speaking in English.'

The Commandant had turned from them to look into the darkness outside, so Del Renzio quickly sloshed some more champagne into their outstretched glasses. Von Mansdorff's voice had gone into his throat. 'I'm as much a prisoner here as you chaps are . . . But!'

Van Reine couldn't help it: he burped.

'I, gentlemen, am in charge. I know . . .' And perhaps now the brandy and the champagne he had consumed – perhaps, too, his sense of guilt at his treatment of Muller in the light of the man's loss; perhaps they were the cause of his tongue taking flight. 'We are soldiers,' he went on. 'You, me, all of us who are here – even poor old bloody Muller. He saw that other war. We are all soldiers, and we are trapped!'

Von Mansdorff swung on them. 'Don't any one of you dare! I already know all about you, Del Renzio, Count Antonio Del Renzio. And I know about you, Jordaan . . . About you, Van Reine, I know that we have more Dutchmen fighting for us than are fighting for the British . . . Understand that. I know!'

The party would appear to have been over. But no. Von Mansdorff was not displaying the exhaustion that would have shown in most men. He sat, rather heavily. 'More champagne, Jordaan . . . This time you serve. Your friend, Del Renzio, is a comic. This is not a time for comedy. You serve.'

So Jordaan took another bottle, opened it, and served.

'Sit down, gentlemen.'

They found chairs and sat.

'When I was a Cook's courier, I knew many British. I liked the women, even the cor blimeys. The men I thought to be rather foolish.' Von Mansdorff chuckled. 'As a matter of fact, I still have my little black book. If it were possible, I could be fucking in every corner of England – to say nothing of Ireland, Scotland and Wales.'

Now all of this was rather disturbing to the three who were listening. None of them quite knew how to respond. It was Jordaan who took the initiative. 'Commandant, it is difficult for us to know how to carry on this conversation.'

'I understand.'

'The limits of our conversation with you, our enemy, are to provide you with our names, ranks and numbers.'

'I already know your names, ranks and numbers.'

'Then how do we proceed?'

'You drink my champagne. So could your Wing Commander. But he looks as though he would break if he bent and broke his glass arse.'

At that they laughed, not out of any disrespect to Glaisop. But the remark did have a certain relevance.

Fleetingly, for Jordaan, there was a memory of a train journey from Newmarket to London when in an over-crowded train he stood exhausted in a corridor to watch a large bookmaker wrapped in a cashmere coat of light fawn with a belt around his enormous waist and a ripened blonde lady sitting opposite him. The man was obviously making his way back to the big city after a day at the races, while he, Jordaan, was still wearing the sweat of the afternoon's battle. He had decided then that his enemies were everywhere, as were his friends. 'I thought,' he said to Von Mansdorff, 'you were a member of Oxford University.'

'I was . . . But an indiscretion with a nurse put an end to that.'

'Was that when you became a courier?' It was possible now to talk like that.

'That, and many other things – until I found my vocation as a soldier. Drink up, chaps. This is my first night here, and I hate the bloody place – as I'm sure you do. But . . . Jordaan I have read your file. I know of your reputation as a potential escaper, and I can assure you that if you try it again and fail, I'll have you shot.'

'I'll try not to fail.'

'Hah . . . Drink up, chaps.'

When the three eventually left they were confused. 'God, what do you think,' Van Reine asked.

'Don't know. What do you think, Tony?'

'I don't know. Maybe he's flack happy.'

Their confusion followed them as each made his way to his bed. But sleep cancelled everything.

Von Mansdorff too fell asleep – at his desk. It would be easy to say that the man was consumed by self-pity. That was not true. But he was immersed in a dream of long ago. He was young and at home. His brother and Ilse were there. He and Ilse were laughing at his brother, and yet in the dream there was no clear reason why they should be. There were rats in the dream when his man, Muller, placed a hand on his shoulder. It was Muller who dragged him to bed.

5

Jordaan was in the track suit which little Mitchell had made for him from a couple of grey blankets. Considering everything, it was not at all unsmart. But they laughed at him, Del Renzio and Van Reine, each time he passed them as he made his circuit of the galloping footballers lunging at each other in the exercise yard. 'It's the thing, lads,' he gasped '. . . the only way to get the booze out of your system.'

Van Reine chuckled. 'He should keep it in his system. It may be a long time before we get any more.'

The Dutchman hated exercise almost as much as his Italian friend. They looked at each other and smiled. Then they turned their eyes to Jordaan, sweating his way around. 'He's quite a character,' Van Reine suggested.

'You're right . . . I wonder why he's doing all this running. Is he building up some kind of pattern to confuse them? Something he will suddenly break.'

'With that kind of man you can never tell.'

'He'd tell us, surely.'

'No.'

Del Renzio, who was not yet thirty, had seen many men in very many strange circumstances. 'What do you really know about Jordaan?'

'I know about him what you know about him.'

'No. I mean his background.'

'I know he's a killer.'

'But before that . . .'

Van Reine paused, with his eyes on the running figure

of Jordaan on the far side of the exercise yard. 'I think he was always a killer. As a little boy, I can imagine him pulling the wings off a half-dead fly.'

The Italian laughed dryly. 'I did that . . . But only to little flies. I'm off.'

'Aren't you coming to my lecture on Bali?'

'The one about its equable climate, its fertility and the beauty of its women. I've heard it six times.'

'Ach, it's good for them.' The Dutchman's shoulders shook as he laughed within himself. 'When I give them the bit about the women, it gives them a splendid resurrection. Resurrection, is that right?'

'That's right. I'm off to sick-quarters . . . Got to think about the gin supply. After the war, I think I'll go into business . . . Del Renzio's Italian gin . . . Good, eh?'

'I'll stick to Dutch gin.'

On the other side of the yard, Von Mansdorff was being as affable to Wing Commander Glaisop as his hangover would allow. After an initial greeting he looked for a few moments at the exertions of those kicking a ball about until he spoke against the shouting, jeering, cheering of the players, 'I'm very much a new boy at all this, Wing Commander. Muller here is showing me – how do you say? – something of the ropes.'

There was no smile from Glaisop. He said, 'I imagine you'll become used to it, Major.'

'Hah, that's something I have no intention of doing. Good morning, Wing Commander.'

With Muller at his heels, Mansdorff was off.

They looked in at sick quarters where a dozen men were in bed in a long, stark ward. Von Mansdorff halted when he entered the room as an orderly hurried towards him to halt stiffly at attention.

'You are . . .?'

'Molder, Herr Major.'

'You are in charge here?'

'Oh, no, Herr Major . . . Lieutenant Stumpe is in charge. He comes every other day from our hospital in Halle – unless there is some kind of emergency.'

'So there is no resident doctor.'

'That is correct, Herr Major.'

'Are any of these men seriously ill?'

'Not really, sir. Stomach upsets; slight toxic conditions. That kind of thing. One of them. The Scotsman Maclachlan, is in some pain. He's had surgery for the removal of shrapnel from his hand and thigh. He's in some pain.'

'Take me to him.'

Deferentially, nervously in fact, the orderly led the way to the Scotsman's bed. The man was, as they all were, in his twenties. It was obvious that he was in extreme discomfort. As Von Mansdorff arrived at his bedside only the man's black hair could be seen above the bedcovers.

'Mac,' the orderly, Molder said, 'the Commandant is here.'

With his good hand, the Scotsman drew down the covers to reveal a sharply featured face with eyes drawn tightly at the corners.

Von Mansdorff smiled. 'As you can see, I know something about hospital beds . . . You've been having a bad time.'

The Scotsman, with an element of disbelief in his voice said, 'Not too bad, sir.'

The Commandant looked at him. His mind was reeling with memories of his own experience. There was nothing he could say that would have any meaning. So he said, 'Good luck, Jock.' And at that the Scotsman's eyebrows were raised.

With Muller he went everywhere, even into the boiler

house. And yet it was a pretence. About this place, h cared nothing at all. Everything about it, the wooden structures they lived in and ate in and were sick in had about them a quality of weakness. All of it was a creation that could have been swept away with a strong enough wind. He had the feeling of having stepped off the sureness of the life he had found on to a rotting platform. Somehow, somehow he would have to get away from this place and back to where a man could die decently.

'Muller,' he said as they walked away from sick-quarters, 'I want you to assume to a much greater extent the day to day running of the camp. I will deal with the issues that you consider to be important, but in the main you can have much more of a free hand than I imagine you have had in the past. I can help you, Muller. But you must go home now, to Augsburg to look after the affairs of your family. When we have completed this little journey of ours you will go home.'

'Thank you, sir.' In Muller's experience, it had never been wise to trust any *real* officer. He had always known how they had looked upon his own kind. He had also heard that even the Fuhrer himself did not trust them. Maybe this one was different. But it worried Muller that Von Mansdorff could speak English so well, and that he appeared to be too sympathetic to those who were his prisoners.

When they arrived in the Mess Hall, Van Reine was in the middle of his lecture on Bali. Seeing them enter from the far end, Van Reine hesitated before saying, 'Gentlemen, the Commandant.'

There was a desultory rustling as they struggled to their feet.

'Please, gentlemen, sit down,' Von Mansdorff commanded. Then he added, 'Carry on, Van Reine.'

‘Well, as I was about to say, Hinduism reached Bali in the seventh century – or was it the sixth?’

‘The eighth,’ someone called out. ‘Go on, Dutch. Give us the bit about the women with their bare tits.’

‘We’ll get to that . . . Now, pay attention.’

From behind them Von Mansdorff smiled, and then, with Muller, was gone. They were a lively lot, he was thinking, these fliers with their wings clipped. Different, very different from the men he had known during those months in Russia, but not quite so different from the men who had swept through France in forty. Russia was the grey cloud towards which you had to move always with the feeling that it would envelop you. Russia was filth and blood and confusion. Walking with Muller on the way back to his office there was for a moment in his mind the flickering image of some of the faces he could remember from those days. Somehow he would get back to them.

In his office he told Muller to make arrangements to leave immediately, but Muller surprised him. ‘Sir,’ the man said, ‘would it be all right if I went tomorrow?’

‘Why, Muller?’

‘There is something I have to do. It’s different, sir.’

‘What do you mean?’

‘One of my men – amongst the British – has discovered homosexuality.’

‘So . . .’

‘I have planned that tonight I should catch them.’

Von Mansdorff laughed. ‘Are you surprised at such a thing in a place like this?’

‘I hate such people.’

‘Muller . . . Muller.’ Mansdorff laughed quietly. ‘Is it our business? Isn’t this something for the Wing Commander? Do we really care if the British fuck each other to death? Tell me what you know about this business, and then be on your way. You have a family to see in Augsburg.'

So Muller told him and was gone.

When the mid-day roll call had taken place, the prisoners were released to make their way to the Mess Hall. Von Mansdorff stood at some distance, watching them drifting away in their groups and wondering which of them might be the deviants about whom Muller was so concerned.

When it occurred to him that it might be an idea to have a look at the food they were eating, he met Wing Commander Glaisop as the man was making his way towards his own quarters. 'Ah, Wing Commander . . . Something has come up, as you say. Would it be convenient to have a chat in my office later this afternoon? Say about four thirty.'

Glaisop's eyebrows wrinkled, '. . . Certainly.'

'Thank you, Wing Commander.'

Von Mansdorff saw the food they were eating, and was aware of the mistrust with which they were looking at him as he walked around the long, echoing room. By the time he left – and he had spoken to no one – he had decided where he would install the bar he had decided to provide for them.

Having eaten, the Commandant lay down on his bed. He was a tired man. Somehow he would have to gather together whatever strength was left in him, for in his imagination he could almost feel the tremor of the world as it was outside this dreadful place. The trickle of determination which was in his gut made it impossible to sleep. Endlessly smoking, he lay there allowing himself to remember. He remembered Ilse until the thought of her made him swing his feet to the floor. He would write to her.

'My dear Ilse,

How is Dino? I say this to be rid of him from my thoughts. Forgive me. I know your husband is a fine fellow, but it is you whom I love.

Ilse, they have put me in a prison – as Commandant of a camp holding British airmen. Or rather a somewhat motley collection of those who have flown with the British. I even have one here whom I believe is the black sheep of a distinguished Italian family, one Del Renzio. Perhaps Dino knows him. But there are all sorts; Dutchmen, South Africans, one or two Frenchmen pretending to be English. I think of them as my cage birds. Mostly they are very young, and strangely it is difficult not to have a sneaking regard for them – which I suppose is wrong, for they are still the enemy.

My darling, how goes the war with you? You worry about your husband I suppose. But don't, Ilse. If I know Dino, he's probably training horses or organizing the Duce's social life, which from what I hear will be tiring but hardly dangerous. Although he could slip in someone's bath for instance – I'm sorry, darling. I'm sorry. I really do like your Duke. He can be very funny.

Dear Ilse, I'm miserable. This place must be like one of those camps for Jews and Communists I've heard about – except that my birds are protected by the Geneva Convention. But it is all so different from the war I have known. I must, I really must get out. And I will get out.

Darling, on my way here I would have made an outrageous detour to see you, but I got drunk instead. Do you forgive me? In any case I look so awful. I think that was really why.

But Ilse, in writing to you like this – and I had meant to be so profound, but possibly cannot – I'm at least remembering what we were like when we were young. I think I'll get drunk again, and then I'll cry. Is that all right?

Kisses,
Rudi.'

He reached for a pen, but there was none. So he cursed and called for an orderly just as the man he wanted knocked on the door of his room.

'Come in!'

'Herr Major . . . It is almost four thirty.'

'Oh yes.' The man was a somewhat undersized Saxon with a heavily waxed moustache, curled at the ends in the fashion of the first war. Von Mansdorff had not troubled to discover his name. He called him 'Adolph'. 'Adolph, do you have a pen?'

'Herr Major, I do not have a pen.'

'All right, all right . . . I'll go to my office.' He had almost forgotten he had said that he would see the Wing Commander at four thirty.

Glaisop had the look of a troubled man when he was shown into the office. A cursory salute was offered, and in return Von Mansdorff gestured towards the chair in front of his desk. This time Glaisop sat down. In the pocket of the tunic he wore, he fumbled for his re-assuring pipe.

'Smoke, Wing Commander,' but as Von Mansdorff lit a cigarette, Glaisop simply held the empty bowl of his pipe. 'Wing Commander, this is a somewhat delicate matter, and I'm sorry to have to bring it up so early in our acquaintance.'

Glaisop's eyebrows narrowed across the bridge of his nose. Von Mansdorff, looking at him, was suddenly aware that his opposite number had rather a good face. It was not fleshy, and the line of the jaw was firmly defined. In the brief silence between them, the German wondered if in other circumstances they could have been friends.

'Something is wrong?'

Von Mansdorff cleared his throat. 'I would be inclined to think so.' And at that he stood, turned his back on Glaisop to look at some prisoners wandering aimlessly across the compound. Then he turned again. He spoke quickly, as though anxious to be rid of the words, 'My man Muller tells me he had discovered what might be described as a nest of homosexuality amongst your men . . . Not a large one, apparently, but it is there – alive.'

Glaisop dropped his pipe – possibly intentionally to cover his confusion – for when he returned to a sitting position his face had visibly reddened. 'I . . . I find that hard to believe.' It was rather a silly thing to say, and he knew it.

Von Mansdorff smiled. 'In a place like this?'

'What do you intend to do?'

Von Mansdorff's face straightened. 'I intend that *you* should do something. They are your men. The crime – if we can call it that – is social, rather than military. I, if you will permit me, will provide you with the details Muller has given me, and then, my dear Wing Commander, you can decide whether or not you take any action . . . Please believe me, I can appreciate your difficulty.'

Glaisop had never been in such a situation. The mere suggestion of what he might be having to face was one which to him was revolting. 'I . . .' He hesitated.

'Wing Commander Glaisop, if you decide to do nothing then I will be left to decide whether or not this situation is one which is affecting the good running of this camp. The decision is yours, or it is mine. I am offering you the choice. May I tell you what Muller has told me?'

'Do.'

So Von Mansdorff told him, and when he had Glaisop stood, excused himself, and made his way back to his quarters. On his way there he met a youngster called Chalmers, and, quite without thinking, he said to him, 'Tell Squadron Leader Jordaan I want to see him in my quarters immediately.'

Chalmers acknowledged the command before hurrying away, while Glaisop stood there, thinking how much he hated this situation into which he had been thrust. At school he had been aware of the sniggering, muted fumblings around him, but as he had grown he had come to know that all that boyish nonsense had nothing to do with homosexuality. This was different. The thought of grown men behaving as Von Mansdorff had suggested they were was hideous. In his room Glaisop looked at the photograph of his family frozen in its frame, and remembering, he became, momentarily, aware of the suspicion that the trappings of honour which sustained him day by day were only of his own making. My God, how he hated this war.

Maclachlan, the Scotsman to whom Von Mansdorff had spoken in sick-quarters – had been released and assigned to a bed in Jordaan's block. There was always an excitement in the arrival of a new man. But this man, still bandaged, was tired. Jordaan ushered away those who had gathered around Maclachlan's bed.

'What's your name?' Flash asked him.

The Scotsman, untrusting, had looked at him first, as though assessing Flash. When he had decided he said, 'Maclachlan, Flying Officer Maclachlan, sir.'

'My name's Jordaan. Don't worry about the sir.'

The man wriggled his body as though in agreement.

'How are you feeling?'

'Not too bad.'

'It's a bugger, being in the bag. I'm sorry.'

'It's not, sir. It's great. You should see it out there.'

'What do you mean?'

The Scotsman breathed deeply, almost displaying an impatience. 'Have you got a fag, sir?'

Jordaan produced a cigarette for the man, and when it had been lit for him, the Scotsman said, 'If you knew what a job I had getting in here, sir, you wouldn't say that.'

'Are you tired, Maclachlan? Would you rather I went away?'

'No, sir. It's all right. I'm all right.'

Flash, sitting by the man's lower bunk, wondered if perhaps the chap was in some state of mental confusion. But no, apparently Maclachlan wanted to talk; not to a huddle of them as had been there before, but to one person. 'Christ, it's great to be here in this bed. It's great to know they can't get at you.'

'Who?'

'Them out there . . . What Squadron were you in, sir?'

'I wasn't. They got me on my day off.'

Maclachlan turned his head, unable to understand.

'I was on seventy-six . . . It was the bloody stupid pilot who fucked us up . . .'

'What were you?'

'Navigator.'

Jordaan realized that it had not occurred to this man that there might be any other type of aircrew outside of Bomber Command. But he said nothing, and the man went on talking as though to himself, even when he asked Jordaan where he had bought it and Flash had told him. 'They hit us at Frankfurt, but it wasn't too bad . . . Maybe they hit him, but I told him, I told him to look out for Koblenz on the way out. We could see it, we could see the bloody place, but he went straight at it. You could see their searchlights. I told him . . . I kept on telling him, but he went straight at them. We were on fire, and they hit me. I was full of shrapnel and I couldn't see . . .'

The man was silent then, lying on his back and staring up at the bunk above him. Jordaan put a hand on his forehead. There could have been a slight fever, but nothing much. He waited, saying nothing.

'. . . When I hit the ground I could see, but there was nothing there in the darkness until I heard those fucking dogs. I don't know whether he got out or whether any of them got out. The bastard didn't deserve to . . . Maybe he was hit . . .'

Jordaan was wondering if he should get Del Renzio. Maybe he could get something from sick-quarters. But when the Scotsman started talking again he stayed.

'Christ, those dogs . . . I got out of my harness and just moved. Then I fell into the bloody water . . . I didn't know that dogs couldn't smell you in the bloody water. Did you know that?'

'Yes. I knew that.'

'I didn't. It wasn't deep, so I just went on. I didn't care if I drowned. I'd rather have drowned than have those bloody dogs get me.'

'What happened?'

'I was lucky. I was dead lucky . . . That's what I was. I was dizzy, though, and hellish sore . . . Couldn't hardly walk when I got myself out of that water. But I could still hear them and their dogs right until I got to the village. I think it was a village. If I hadn't knocked on the right door they'd have had me. I didn't know it was the right door. I was just so tired I couldn't go any further . . .'

'Why was it the right door?'

'There was a soldier there, a real soldier. He was home on leave, and it was his mother who opened the door to me. She was frightened. I remember that . . . She was frightened by the look of me. I must have been a helluva sight. He was a good lad, that. Gave me a drink before he called the right people. If the other lot with the dogs had got me, they'd have cut my balls off.'

Jordaan smiled.

'Even then they left the shrapnel in until they had finished interrogating me. God knows what I said to them. I was screamers . . . It was amazing. They knew the name of my Winco and the Flight Commanders. They even knew the name of the pub we usually drank in.' Maclachlan raised himself on one elbow. There was a puzzled expression on his face. 'How the hell would they know all that, sir?'

At that, little Chalmers, whom the Wing Commander had sent for Flash, was there. 'Wing Commander Glaisop wants you, Flash . . .'

'Really . . .'

'He said he wanted to see you immediately.'

'Fuck him . . . Right. Are you all right, Maclachlan? Is there anything you want?'

'I'm all right, sir. I'm just tired. I must be all right. They let me out, didn't they?'

'Of course . . . see you later.'

Glaisop was standing before the unlit stove in his room when Flash Jordaan entered. When he looked at Flash and nodded in acknowledgement of the other's salute there was nothing in his expression which conveyed the concern he was feeling. He asked Jordaan to sit down, and then he himself sat on the edge of the table he used as a desk.

'Trouble, sir?'

'Afraid so, Jordaan. I don't quite know how to put this. It's bloody awkward . . . I'm really asking for your help.' There was a dispassionate quality not only in Glaisop's voice but in his whole attitude which was probably the result of his years of training. He was capable of ignoring the fact that at their last meeting he had lost his temper with the South African. So now, in that calm, measured voice of his, he went on. 'Von Mansdorff tells me that two of our chaps are indulging in homosexual acts . . .'

'Oh, Christ . . .' Jordaan laughed. 'You mean Mr and Mrs Templeweed . . . Everyone knows about them.'

'Come now, Jordaan. This is not a laughing matter.'

'I know that . . . But I'm afraid I don't particularly care what people do with their bodies – providing they don't annoy me with them.'

'Come, man . . . You know very well that Templeweed and his friend – by the way. Who is his friend?'

'We call it Lilly Langtry.'

'What's his real name?'

'Torrance . . . A wireless operator from Coastal Command. Perhaps they pick up sailor's habits.'

Glaisop resisted a smile. 'They'd be drummed out of the Service in normal circumstances.'

Flash lit a cigarette. 'We can't very well drum them out of this place.'

'No, that's true.' And at that Glaisop did smile. 'But the ball's in our court. Von Mansdorff told me that if we don't do something about sorting this thing out, he will.'

Jordaan's eyebrows came down at the corners as he seemed to swing himself to his feet. 'What's he going to do about his own men?'

'What do you mean?'

'I mean that there are bloody few stiff upper lips outside

of this room – in this camp that is. There are all kinds of nut cases in here – and every day they get worse. Man, think of the situation they're in. All the basketball and football and endlessly repetitive lectures won't change them. All these poor bastards can do is hope this bloody war will be over and they'll get out before every one of them goes stark raving mad. These two, Templeweed and his friend, have at least provided comic relief.'

'But you say they're involved with the enemy. Why wasn't I informed?'

'No one – certainly not I – can prove that. I said what I said because of certain observations I've made. I've noticed little things. If I'd told you, what the hell could you have done?'

Glaisop walked slowly across the room. Then he turned, looked through the dusty windows and started to fill his pipe. Jordaan waited. There was nothing more he was about to say then. But when the pipe was lit to his satisfaction, Glaisop said, 'It makes sense. When Mansdorff told me what his man Muller had said I couldn't understand how they would be able to use an empty cookhouse for their . . . their goings on. But if Germans are involved, that would explain it. Wouldn't it? Don't you think so, Jordaan?' Glaisop spoke as though he was glad to be clutching at something.

It was obviously essential that Von Mansdorff be told immediately of this new development. Glaisop's blood was up, for to him there was something like satisfaction in the prospect of some of Mansdorff's men being involved in the mess. No caution such as Jordaan was for once suggesting was acceptable. No, Von Mansdorff would be told immediately – by them both.

'But it's only a suspicion on my part.'

'I realize that, Jordaan, but in a situation such as this I trust your judgement.'

'What!'

'I . . . I mean . . . that in some things you're probably more worldly than I am.'

Von Mansdorff was at his most urbane when they entered his office displaying the strictest formality.

'Gentlemen, how nice to see you. It's such pleasant surprises that make life in this place bearable.'

Standing alongside the Wing Commander, Jordaan couldn't resist it. He said, 'Or unbearable.'

Von Mansdorff's one workable eyebrow shot up. He looked from one to the other with the lower part of his face as expressionless as a battleground could be. 'Why are you here?'

Glaisop spoke. 'It's regarding the matter we spoke of this afternoon. Squadron Leader Jordaan here has acquainted me with certain aspects of the situation with which perhaps you are not aware.'

Von Mansdorff's head leant forward and to his left. 'Really . . .'

'Jordaan, perhaps you had better tell the Major of your suspicions.'

Jordaan looked to Glaisop, then to the man behind the desk. For some reason in the moment before he spoke, Flash was suddenly aware of the German's elegance. The comparison with the appearance of himself and the Wing Commander momentarily toppled him. There was a hesitance when he spoke. He was conscious of his own vulnerability. 'I suspect, Herr Major, that some of your own people are involved.'

'Germans are involved . . .?'

Glaisop broke in. 'How else would this business be

taking place on the premises you mentioned? It occurred to me when you told me.'

Von Mansdorff's face darkened. 'Sit down, gentlemen, sit down.'

'You realize I'm basing these suspicions only on observations I have made throughout the past months. It's . . . It's pure speculation.' Jordaan felt almost sorry for the man opposite him.

Von Mansdorff raised himself in his chair, breathing deeply. He was silent for some time. Then he leant his chin forward into his good hand, his only hand. He stood to slap his desk. 'These observations . . . No, no, no . . . I know what you mean. My God, I'll gut this thing. I'll tear the entrails out of their filthy performances . . . Pour me a cognac, Jordaan. Pour yourself one.'

When Flash went to the drink, he turned to the Wing Commander. 'You, sir?'

Glaisop shook his head.

'Do you mind if I . . .?'

Glaisop shrugged.

'Excuse me, gentlemen. Excuse me. I must attend to this.' Hurriedly, when he had swallowed the drink Jordaan had poured for him, Von Mansdorff swept from the room. The man's anger seemed to have gripped him.

Flash poured himself another brandy as he said, 'The cat's among the pigeons.'

'Watch that stuff, Jordaan.'

'I will, sir. Have one?'

'Thank you. I will.'

They were having yet another when Von Mansdorff slammed back into the room. 'Right, gentlemen. Everything is arranged. At seven we strike. Which of you, or are both of you going to join me?'

Glaisop said, 'Jordaan will be with you.'

Flash Jordaan's flesh squirmed when he saw the targets of their invasion. The blood seemed to rise towards his throat, almost choking him, but in moments when they were being dragged away Von Mansdorff in a voice held tightly in his grip, said, 'A drink, Squadron Leader?'

6

For Flash Jordaan the pattern of his existence was becoming smudged by the erosion of month after month in that place. Twice in the year he had been there he had escaped, and twice they had brought him back. Then there had been on each occasion the initial sinking of hope, but it had been relieved by the lingering sense of challenge which each adventure had brought. He had swash-buckled again. He had been able he felt, in his way, to help those others who had seemed to be so very lost. But now he was tiring, and in spite of the huddle of all those around him he felt himself to be increasingly lonely.

Perhaps the feelings within him were aroused by what he saw of the others. It was strange, he often reflected, how those men who within their own squadrons had seemed to be sustained by such a sense of camaraderie should now in this situation be so different.

When each man arrived he was delighted to be with his own kind, but gradually when the relief at being alive was over, they seemed anxious to hide within whatever individuality they had. Even the jokers were in the main left to laugh at their own jokes.

Only the rough scramblings of their football matches and the thudding of their energies against each other seemed to bring any kind of relief. Jordaan himself, as he did every morning, had just emerged from a shower after completing twenty circuits of the exercise yard when he flopped down where Charles Seymour, the tall, languid young man who had been reading Medieval History at Oxford was drinking tea as he read a Penguin edition of 'The Quest for Corvo'.

'Can I have a mouthful of that?'

'If you've got a cup,' Seymour said in his slow, drawling voice. He didn't look up.

Flash returned with a tin mug, and Seymour, with only the most casual glance at the thing, poured some tea. 'There's only tea,' he said.

'That's fine.'

Jordaan tasted the tea and winced. 'What you reading?'

Seymour held up the book.

'Never heard of it. What's this stuff you're writing?'

'My second novel.'

'What happened to the first one?'

Without changing the blankness of his expression, Seymour said, 'It's under my bed.'

Flash lit a cigarette. It was of a German variety which he had been given by Von Mansdorff. 'You mean you're prepared to go on and on writing just to put it all under your bed . . .'

'It's better to live in a world of your own than to live in this one . . . I intend to take it all with me when I get out of this place.'

Jordaan looked at the long, almost gaunt face of Seymour whose hair was constantly falling over his eyes, so that the continual act of sweeping it away had begun to resemble something like a nervous twitch. 'Get out of this place?'

'If I can. I want to be in at the kill when we invade France.'

'In Hurry Bombers like before?'

'If possible.' Seymour smiled. 'It'll be one of the great battles of history, and fundamentally I'm an historian.'

Looking at him Flash believed him. Within the quietness of this young man there was desire, so to hide the confusion he felt at having mis-read Seymour he said quickly, 'Hear we have a new intake arriving.'

'Bomber Command. They're stepping up the pressure. We'll be having lots of them.'

'There'll be no room.'

'They'll probably stretch the place. They'll make room.'

'Probably.'

On his bunk, when he had changed into his old battledress, Flash lay with one hand behind his neck, the other stroking at the blond moustache without realizing he was doing so. He was thinking about what Seymour had said about living in a world of his own. But the boy had not been quite right. In fact he was getting his own world *out*. Flash knew he couldn't do that himself. Everything stayed within him until he battered it out.

Into his mind from long ago there leapt an image of himself. He liked remembering things, and he liked pinpointing a memory in its exact position in time. Would he be sixteen or seventeen? Perhaps he was just about to be seventeen. He was on the farm on which his father had settled when he had pulled out of Northern Rhodesia and moved south to the Northern Transvaal.

God it had been good to be there, even with the old man as he had been. He was remembering as he lay there the day on which old Mawli, his father's man from better days, was holding the roped and bare-backed little Arab pony he loved while he was trying to leap on its restless back as he had seen Hollywood Indians do on the movies. Three times the horse had slid him over, until Mawli was pained with laughter. 'Little man, little man . . . you make him frightened. He thinks you're gonna hurt him.

He's not that kinda horse. This is a special kinda
You know that, little man.'

It was just about then that they heard the shot
inside the house. Flash could remember his fear. Then there had been two, three more shots.

'Don't worry, little man. He hasn't killed himself. There would only have been one bullet.'

Flash remembered leaping from the horse and running into the house with old Mawli following him. He had burst into the big room on the ground floor, and somehow he could still hear the crash of his boots on the polished wooden floor. It was a place littered with the remnant trophies of his father's life.

'For Christ's sake . . . for Christ's sake, dad, what have you done?'

His father's dead head, open-mouthed, a pulped mess on one side, lolled lamely. A rifle had slipped across his body. On the wall above the fireplace the portrait of old Gus, his grandfather; he who was so proud of his fight against the British at Majuba Hill, was shattered in its frame, as though the likeness was itself a victim.

But brush away all that for Millie Gordon. With the thought of her his body still tingled. Millie of the thighs, and the long, sun-washed hair. Oh, Christ, to reach for her again.

She had been the wife of old Findlay Gordon; he in his sixties, she about thirty. Her husband had been neighbour to his father and old Gus. Flash's brow wrinkled with the thought that she must have been watching him growing, waiting for him. Almost every day he had ridden with her across the low veldt which had no boundaries. On a horse she was a fury of a woman. Even his Arab was no match for the big black stallion she rode so intensely.

He remembered the blazing day when she had come

near to frightening him. He had been standing at the paddock gate, waiting for her, when she had ridden at him to halt in a slither of dust and then slip from the lathered, quivering beast. 'There's such life in him,' she gasped. 'I love him.'

That must have been the day when there had been a beginning between them. Old Findlay had taken to spending a great deal of his time in Pretoria, but inevitably there had come the day when he wasn't where he should have been, and, lying there on that bed, Flash suddenly laughed at himself and the memory of scuttling bare-arsed from the stable as the old man lashed out at him with a rhino whip. Somehow he had made his way to his friend Bobby Wardroop's place, and it was then, after he had soaked himself in the big wooden tub in Wardroop's father's yard, that they had decided to make their way north. After all, it had been in the north that old Gus had made the fortune he had eventually lost.

Van Reine said, 'What's funny?'

'I was laughing at me.'

'You're right. That's funny.'

'No . . .' Flash shook his head, still smiling. 'I was thinking of the first woman I ever had. She was a helluva woman.'

'Woman . . . How could she be a woman?'

'She was. She was about thirty . . . I was about seventeen maybe . . .'

'You were lucky . . . Mine was a girl, but come to think of it,' the Dutchman mused, 'maybe she was a woman too. She said a very strange thing to me which it took me years to figure out. She was English. The English are a funny lot.'

'English?'

'I was in England as part of my pilot training – in

Bournemouth . . . It was in a park in Bournemouth . . . Summer it was.'

'It's always summer in parks. You hold hands in winter.'

'No . . .' The big Dutchman's throat rumbled in pleasure at the memory. 'No, Flash, I had done all the Protestant things . . . I really thought I had done all the things, but I hadn't. She was the first woman I ever really had known.'

'What do you mean?'

'Knew, I mean knew.'

There was a quickness in Jordaan's reactions which could confuse people. He used it then. 'You mean you loved her?'

'The only woman I ever really loved I think was my mother, and I'm not so sure about that . . . Shut up, Jordaan, for Christ's sake! I'm telling you a story about *me*.' Then Van Reine laughed. 'Do you know what she said?'

'How can I, idiot? What did she say?'

'Hah! When I didn't know what was happening to me, and it was all about to happen, she pulled me closer to her and said, 'It's all right, darling . . . I can't have babies . . . Neither could mummy.'

'What?'

'It took me years to figure that one out.'

'She was adopted.'

'That's right. Her name was Snowina McCann.'

'I don't believe it.'

'It's true.'

There was a movement towards roll-call. No one announced anything; no bell rang. It was as though through the steady rhythm of their days there was something to which they responded without thought.

Von Mansdorff was there, making his major appearance of the day. If anything his presence was somewhat more solid than it had been when he had first arrived. His health undoubtedly was improving. But perhaps only Jordaan, and maybe, Del Renzio and Van Reine, knew something of the true state of the man's morale.

The bar in the dining hall which the Commandant had installed had been a great success with the inmates. Even Wing Commander Glaisop had been forced to agree with Von Mansdorff that there was less tension in the atmosphere of the camp – although he had only visited the place once in the couple of months it had been open. But Von Mansdorff was frequently seen there; once indeed with old Muller and the two other aging subalterns who were under his command. That had not been a happy idea. Von Mansdorff's Germans had been embarrassed, perhaps because they thought the occasional laughter of the English was directed at them, and as they stiffened, unable to leave until they were dismissed, the English themselves had gradually drifted away until only Jordaan and Del Renzio, Van Reine and a couple of Irishmen were left.

Perhaps that occasion had been the beginning of the sense of separation Flash had begun to feel from those he had known longest. Mathers, the Fleet Air Arm man and little Chippy Carpenter, even they seemed to exhibit a certain coolness towards him.

At first he had imagined himself to be going 'stir-happy', but when he began to notice that many days would pass before Glaisop would address him directly he became certain that they were placing him in isolation. Confirmation came when Glaisop summoned Flash to his quarters.

The decision had obviously been arrived at with some

difficulty on the Wing Commander's part. As always there was the unlit pipe, but now, when Jordaan entered, Glaisop stayed still for some moments at the window with his back to the door. When he turned to the South African there was something more than the customary seriousness in his expression. The heavy brows were drawn together; the mouth, before it opened, was set in a line hard enough to suggest that he was chewing on his teeth. When he spoke his voice had hoarsened. 'Jordaan, there's no point in beating about the bush. I'm concerned.' He halted there, as though finding it difficult to say what he was concerned about.

'About what, sir?'

'About all this damned fraternization with those Germans.'

'Fraternization . . .'

'Yes, just that! I can tell you that a lot of the chaps don't like it. And I don't like it . . . In fact I forbid it.'

'On what grounds?'

'On . . . On the grounds that as a serving officer of the Royal Air Force, your first duty in this place is to escape. That's your first duty, Jordaan – not to fraternize with those bloody Germans.'

Jordaan felt peculiarly calm as he said, 'I have done – twice. How do you know I'm not planning to escape again?'

'You know perfectly well that all escape attempts have to be approved by the escape committee. Mathers is head of that Committee . . . You've submitted nothing to him.'

Flash ignored that. He had no plan for escape. Instead, he said, 'When I was shot down in Northern France, the chap who shot me down had lunch with me – after a great many drinks. I found them a most convivial bunch. Was that fraternization? Should I have refused to drink with them just because they were lucky enough to have shot me down?'

'Quite different . . . You were simply responding to a front line squadron's hospitality.'

'I would say that from the look of him Von Mansdorff is a front line soldier.'

'The situation is entirely different, I tell you. You are a prisoner of war.'

Jordaan smiled, and that smile must have irritated the other man. 'I can tell you, I was very much aware of being a prisoner of war when I had lunch with that bunch.'

They looked hard at each other until Glaisop said, 'Jordaan, if you choose to join issue with me, I'll break you. This war won't last forever you know.'

'Let's hope not . . . Let's hope we win.'

'By God, *you* won't.' Glaisop was angry now. 'I'll see to that when I get the chance.'

'Is that all, sir?'

'For now, Jordaan. For now.'

More than a week passed before Flash told his friends Del Renzio and Van Reine what had happened with Glaisop. He had been troubled by what the Wing Commander had said. The imputation that they were labelling him as some kind of traitor was something that his sense of self-mockery could not quite cope with. The three of them were drinking during the opening hour of the bar, and they had been doing so for most of that hour's duration when Van Reine said to them, 'Is there something wrong with us? I have the feeling that these little boys are avoiding us.'

Del Renzio stifled a laugh, and as he did so Jordaan was about to tell them what had happened between himself and Glaisop when Von Mansdorff walked in. The German surveyed them with something of a proprietorial air as he approached the bar. A big Irishman called Fahy was the fourth of their group.

'Good evening, gentlemen.'

'Good evening.'

'How is the beer?'

'Good . . . all right.'

It was Del Renzio who said he couldn't stand beer. But he wasn't complaining; he wasn't complaining, he was quick to add. Von Mansdorff, and then, when he had a beer served to him by the Englishman who was acting as duty barman, he turned to Jordaan. 'Our chess game,' he said, 'has been static for almost two weeks now . . . Should we resume it this evening?'

Flash smiled, but there was hesitation in his expression.

'No?' Von Mansdorff turned to the others. 'Your friend is quite good, but I think he's afraid that he'll be shot down again.'

To cover his thinking, Flash drank slowly from the tankard he was holding. He appeared to ignore the others as they made their comments. 'Go on, Flash. Keep the side up.' Del Renzio laughed and came in to say, 'The Major is our host. You mustn't . . . What is it you say? . . . You mustn't be churlish.'

'That's true,' the Irishman offered. 'And you might get a decent drink as well.'

Flash looked at them, his friends, and then at Von Mansdorff. He waited for a moment until the acting barman had receded, and then he said, 'I don't think the Wing Commander approves of what he calls fraternization . . . He wants to go on fighting the war without any weapons . . . In fact I know he doesn't approve. He told me.'

Del Renzio laughed. 'What about us? We've had a drink with the Major here.'

Jordaan's eyes turned to the Italian. 'You don't count. You're wogs . . . Paddy doesn't count. He's an Irishman.'

'The bastard!' Fahy gulped down some more beer. 'If it wasn't for the Irish there'd be no bloody Air Force.'

'Well hardly, Paddy.' Jordaan was still examining in his mind the situation in which he was finding himself.

'It's a bloody fact. What about Finnucane?'

'That's what I mean. Hasn't he killed himself?'

'So . . .' Von Mansdorff ordered some more beer. 'Our game of chess has come to an end.'

Jordaan's expression was troubled, thoughtful; uncharacteristic of anything they had seen him display before. 'No,' he said suddenly, 'I'll carry on with our game.'

'When?'

'Tonight if you like.'

When he was seated opposite Von Mansdorff in the latter's quarters, Flash played with as much concentration as he could gather. The room had changed since the Major had first arrived. Photographs of his family decorated the walls, and, dominating the place, was a watercolour showing the edge of a lake with behind a long, rolling parkland half-screening the outline of a house. The house appeared to be large, and faithful in its outline to the Teutonic tradition. It was Von Mansdorff's move, but he was aware of his opponent looking at the picture. 'That's where I grew up. It is the house of my family. I was very happy there as a boy. My father threw me out . . . But maybe I'm allowed back now. Don't know. Maybe I don't want to go. You like this cognac?'

'Mm. Splendid.'

'A man who served with me in France is now butler at a shooting lodge which the Reichsmarshal keeps near here. He gets it for me . . . The Reichsmarshal no doubt got it in France as one of the fruits of our victory . . . But wait . . . wait, Jordaan. I also have some of the Reichsmarshal's champagne – which is splendidly victorious fruit. Nineteen thirty-six. Very good year. We'll have some . . . We'll make cocktails.'

When Von Mansdorff had left the room, Flash was able to appreciate the changes the German had made. Gone was the stark issue furniture which had once been there, and in its place were pieces which suggested a heavy comfort. Somewhat lush perhaps for Flash's own taste, but welcome in that place.

Flash stood before a gilt-framed photograph of a young woman which had been placed on the desk the Commandant had acquired. Loose ash blonde hair, flecked with something lighter, framed eyes which in the black and white picture appeared to be grey. The head was held in charm above a strong aristocratic neck.

Von Mansdorff re-entered with an enormous bottle of champagne. 'You like her?'

'Your sister?'

'My cousin . . . That's Ilse . . . I've been in love with her all my life. She's married to an Italian Duke. He's a good idiot; quite funny . . . Totally unworthy of her. Jordaan, open this. I no longer can. It's one of the things for which I'll never forgive the Russians.' He held out the bottle.

There is a certain exhilaration to be had from looking at a glassful of champagne spiked with a decent brandy. They both felt it as they held up their glasses. Von Mansdorff said, 'We should drink to Reichsmarshal Goering . . . But no. You can't do that. I will.' As he held up his glass he smiled and said, 'God bless the fat man's forethought.'

'And God bless his butler.' Flash said it, and at that they laughed before they drank.

'Aah . . . Splendid. It must be an essential aspect of German policy to keep the French happy. A nation which makes such champagne can't be all bad . . . You like Ilse?'

'She is very beautiful.'

'I know. She is the only woman who has ever made me feel utterly alone. Why is that, Jordaan?'

'Maybe because she reminds you that we are all alone. Maybe that is the meaning of loving someone.'

'Christ, I hope not.'

'It could be, Rudi.'

'You call me Rudi.'

'It's the champagne.'

Von Mansdorff seemed to swell with pleasure. 'Ah, Jordaan, how good it would be to be out of this place. War, I don't mind. Even with all its stupidities you are part of an overall purpose. Before I joined the Wehrmacht I had never known that . . . But here – this is a place for hiding. I must get out . . . I must get out. I will go to Berlin and shake that damned brother of mine by the neck until he does something.'

'Your brother . . . What does he do?'

'He's a decoration at Luftwaffe Headquarters . . . Did quite well in Spain I think, but nothing since . . . He's clever, my brother – loathfully clever. Oberst, The Graf Von Mansdorff. He knows them all.'

Flash, confident now in the company of this man, touched up his glass and proffered the bottle to Von Mansdorff. 'I had great fun in Berlin.'

'You know Berlin?'

'Well, I spent six weeks there once with a friend of mine . . . Great fun. Helluva place in those days.'

Von Mansdorff was amused. 'When was this?'

'Thirty-six, thirty-seven.' Flash's head drooped as he

thought of himself and Wardroop. Bobby was dead now. The big hunk had killed himself in a Tiger Moth. It was the only death Flash Jordaan had ever really cared about. Not that the hurt itself had been so great. Even in those early days most of them had been steeled for that: more it was a feeling of shocked surprise that big Bobby was no longer there.

'You were on holiday in Berlin?' There was a light curiosity in Von Mansdorff's voice. 'Here, man, drink.'

Flash went on to tell of how he had got himself with Wardroop to Berlin. He told of their leaving home, and when he digressed to tell of the immediate reason for his leaving, Von Mansdorff heaved with laughter until he was wiping his good eye with a sleeve.

'You used whips in those copper mines?'

'Well, we cracked them. Sometimes we used them. We were gangers. That was our job . . . Bloody hard work. We sweated when we were in those damned mines. But it strengthened us. It taught us not to turn our backs on any bastard – black or white. But none of it mattered: we had a goal. We knew why we were there.'

The German laughed. 'To get away from that old husband.'

'No, no . . . To get ourselves five hundred pounds each and get ourselves to Europe.'

'And you did.'

'That's right. It was Cairo first, and then we picked up a boat in Alex and worked our way to England. I remember London seemed to bore us. It was full of things and no people . . . Well, millions of them, but they all seemed to be the same person, someone we didn't know. It was Paris and Rome and Vienna and Berlin for us: that's where we went. We had a helluva time. But Berlin bust us. Jesus, I had never imagined such goings on were possible with the human race. A zoo would have been more acceptable to the kind of people I knew at home. But we loved it for a time. When we got back to England we were flat broke – penniless, not a dinar between us.'

Flash laughed at the recollection. 'We went to South Africa House and tried to get ourselves signed on for the maiden voyage of the Queen Mary, but they told us that the Queen Mary was full of bums like us. All they could do was get us into the Air Force – with a brush in our hands.' Flash looked up at Von Mansdorff. 'So here I am.'

'What about your friend?'

'He was killed in training.'

For some long moments Von Mansdorff looked at Flash. 'You know,' he said eventually, 'your story is very similar to mine. You liked being in the Royal Air Force?'

'As far as I know, I'm still in it.'

'Of course.'

'. . . I can't imagine doing anything else. For me there is nothing else. There never will be. I love this war.'

'But for you, Jordaan, the war is over.'

'No, no, no.' Flash stood to help himself to some more wine.

'Stick some cognac in it.'

'Good idea . . . You?'

Von Mansdorff nodded as Flash went on to say with some enthusiasm, 'The war isn't over for me. When we've beaten you, there'll be the Japanese to beat. Christ, man, there'll be enough work to keep me going for years.'

'Hah . . .' At that the German was much amused. 'You are very funny. You are very funny, Jordaan. I like you . . . I really do like you.'

They drank on and they talked on. More champagne was opened, and the talk became a mélange of their experiences, which, as Von Mansdorff had said, were remarkably complementary. Mansdorff told of his wanderings after being sent down from Oxford, without bitterness. Perhaps it was that, the man's capacity for laughing at his own youthful foolishness, which drew Flash towards a sympathy for him. Somewhere in that evening – perhaps it had been when Flash had been talking about old Gus, his grandfather who had fought the British at Majuba Hill – Von Mansdorff had leapt to his feet with gusto. 'Jordaan, you're a mercenary. Do you realize that? You're a mercenary.' Then a serious blankness replaced his expression.

'I'm an officer in the Royal Air Force.'

'Quiet . . . wait! Flash, think . . . wait!'

'I think I'd better get to bed.'

'Hold on – wait! Flash, think of this . . . It's the one guaranteed way we have of getting out of this place . . .'

Flash shook his head and laughed. 'Are you going to give me a pass?'

'Wait, wait . . . Think . . . This could get you out of this place – and it could get me out too. This idea could get me out, Flash. Flash, why don't you fly for the Luftwaffe?'

'Major, you're drunk. We're both drunk. We have to be.'

Von Mansdorff, talking all the time with enthusiasm of his idea, walked Flash back to his hut. At that time of night it was necessary.

7

Flash made his way through the heavy smell of their sleeping bodies to the cubicle which he occupied at the far corner of the hut. He tried for a time to think of the ridiculous suggestion Von Mansdorff had made, but it was impossible against the weight of the drink he had taken.

But in the morning as he washed and ate and exercised, the words of the Commandant were still beating in his brain like a pulse. So it was all through that day, and for days following. He heard the voices of the others, but only one voice was reaching through to him, and it was saying, '*Why don't you fly for the Luftwaffe?*'

Of course the whole idea was a nonsense; unthinkable. Once or twice Del Renzio tried to draw him on the question of what was troubling him, but he would say nothing until in the end Del Renzio left it to the possibility that he was suffering from the periodic fits of depression which attacked all of them from time to time.

And in a way Del Renzio was right, for alongside the troublesome words Von Mansdorff had spoken, there was in Flash Jordaan a despair which recurred more and more. There was not only in him a need, as it were, to shake the bars of his cage; there was lying low in his gut an ugly residue. It would have been so easy, as so many of them seemed prepared to do, to say to himself, 'It's over; for me it's over.' In that place, by the simple process of doing nothing except wait, a man could stay alive, but life for Flash was something which whipped through his nostrils and lusted in his veins. He had grown that way, strong and running, alive with the smells and sounds and quickness of those other creatures who had shared his father's land. He could even remember the smell of his own earth. But for him there was something else: he was drawn towards a death which he couldn't believe to be his. Someone else would die, as his friend, Wardroop, had died. But not he. He would flirt with it, cheat it if necessary, but it would not claim him yet. Death was in the far distance.

In the evenings in those days he was less and less inclined to visit the bar they had labelled 'Chez Mansdorff'. Not only was he becoming more and more aware of the rejection offered by so many of the others – and in any case that was not something which particularly troubled him – but more necessary was the need to think through this notion of Von Mansdorff's.

Had the man been serious? Or was the idea something which had come out of the drunken ramblings they had been indulging in and was now forgotten by the German? In those late spring evenings he would walk endlessly around the compound trying to reduce the problem to its essentials. Again and again he hammered at it all. Already he had escaped twice, and after recapture on the second occasion when they had dragged him almost unconscious and rotten in his own waste from under the coal in that railway waggon which unfortunately had been travelling east instead of west, they had threatened to shoot him if he attempted to repeat the performance.

To take the problems in their order of precedence, surely the first to be solved was that of getting out of the damned camp. If Von Mansdorff had meant what he said, and if such a thing were possible, that could certainly be a way of staying out. Once out, it might be possible to make some kind of plan for himself: then anything might be possible. But if it weren't, and if he had in fact to fly for the Luftwaffe, could he do that? Von Mansdorff had said he was a mercenary. Was he? He was a South African who had flown with the British Air Force, and was now a prisoner of the Germans. His own people had fought the British; his grandfather had fought them, and his father had fought for them. What the hell did it all mean? Had he ever felt hatred for any of those Germans he had killed? Never. He had been one man trying to kill and survive. The killing was a consequence of what he had been trained to do.

Sometimes at night, Flash, in his imagination could fly again. Sometimes, looking into a glass, it was easy again to feel the thread of power in his hands and experience that mysterious lifting of the spirit which is known only to those who fly alone and know the freedom filled with threat which is in all that sky that never embraces as does the cloying realities of the earth. There was something like real pain in those imaginings. By the time he knew the need to speak to Del Renzio again the urge to be away and flying was close to the edge of obsession.

'I thought you'd given up drinking,' Del Renzio said when he joined him. Del Renzio was standing alone at the bar.

'Ach, this place . . . Where's Van Reine?'

'He and Paddy are having a bath. They think it's the best time to have one – when the bar's open . . . I think it's a waste of good drinking time.'

When Flash said nothing, the Italian asked him, 'What's wrong?'

Flash looked around. There were now three other people at the bar. 'Let's sit down. Do you mind?'

'What the hell's the matter with you, Flash?'

Flash picked up his drink and moved to an empty table close by a window. The Italian followed. 'Christ, Flash, what's the matter with you?'

Jordaan raised a hand to silence him. 'I want to talk to you – I need your advice.' His eyes wandered around the room. 'Have you noticed how unpopular we've become? Glaisop's right. This lot seem to think we've joined the other side.'

'What other side?'

'The Germans you fool.'

'Ah hah . . . But my lot joined them a long time ago.'

'Don't think they don't know it.'

Jordaan looked hard at the darkly handsome face of his friend. If someone hadn't broken Del Renzio's nose at some stage, his features would have been too regular. 'Tony . . .' Even then, at the brink of confidentiality, there was the question of whether he could trust anyone in that place.

'What's wrong, my friend?' Del Renzio lightened his voice. 'Don't tell me. I know . . . You've fallen for one of those blokes you saw being clobbered a couple of weeks ago.'

'Oh, shut up.'

'Well, then, tell me.'

Flash looked away from his friend's face towards nothing in particular. Beneath the moustache, his lips were tightened.

'Tell me, Flash. Why do they call you Flash?'

'It was my father's old black servant who called me that. Wardroop picked it up from him, and he brought it with us to the Air Force . . . Tony, Von Mansdorff said a crazy thing to me the other night.' At that he paused.

'Was he drunk?'

'Yes.'

'But he drinks well.'

'That's true . . . He suggested he could get me out of here if I joined the Luftwaffe.'

Del Renzio's voice was steady. 'Why would he say a thing like that?'

'Tony, Von Mansdorff feels as badly as we do about being in this place – maybe worse. It's an offence to everything he values and has come to believe in . . . this place, doing the kind of job he's doing now . . . This notion of his sounds pretty weird, but if you think about it, it's not so stupid. If he could get someone to defect, it might get *him* out. That's what he's after. If he pulled it off, Tony, at least it might remind someone that he was still around.'

'Von Mansdorff's problem is that he's only got one arm and one eye.' The Italian spoke as though he were thinking into himself.

'But you must agree. He has something of an idea.'

Del Renzio nodded. 'Would you do it?'

'That's what's been bothering me for days.'

'You haven't seen our man since . . .'

'No.' Flash sipped slowly from his glass before saying, 'Would you, Tony?'

The Italian shrugged. 'I'm different. I owe less allegiance to the British than to the hole in my arse. There are those who would say now that I'm a traitor . . . Do you realize, Flash, that the regiment in which I grew up is fighting the British now?'

'Of *course*. Of course they are. But what about Spain?'

'Spain . . .' Del Renzio smiled thoughtfully. 'Flash, as a young man in the smartest regiment in the Italian – cavalry that is – I had a family that was rich. It still is, as far as I know. Don't forget we were Badoglio's own regiment. That was why he wanted us in Abyssinia when he was appointed Commander in Chief there. I just refused to slaughter those poor black bastards.'

'Why hadn't you joined the Air Force?'

Del Renzio laughed. 'Socially unacceptable. So is yours. I could afford to fly privately . . . Flash, I became one of the best aerobatic pilots in Italy, and, believe me, my friend, that's saying something . . . So, if some character comes along when you're broke and working as a barman in Casablanca, you listen to him. You take the money. That's what Spain was all about.'

The long, bare room in which they were sitting was filling now with some of the newer faces; younger, different faces. There seemed to be an earnestness in the expressions of those Bomber Command people who were beginning to join them in such numbers. It was something Flash Jordaan couldn't remember in those he had flown with. He looked up quickly. 'Another drink?'

'I'll get it.' The Italian moved to get up.

'Tony . . .' Flash gripped the other's forearm. 'Tony, would you do this thing Mansdorff's suggested?'

'Of course I bloody would.'

It was some days later that Del Renzio came to Flash with the news that Von Mansdorff wanted to see him in the Commandant's quarters that evening.

'Are you sure?'

'*Yes*. There I was happily brewing a tubful of Del Renzio's hundred proof ginny gin when the bastard suddenly appeared. Mother of God, I died, Flash.'

'What did he say?'

'Nothing. All he said was that I should tell my friend Jordaan to be at his place this evening. That was all he said . . . He went away. I couldn't believe it.'

Later, when Jordaan presented himself at the Commandant's quarters, Von Mansdorff appeared to be in great form. When the orderly had shown Flash in and had left, the German swung around, beaming. 'Ah, Flash . . . good to see you. I have news for you. But tell me, tell me first if you have thought of the idea we had that night.'

Flash nodded. He was unsmiling, for even as he entered that room he could not fully embrace the enormity of the plan Von Mansdorff had suggested. He looked hard at Von Mansdorff standing there, almost glittering in that uniform of his. For a moment there was a feeling close to inadequacy.

'Have some schnapps, my friend . . . This is excellent schnapps.' Von Mansdorff held out the neat little glass, and Flash drank from it quickly. 'Another?'

'No . . . No thanks. Not now . . . I'll have a glass of your beer.'

'Good. Sit down, Flash.' Flash sat while his host remained standing. '. . . I have been thinking a great deal . . . Before you say anything let me tell you that I have been thinking a great deal. I am aware, Jordaan, of the difficulty there is in this plan of mine – for you that is.' Von Mansdorff poured himself another drink. 'But I think you should remember that many men have changed sides in wars. Many men.' He laughed quietly. 'It is even said that the Russian General, Timoshenko, is an Irishman, Tim O'Shea, who deserted from the Dublin Fuseliers at Archangel in nineteen nineteen.'

Flash stood and took a couple of quick paces away from the fireplace without a pause. 'It's not the rightness or the wrongness that I think really bothers me. It's more that I don't think I've ever made a decision in my life. I didn't leave home – I fled. I hadn't thought of joining the Royal Air Force . . . If Wardroop and I had been able to get a job on the Queen Mary, we'd probably have jumped ship in the States and taken a look around there. You see, I've never really made a decision in my life. I've simply reacted to a set of circumstances.'

Von Mansdorff dusted the empty left sleeve of his tunic. It had become a habit of his; something of a nervous tick. 'If, Jordaan, you were to do the thing I'm suggesting – if I could make it possible that is – wouldn't that be exactly what you'd be doing, reacting to circumstances? Look at it, man: the present prospect is that you'll rot in a Godforsaken hole like this for years. If Germany wins – and if you look at the facts that must be more than a possibility . . . Flash, we're now in the first half of forty-two; the finest Army in the world controls all of Europe – with England snapping at its heels like some little terrier dog . . . All right, the Russian climate has made things more difficult than had been planned. But, I tell you; I've been there – they will crack. It may take time, but we will crush them.' Von Mansdorff's enthusiasm was taking flight. 'Are your South Africans fighting in Europe? No. Are they fighting with enthusiasm in North Africa? No. And your friends, your Italian friend – are his people fighting in Russia? Yes! And the Dutchman: his people – yes! Even your Irishman, Fahy . . . We have his people there. Are you aware, Jordaan, that we have something called the Britannia Legion deployed in Russia . . . Not that they're first rate troops, but they're there.'

'I'll go.'

Jordaan spoke quietly. And the words slipped out so easily that he didn't feel himself uttering them.

Von Mansdorff smiled; the eye gleamed, and as the skin around his mouth folded there was a handsomeness in his expression which was unique. 'Now I will tell you my good news – I am going to see my brother in Berlin. And I will tell you more.' Von Mansdorff paused, like a man waiting to strike with the maximum effect. 'Since we talked that night I have expanded my idea considerably. What I am going to propose in Berlin is not that you, one lone Royal Air Force fighter pilot, defect to the Luftwaffe. I am going to propose, my friend, that you lead an entire Squadron of ex-British fighter pilots against the Russians. Do you hear? *Against the Russians.* There – if it troubles your conscience to fight against the British, fight against the Russians. Do you hear? Against the *Russians*. It will be the greatest propaganda stroke of the war. Hah! You think so? How . . . how about that? Let's drink to my genius. I'm a genius, Flash.'

Flash smiled. 'I know.'

'Of course, I'm not serious.'

'I hope not.'

'Good then . . . What do you think?'

Flash shrugged. 'I think it could work. It will be difficult to convince your people, though. A lot of equipment will be involved. You're not talking about a company of pioneers.'

'Yes, I know. It will be difficult, but I have – I really do have – friends in high places. Let's drink to the success of our plan. Heinrich!' Von Mansdorff bellowed the name of his orderly. 'There is much of which we must think. Flash, would your friends be prepared to form a nucleus? Are they good enough?'

'They could be.'

The orderly appeared and when he did, he was told to fetch some more champagne. With Von Mansdorff there was always this drinking, but Jordaan was pleased to go along with him – and with the plan, although he couldn't altogether believe that it had a solid foundation. But there was nothing to lose by waiting, and there was a certain gratitude in Flash for the surging thrill he knew with the thought of being out of that place and perhaps even flying again. But maybe, just maybe the whole thing might be possible. He would wait.

'There is one thing,' Von Mansdorff said when Heinrich had poured some champagne and was gone.

'What's that?'

'Don't mention any of this to your friends. I will talk to them individually.'

Flash nodded, and they went on to discuss the problems. Von Mansdorff was leaving on the following day, and he did not expect to return with any kind of concrete answer: that would take time, and there would be a certain delicacy required in presenting the scheme. That would have to be carefully observed. For one thing, it would be necessary to make someone else look clever, and it might be difficult to find the right person. Even if and when they received an affirmative, there would be certain difficulties in getting those involved out of the camp without arousing the suspicions of the others. But all could be overcome when the time was ripe. Something like relief was in Von Mansdorff's voice when he said slowly, 'You know, my friend, I have a strange feeling in my gut. Always I have known that somehow I would get myself back . . . Oh, I know that in my condition it would be difficult to convince them that I could do my old job . . . I understand that. But I could transfer to the Luftwaffe and be adjutant – watchdog if you like – with this squadron I'm proposing they form. I could be there to see that nobody is stupid. What do you say? . . . Play silly buggers, eh?

Flash laughed. There was already a feeling of growth in him which was almost physical, of being away and airborne. He was allowing the thought to run around his imagination as he might have savoured a glass of good wine before swallowing. 'If it comes off, I'll die of disbelief I think.'

'That's something you haven't considered. There's a very strong possibility that you could get yourself killed.'

'That's true. It's never been something that's worried me.'

'Good . . . good. Who the hell wants to die in his bed like some old woman? Tell me, Jordaan. Where does the name come from?'

'Huguenot . . . They fled I believe to England at first, and then to South Africa. They've been there – I don't know – two, three hundred years.'

'You're a Frenchman.'

'No, South African . . . Very South African.'

'No matter; soon if everything is well, you'll be a man again. And that's what matters, Jordaan – being a man. Tomorrow I'll be a man when I get away from this place, and just the thought of that – even if it's only for a week or two, is wonderful. I've lied, you know: I've told them that it is necessary for me to see my specialist in Berlin. Instead . . .' He laughed suddenly. 'I'm seeing my specialist brother. He's a specialist in self-importance.'

'You think he could have you transferred to the Luftwaffe?'

'Of course he could arrange it. My dear man, you must realize that the majority of Luftwaffe staff are ex-Wehrmacht. There were simply not enough people in the Luftwaffe with any kind of staff experience. It could be routine – if my bastard brother will go along with me.' Suddenly his thoughts switched direction. 'Would you like to eat some decent food to celebrate all we have been discussing. Of course you would – Heinrich!'

When the door opened Heinrich was told to bring some food, something simple, like a little cold chicken and some sauerkraut. '. . . And wine, Heinrich. Bring some more of that champagne.'

Until Heinrich reappeared with the food they concentrated on finishing the champagne they already had. Von Mansdorff's eagerness was transmitting itself to Jordaan. He had already ceased to think that nothing would come of the plan. It was easy, there in that room with decent food and wine to believe that everything would be as they wanted it. They laughed a great deal but behind their conviviality there was in Flash Jordaan a growing awareness of that loneliness which lay within him, a flaw almost, usually dormant, and something which he never discussed with anyone. It was almost a physical ache which could only be salved with laughter. He laughed then with Von Mansdorff.

The drink, as it can do, was affecting him perversely. Wardroop's death came back to make him angry. But he hid his feelings from the German, thinking instead of space and times of long before. But there was a moment now when he could laugh at the memory of walking unwittingly into the tent of the sixteen year old Wardroop to find him masturbating. He had promised, sworn never to tell anybody when Wardroop had explained that everyone – even he, Jordaan – had this slime thing in them. Slime, God! But the shock had been like crashing through a doorway into life. Now it was funny.

'Jordaan . . . Jordaan, listen . . .' Flash jerked into attention. 'Jordaan, I'm not going straight to Berlin and my brother. I'm going to spend a few days at Ilse's place in the Forest.'

'Ilse?'

'She is my love, my cousin.'

'Good.'

Now it was into the night, and from then on nothing

made much sense. But there was conviviality. They parted as friends, and as Flash Jordaan eventually lay down there was a release in his body which seemed to tell him that he could be committed. As he felt at that moment of the night, there was a welcoming temptation in the thought of all that space which stretched towards the east, endlessly.

8

Ilse was playing with the dogs by the lakeside when she first heard the crunching of the car's tyres on the gravel of the driveway. At first, laughing with the dogs, she did not pay too much attention: there was nothing unusual in the arrival of a car, and her eyes were for some moments bedazzled by the glare from the lake. Then when she looked again she saw him alighting from the car, and she ran with the dogs chattering away at her heels. 'Rudi . . . my God. Rudi . . .'

With his good right arm he clutched her, and in his laughter there was all the heart she had ever known to be there. She was a little afraid to break from his hold and really look at him. It was two years since they had met, and although they had written to each other and she knew he had been hospitalized, he had never mentioned the extent of his injuries. Once there had been a brief letter from his brother, Paul, but he had only told her that Rudi had been rather seriously wounded on the Russian front, he had made no mention of where his brother was, not even when she had written to ask.

Von Mansdorff released her and looked again at the ash-blonde hair and the grey eyes with their gleam of melting ice. He held her again with his good arm to relish the strength of her back before burying his face in the long, smooth neck. 'Ah,' he gasped when he had released her and had looked up at the sky, 'it's good to be back at Freudenstadt. Let me breathe the place in . . .' And, vigorously, he began breathing with the exaggeration of a little boy who has been told to do so.

'Ah, Rudi . . . Let me look at you.'

He laughed. '. . . Not advisable, my darling.'

She bit her lip with the suggestion of a tiny embarrassment. 'You must be tired.'

'Thirsty.'

'Ah, Rudi . . . It's good. You are the same.'

Without taking his eyes from her, Von Mansdorff touched the dogs fussing around his legs. 'Ah, Hans' – he nodded at his luggage – 'leave that. Someone will take it in.' Von Mansdorff turned to his cousin. 'Ilse, could you find a place for Hans here for the night. He's driven a long way. It would be better if he went back in the morning.'

'But, Herr Major, what about Berlin?'

'It's too far. I'll go on from here by train.' And as he spoke, he smiled to himself, for he had been aware of the man's desire to stay away from the camp as long as possible.

Holding his arm with both of hers as though afraid that he might escape from her, Ilse asked him, 'You are going to Berlin, Rudi?'

'To see your cousin. The one who calls himself my brother. I think we have business to do . . . I *hope* we have business to do.'

'How is Paul? I wrote to him about you, but he didn't answer. I don't understand.'

'He's very busy, flying his desk up and down the Unter den Linden.'

'Oh Rudi. Paul is the kind of man who would take this war very seriously.'

'Of course, my darling.' Von Mansdorff laughed. 'That's because he's never seen it.'

They entered Ilse's salon by way of the high French windows, and when she had rung Von Mansdorff immediately recognized the ageing servant who answered her call. 'Ah, you still have Angostura.'

Ilse laughed. 'Augustine . . .'

The servant laughed in a way which accentuated the rather gaunt structure of his face and, after bowing discreetly, merely said, 'Herr Major . . .' He had fought in the Spanish Civil War as a Republican, and after having been taken prisoner, Ilse's husband had requisitioned him as a personal servant. He still was.

Ilse asked the man to have the Major's things taken to the Duke's room, and then asked him to bring drinks. 'What would you like, Rudi?'

'A glass or two of champagne to freshen me, and then perhaps a little cognac to relax me.'

She laughed at him with a kind of delight in her expression. 'You were always so practical.'

'My dear . . .' Von Mansdorff walked towards the Spanish servant and allowed Augustine to remove the greatcoat he was wearing. 'Thank you, Augustine.'

'Major.'

When the man had left the clean elegance of that room, Von Mansdorff breathed deeply as he looked through to the trees. He was remembering the years when they had been young and this had been the house of her father, he who had been the friend of the Prince D'Orsini, the man whom Ilse's father had always described as the most civilized individual in Europe. He it was, this D'Orsini, who had arranged Ilse's marriage to her Italian Duke.

D'Orsini had indeed been a most civilized European – civilized enough to still be running his own estates in his own way, and able to behave with great subtlety towards

Mussolini, as though the man was a butcher's boy who had lost his way.

'How is Dino?' Von Mansdorff had turned from the window.

'He laughs.'

'Where?'

'In Rome, mostly.'

'Why aren't you there?'

'It would be bad, I think, if I laughed.'

'This was, do you . . .?'

The doors opened, and Augustine was there with a tray and the drinks. He placed the tray and said nothing. There was a suggestion of genuflection, and he left.

Von Mansdorff looked at the champagne. He moved towards it in its bucket, and then he paused. He said, 'Do you believe in this war?'

'I don't know. I believe in Germany.'

'Do you believe in your husband's Italy?'

'I believe that Italy is eternal.'

'Good. I am with you. Tell me, my darling Ilse, if I sleep in the Duke's room, does that mean that the Duchess sleeps with me?'

'You are still a boy, Rudi.'

'I love you.'

'I love you. When we have had some champagne, I will ask you the meaning of love.'

She smiled. She laughed.

'You know before the champagne?'

'Yes, Rudi. I think I do.'

'What is it?'

She paused and then said, 'I think it is mutual comfort.'

'How dull. What has become of my Ilse? Love, my darling, is death!'

'Have some champagne, Rudi.'

He smiled, and in the smile there was everything he had ever come to know.

With his right hand, and with some carefully prepared organization of his faculties, he poured two glasses of champagne. When he had given one to Ilse, he took his own, and then, as he looked into her eyes, he said, 'We have been so fortunate.'

The remaining days touched a delight he had forgotten. They more than walked through the glory of those lightly perfumed trees; they drenched themselves in all the goodness of the senses.

There were moments, though, usually when he was walking the dogs and Ilse was off thrusting her horse into odd spurts of gallop, when Von Mansdorff knew a trickle of doubt when he thought back to Jordaan.

Could it be that Jordaan was in some way using him? Was it possible that in his own desperation to get away from Leinefelde his judgement had been weakened? Was it possible that he was indeed the fool his father had always said he was, that the old man had been right?

There was the day when he was almost home from the walk he had taken with the dogs, and, tired – although he would not have admitted this to anyone but himself – he sat by the lake which was largely ornamental, staring into the lapping water as though looking into himself. Could it be that that bastard, Jordaan, was planning some elaborate escape attempt, and was his acquiescence merely a ploy? Jesus, God, if that were true, he was ruined.

And then, being the man he was, he lay back on the soft grass with a gloved hand behind his head to think of Jordaan and the others he knew: Del Renzio, Van Reine, the Irishman, Fahy. There was a Frenchman, too, a silent, dark young man called Oberlin who appeared to be thoughtful. Maybe he . . .

His mind flipped to thoughts of his brother, Paul; and of the tactics he would have to use in approaching the man. He could see Paul and the untempered arrogance he wore sitting behind that desk of his at Luftwaffe Headquarters in Berlin; and he could imagine the cold insolence he would display if he were approached with anything like clumsiness.

The dogs stirred at the approach of Ilse on her horse. He sat up to see her approaching, straight-backed astride the beautiful beast and smiling.

'Rudi, you were resting. I have disturbed you.'

'You never disturb me.' Von Mansdorff struggled to his feet and moved to stroke the horse's neck. Then they walked slowly towards the house with Ilse holding the horse while her other arm was entwined in his. Neither said much. They laughed a little at the dogs scampering around them. But it was enough for him that she was there, and she sensed this.Throughout the days they had been together she had known that something was troubling him, but she knew too that if he felt the need to speak he would do so.

When the groom had taken her horse and they were walking alone towards the long terrace which fronted the house, Von Mansdorff said, 'Would you mind if I slept a little in my room this afternoon?'

'My dear . . .'

'Sometimes I still get a little tired.'

'Of course.'

'And do you have anything in the house – maybe something of Dino's – which I could wear this evening instead of this uniform?'

'Of course . . . I'll have Augustine adjust something for you. Perhaps he's a little taller than you are.'

'Never.'

She released him to look at him. 'Maybe a little longer in the arm or the leg.' And then, realizing what she had said, she threw her arms around his neck. 'Rudi, I'm sorry. I'm so clumsy.'

'No, no.' And he kissed her on the cheek.

At lunch he drank lightly. Somehow that day it seemed enough that he should listen to the tinkling of her talk, which was intentionally inconsequential. When he excused himself, Ilse felt as though he had not been there.

It was a long time before he slept, lying on her husband's bed . . . for his real reason in wanting to be alone had been the need to think. On the next day or on that following, he would have to leave for Berlin and the confrontation with his brother.

Away from Leinefelde, his plan had become increasingly outrageous, the more he thought of it. It had seemed so simple, back there in the isolation of that place, but as he lay there one thing did gradually become clear. If he were to achieve anything – and he was determined to press ahead with the scheme – it would have to remain simple. And that meant by-passing the bureaucracy in Berlin and dealing only at the highest level. It would be the function of his brother to make that possible. Paul had the social background, but he didn't have the power.

It was with that thought that Von Mansdorff finally fell asleep. Augustine awakened him when he entered with the evening clothes belonging to Ilse's husband. They had been modified, for Ilse had been right: her husband was slightly taller than Von Mansdorff.

'I'm sorry, sir. Did I disturb you?'

'Ach . . . It's good, Angostura.'

The misuse of his name did not exactly please the Spaniard, but when he returned with the two beers Von Mansdorff had asked him to bring he was smiling and hurried to help the German to extricate himself from his tunic. But Von Mansdorff would have none of that. He was determined to master the technique of dressing himself with one hand. 'No, no,' he insisted. 'Have a beer. One of these is for you.'

The man smiled as he raised the glass to his lips. 'Gracias, señor.' And he watched, fascinated, while Von Mansdorff removed the rest of his clothes as though there was no one else in the room.

It was only when he had showered and shaved and was dressed except for his shoes and a collar with its black tie that the Major had to curse with the admission of defeat. He rang for Augustine.

But when the man had finished with the shoes, and had fixed the collar with its rather elegant black tie, Von Mansdorff smiled at himself in the mirror. 'What do you think, Angostura? Good, eh?'

'Si, señor.' The Spaniard pointed to his own left eye. 'This helps . . . Very good.' He was referring to the black eye-patch Von Mansdorff wore.

'Yes . . . Yes, maybe you're right.' But the consideration in the comment escaped the servant.

He was sipping some gin in the salon when Ilse came in behind him. She smiled when he turned to her. 'But who is this man? Have we met before?'

'Many times.'

'Rudi, you look splendid. I didn't realize my cousin was quite so handsome.'

'Nor I that you were quite so beautiful . . . I lie. I did know, but tonight you are ridiculous.'

'Ridiculous? I bought this on my last trip to Rome. You like it?' She held out the skirt of the gown she was wearing for his inspection.

'It is quite beautiful. But you don't need it. I would rather see you naked.'

She laughed. 'Think of the servants.'

In the dining room, which was less than Ducal – for this was Ilse's family home, not the Duke's; that was in Italy, and had all the crumbling grandeur of a renaissance palace – they looked at each other from either end of the table and laughed repeatedly at the intimate jokes which were almost the basis of their knowing each other so well and so long. Especially they laughed at the miseries they had perpetrated on Paul, Von Mansdorff's brother, when they were children. 'Paul never seemed able to laugh,' she said at one point.

He cleared his throat and drank. Then when he had looked at her for a moment with his head lowered, he said, 'I hope he doesn't laugh when I see him in Berlin.'

'Why?'

'Your food is still excellent,' he said. 'There is no war here. This wine, too. It is very good.'

'That is Dino. He's a good husband. He arranges things for me. Then there is the game and the gamekeeper. There is the fish, and there is the farm. May I say something?'

He smiled and nodded.

'You look very interesting with that thing on your eye. Is it all right to say that?'

Again he smiled at her before sipping at his wine. 'I only wear it so that I see half of you. If I saw all of you, I'd be driven to despair.'

'Ah, Rudi . . .'

He stood and moved his chair until he was sitting next to her. He thought for a moment. Then he said, 'There are some interesting people in this camp I run.'

'Sad people?'

'Perhaps in private. Probably more sad than I can

imagine. Some of them are mad with a rage to get out of the place. But there are some who still know how to laugh at themselves, when they are seen. They laugh at me.'

Von Mansdorff began to talk of Jordaan.

'Jordaan? He is English . . .'

'South African.'

He described the lean, blond looks of Jordaan, and laughed a little at the Englishness of the moustache which swept across Flash's upper lip. Then he paused before trying to describe the aggression which he felt to be in Jordaan. It was something, he said, like a spring which was inside the man. There was nothing on the outside which was vulgar. 'He moves,' he said at one point, 'like something from the wild.'

'Why do they call him Flash?'

Von Mansdorff spoke of the old servant who, Jordaan said, had first called him that.

'What is his real name?'

'Christian . . .'

'What? It doesn't sound – what would you say? – appropriate.'

'My dear, we are all of us Christians at this end of the world.'

He talked to her, too, of Del Renzio, and the Dutchman, Van Reine; of the Wing Commander, of Fahy, the Irishman, and of some others. He paused then for some moments as she was looking at him, until sensing that he was about to say something which was important to him, she said, 'Rudi, let's have our coffee and brandy in the salon. It is better, and the coffee's real – thanks to Dino.'

'That bloody husband of yours. I shouldn't drink it – but I will.'

When Augustine had served their coffee, Von Mansdorff told him to leave the cognac, while she dismissed the man with a grateful smile. 'Really, Augustine . . . That will be all.'

Von Mansdorff sipped some coffee, and then poured a little brandy into it. He raised his cup. 'Confound our enemies . . .'

'Confusion to them.' She laughed. 'Rudi, you look like a banker from Hamburg.'

'A bankrupt banker.'

'No. Very successful. Very elegant. I know about such things.'

'Ilse . . .' He emptied his cup and poured himself another brandy before leaning forward with his right arm on his right knee to stare into his glass. 'Ilse . . .' And he turned to her before saying, 'Are you wondering why I am here, and why I am going to Berlin?'

'You are on your way to see your brother.'

'I doubt if I'd go into the next room if I heard him choking to death.'

'Ach, Rudi, don't be too unkind about poor Paul.'

'Ilse, don't laugh at what I'm going to say. I've been thinking of something for quite a long time now. It's not something I could discuss with anyone. But I'll talk to you about it.'

And he started to tell her of the way in which he had found the man he really was when he had become a soldier.

'But surely the Russian front is horrible.'

'Quite horrible – in some ways. And yet, there is something there for me.'

'What?'

'I don't know . . . The sense of purpose, the sharing. I don't know. No one is cheap there. Some are despicable, but no one is cheap – on either side.'

'Life would appear to be cheap, Rudi.'

'Maybe. But living it isn't. I have to get back.' He stood suddenly and turned to her. 'What is there for me here? When this war is over, what do I do? Do I go back to selling bloody Italian cars when I'm not fit even to drive one.'

'There is the estate.'

'Paul will lord it over that. In any case I'm not a farmer, and it would be difficult to shoot wild boar with one arm . . . No, Ilse.' He sat again by her side to take her arm. 'Ilse, don't laugh. I have a plan. Listen to me.'

She listened as he told her of the proposition he was about to offer them in Berlin. And when he had finished, he looked for long moments at the still silence of her face as she was thinking.

He had emphasized the importance of avoiding the bureaucracy and he repeated his emphasis before he said, 'Well?'

Still she didn't move.

'What do you think, Ilse?'

She turned to him and smiled. 'What have you to lose, Rudi? Looking at you, my darling, you could so easily have been dead: you are alive. I'm not qualified to pass judgement on the wisdom of your plan. I accept that you want to get back.' And she looked at him with eyes that were moist and a throat that was tightening as she spoke. 'Rudi, you are so foolish. I love you.' Then she cleared her throat and tasted some brandy. 'Now I must write to Hermann. Tonight . . . tomorrow, I will write to Hermann.'

'Hermann who?'

'Goering, of course. He's our neighbour at that lodge of his ten kilometres away. He's very funny. I like him. He always stays with Dino when he's in Rome. He owes me favours for all the times he's used our villa on the

Adriatic. Once he used to look on me with great affection when I was very young.'

Von Mansdorff took up his drink and moved to the fireplace. 'He listens to everyone,' he said when he had turned to her. 'Hans Jeschonnek, his Chief of Staff, especially. It would be important, Ilse, that I don't go over the heads of his underlings – unless they were made to believe that the idea was his.'

'I know Jeschonnek too. He's a gentleman. Does he listen to Paul?'

'I imagine so.'

'Well then, I'll write to the Reichsmarshal – I'll write to Jeschonnek. Rudi, why don't I go with you to Berlin?'

He thought for a moment. 'No. You write – first to Goering, then to Jeschonnek. I'll handle Paul. His main purpose is to have me transferred to the Luftwaffe. If he's difficult about Jeschonnek, your letter will be helpful . . . Darling, you mustn't come to Berlin. You would distract me if you did. I'd spend all my time trying to make love to you.'

'So . . . Isn't that better than war?'

He laughed. And then he moved to kneel on the sofa on which she sat to take her face gently between the fingers of his right hand. When he had looked at her for a long time, as though it were the first, he kissed her gently on the forehead and said, 'You are such a woman.'

Their talk had eased him, so now he could drink more and they could both laugh as though nothing which was in any way serious had been said that evening. It was late when she said, 'Oh, Rudi, you in that suit, talking of war. It's so crazy.'

He stood to look down at himself. 'You think it's so crazy.'

'After Berlin, will I see you?'

'Ilse, I don't know.'

'Tonight, will I come to your room, or will you come to mine?'

'No.'

She stood to kiss him, and she did with the light brown hair slipping down one side of her face. 'I want to warm you.'

His laugh had no meaning, and neither did he mean it when he said, 'You would melt me. I couldn't have that.' But there was a hardness in his voice when he went on to say, 'I couldn't bear that, Ilse . . . Look at me. Look at the mess that I am . . . I'm sorry, Ilse my darling.'

Later, in his room, he looked at himself in the mirror which was above the fireplace. Then he cursed and tore the collar and tie from his neck.

9

There was a man who worried Jordaan. The poor chap – his name was Purdie – had proved himself to be such a bloody nuisance in every hut in which he'd slept since his arrival at Leinefelde that Flash Jordaan had been forced to allow him a bed in the hut he himself occupied.

The man was tall, and had become gaunt; he had never been seen to undress, and all of his time, when he wasn't talking endlessly at no one in particular, was spent in reading the only book which appeared to interest him. It was an obscure work by some Austrian woman which had been published in New York before the war by a cheap publisher. It was called 'Is Understanding in Depth The Answer?'

Everyone laughed at Purdie, except the few like Van Reine who told him to shut up whenever he opened his mouth. He would sit cross-legged on the upper bunk he used uttering quotes from his book such as, 'Your skin is a prison: the key to the gate is your mind.' This to anyone who would listen.

But it was difficult – and becoming more so for Flash; for a growing number of the inmates were becoming restless at the man's presence. He was undoubtedly affecting their morale, which was low enough in the first place.

Excepting the necessity of his appearance at roll-call, Purdie seldom left the hut, and its shelter. When on the odd occasion he did, people were at pains to avoid him. For he would grab you, literally holding you by whatever you were wearing, and staring into you with those great ecstatic eyes of his, as he insisted on communicating the latest truth that had come to him.

He had done it to Del Renzio one day as the latter was on his way to the gin mill, the name by which sick quarters had come to be known. Del Renzio, who in the previous six or seven years, had seen so much, smiled. He was someone who seemed incapable of being disturbed. Perhaps it had something to do with his breeding, for his family was one of the oldest in Italy. In terms of lineage it pre-dated anything in England which could describe itself as being aristocratic. In Tony Del Renzio the centuries seemed to have produced an individual who was as immune to disaster as a human being could be.

'Hold it. Hold it, Purdie. Take your hands from me. What are you trying to say to me?'

Purdie's eyes were hooded by brows which were exceptionally long for a man who must have been as young as he was. His face searched Del Renzio's.

Del Renzio broke free. 'What are you trying to say to me?'

'I'm telling you that this is the place. We are here. We have arrived. Don't you understand that?'

Del Renzio tried not to smile. He said, 'Yes. Yes, I think I can understand that.'

'We're here!'

'You're right . . . Purdie, can I say something? And, please, I don't mean to be offensive.'

'Say something.'

'Yes . . . Look, old man, you really must take a bath. It's becoming difficult to be near you. Be a good chap . . . take a bath.' And with that he walked away towards sick-quarters. There was a bathful of gin there awaiting his attention, and he was worried at the possibility of some idiot getting into it. It had happened before.

But Purdie had worried him, perhaps for the first time. The man was going to break: there was no doubt about that. He decided to speak to Flash when he had finished his stint at sick-quarters.

Flash himself had been faced that morning by something of a delegation in his hut. They had taken the opportunity of speaking when the man, Purdie, had decided to go out. They'd had enough. And he could understand them, in spite of his laughter. But he couldn't remonstrate: all he could do was to try to instil a sense of the ridiculous into their attitude. And even then he knew he was losing. 'For Christ's sake, chaps, what's the matter with you? The man's harmless.'

'He stinks!' Someone shouted, 'Flash, if you don't do something about it, we will. We'll throw the bugger out. We're all going creepy with that bastard mouthing on and on, and staring at us as though we'd come out from the woodwork. He looks at us as though we're nuts . . . He's the one who's nuts!'

'Hold it!' Flash's voice had deepened, and the smile had gone from around his lips. He was searching for something he could say to the poor bastards, until he picked on one of them. 'Oberlin,' he said – Oberlin was the quiet, dark Frenchman who was an unlikely member of that gathering. 'Oberlin, it would be easier if the Commandant was here, but as you know he's not. I'll speak to Muller. Maybe he can do something . . . I'll speak to the Wing Commander.'

'Ach . . .' The reaction seemed to be spontaneous. Then someone said, 'The Wing Commander will try to plant him somewhere else. You know that no one else will have him, Flash.'

Whoever had spoken was right.

'I'll speak to both of them now . . . Right now. There's nothing else I can do. We can't throw the man out in the cold. You know that.'

'Why not?' a voice said.

'That's enough!'

Before he went to Wing Commander Glaisop, Flash went to Carpenter and Mathers, the two who shared his seniority. Their attitude towards Flash had of course cooled since the arrival of Von Mansdorff, but they agreed with him. The man, Purdie, was sick and should if possible be hospitalized. They agreed that the possibility of Glaisop being able to do anything was remote, but they'd try: they'd go along with Jordaan, and they did.

Dear old Glaisop was of course confused. The difficulty, as he put it to them, lay in the Commandant's absence. He would speak to Muller – of course he would – but he doubted very much if the man was in a position, or that even if he were, he would be prepared to make a decision on his own.

'Why don't we stick Purdie in sick-quarters?' Jordaan suggested.

Chippy Carpenter couldn't resist proposing that Purdie could be Del Renzio's assistant. Jordaan giggled, but there was nothing from the others until Wing Commander Glaisop, sucking rather seriously on his pipe, said, 'Who's to say the man's sick?'

'Their bloody doctor.'

Glaisop looked up and hard at Jordaan when the latter had spoken. 'There isn't a mark on this man Purdie,' Glaisop said slowly. '. . . Not a mark, and if there isn't, you know as well as I do that in their eyes he isn't sick.'

Jordaan suggested that he be marked, but he was cut short by the Wing Commander's, 'That's ridiculous'. So it was left at that. Glaisop would do what he could with

Muller, and if that didn't work – which he didn't think it would – they'd have to wait for Von Mansdorff's return.

With the usual politeness they left the room.

But it was the thought of that room's fixtures, its bareness. The single empty table, the three chairs, the rather pathetic photographs of Glaisop's family were like a weight that Jordaan couldn't lift from his mind.

Jordaan knew a feeling of utter helplessness as the three parted to cross the empty compound with in their ears only the odd spasm of laughter above the bits of voices which came to them like interrupted Morse.

Once or twice Jordaan glanced at the other two as they walked away from him. The only other visible figures were those of the sentries, high above each corner of the place, alone and sunk in an apparent indifference. Looking at the backs of Mathers and Carpenter as they in their turn parted, it struck him as being strange that this place, as opposed to all the other groupings of men he had known, seemed to have the effect of separating them.

Mathers, who was in charge of the escape committee, was obviously working on some scheme. Jordaan could sense that in the attitude he displayed, which was quite different from the air of joviality he normally displayed. And, equally, it was obvious that a South African was no longer to be trusted – especially if he was someone who was not opposed to taking a drink from a German if it was offered to him.

Maybe it had been a mistake to have become quite so friendly with Von Mansdorff, but as he thought of Mathers and a scheme – which no doubt would be another tunnel – he thought of his own attempts. So far the only successful attempt had been Flash's own when he had managed to get himself through the gates by getting aboard the swill truck which left the camp every other day. Even that had failed. You weren't fighting a camp and its keepers: you were fighting a nation of eighty million people, and each one was your enemy.

The whole thing had become a kind of public school game which he had seen blasted out of them throughout the year that had gone, as those who had survived had watched so many of their friends dying. But here in this place with the wire around it, some of them seemed to find some kind of strength in the thought of outwitting their masters. He could have told them, but he never had done.

He could have told them of what it was like out there; of the frozen wet nights, the occasional thirst which could be awful, the gut-gripping fear when discovery lay on the brink. Let them tunnel away and discover for themselves that the wire and those slouching Krauts with their sub-machine guns and their searchlights were only the first hurdle. On his last attempt he had ended up in Murmansk under a waggon-load of coal. For three weeks he had sat on a bed of his own filth. But he had been the only one to get anywhere, and that effort, in the end, had led to nothing. Of the six others who had followed him under the wire, three had surrendered, and three had been shot.

There was confusion in his barrack-block when he returned. It was the noise which first assailed him, for normally this was little more than a steady buzz of talk which sank occasionally to silence as the readers, the writers, and those who gambled for nothing went about their business: but not then. The place had an air of hysteria.

'What's going on?' Flash asked the first man he met.

'We've washed Purdie – scrubbed him.'

'You've *what*?'

Flash pushed through them, silent, his face set in a way

they had never seen it before. Then he saw Purdie, sitting cross-legged on a bunk with a dirty grey blanket around his shoulders. The man looked up at Flash as he approached. He said nothing. The eyes dulled, stared steadily at Jordaan's, and Flash noticed that Purdie's beard was still wet. There was nothing in the eyes, not even reproach. Jordaan swung around on them: 'You bastards,' he cried. 'You pack of bastards.'

It was two days before they found Purdie, who had hardly moved throughout that time. They found him when they had broken down the door of a locked lavatory and seen there the lolling neck, and the now lifeless eyes above the emaciated body which had found death hanging there from the pipe that led to the cistern above. Someone had screamed as he burst his way through to them with his news. But it was Jordaan who held the body while they untied the cord which had killed it. Van Reine, with Fahy and Del Renzio were there by the time he had laid it on the centre of the floor. Then Carpenter and Mathers arrived; for anything which could break the rotten routine of that place made it a kind of holiday.

When the Germans arrived, Muller was with them. Even he fussed. Muller had soldiered in the first war, and he had seen the horrors. But that a man should kill himself when in a war there were so many who were willing to do it for him, that, for Muller, was confusing. Perhaps too, with the realization that this was the man of whom the Wing Commander had spoken a couple of days before as being in need of hospitalization, perhaps that too was troubling. Muller had refused to take action until his superior returned. He said to Jordaan in a halting, unthinking version of English, 'What do we do?'

'Get him out of here. Get a priest or a Lutheran or whatever from Halle, and arrange to bury him. I'll – or rather the Wing Commander – will arrange our burial party.'

Muller set about organizing his men, and the body was removed in a sack.

Wing Commander Glaisop was much troubled when they were assembled in his office. 'This,' he said when he had removed the pipe, 'is the first suicide we've had I think. People have died . . . but not this way. The poor chap must have been very sick.'

'He wasn't sick as such,' Jordaan said.

Glaisop whipped his eyes to the South African. 'He must have been. A man doesn't do a thing like this . . .'

'He killed himself. That was all. He'd had enough. Suicide can be a philosophical statement.'

'That's rubbish, Jordaan.'

Flash shrugged as they went on to discuss the funeral arrangements. There was talk of a priest, and of having the Krauts supply a firing party, but in the end there was no priest and no firing party. Glaisop conducted the formalities, and those who were there, standing at a short distance behind Jordaan, Mathers and the others, had to admit that the old man did the job rather well.

The day was fine, and as Jordaan stood there, looking up as though it was necessary to look away from the words the Wing Commander was using, there was again in him a lessening of the spirit. He tried, against the sound of Glaisop's carefully controlled voice, to think of the man they were burying. He knew nothing of Purdie, none of them did; but there must have been another Purdie, a boy, someone's son or brother maybe. There had to have been, just a few years before, a very young man who had been filled with the eagerness to fly and to fight. But it was difficult to relate anything he had seen of the man to that which he was trying to imagine.

'. . . He was our comrade,' Glaisop was saying. 'Perhaps his personal difficulties in this place were greater than most of us have known . . . But let us not forget that to get here in the first place meant that a brave man had taken off from the earth into that which all of us know to be the unknown. Now we leave him – and let each of us in our way pray that we leave him in peace – to whatever is the certainty of the unknowable.'

There was a silence which was almost audible until Jordaan bent down to pick up a handful of earth which he threw on the bare coffin, and it was when he was doing this that there was a certain movement in those gathered behind him. When he turned, it was to see coming through the knot of bodies there, the figure of Von Mansdorff.

The Commandant nodded without expression when he saw Jordaan. He turned to where the Wing Commander was standing at the head of the open grave. They saluted, and then Von Mansdorff, after looking into the grave, said, 'I'm sorry. Poor chap . . . A stupid way to die . . .'

The two walked off together while the others shuffled slowly towards their own huts. Back on his bunk, Jordaan lay there alone for a long time until Del Renzio joined him to sit there. The Italian expelled most of the breath he held, 'Well . . .'

'As you say . . .' Jordaan didn't move. He said, 'Those bastards killed him you know.'

'I know.'

'Bet you *they* don't, with all their little Englishness.'

'They do, Jordaan. They're just afraid of the things they don't understand. Weren't you once?'

'I was born knowing everything, and if I wasn't my grandfather taught me everything quickly with a kick on the arse.'

Del Renzio almost laughed. 'My grandfather was an old fairy. He used to wear a dress and a tiara at dinner. No one paid any attention . . . But I learned a lot from the servants.'

'We only had one. He was black and very wise. Next to my grandfather I loved him more than any man alive.' Jordaan thought for a moment of the old man, wondering if he was still alive. Then suddenly he said, 'Out of the way.' When Del Renzio had moved Flash swung his legs to the floor. 'I wonder,' he said, when he had settled, 'if our friend's come back with any more news. Have you thought any more about his crazy suggestion?'

'Of course I have. It's not so crazy. It's no more crazy than someone like myself flying for the Republicans in Spain.'

'Maybe a little.' Jordaan smiled.

'Raus! . . . Attention!'

'What the hell's this?' They both stood, listening to the echoing crumpy, crump of boots approaching them. 'It's got to be Von Mansdorff,' Del Renzio said. And it was, with two soldiers a yard behind him.

They stood to wait until he halted opposite them. They couldn't salute, being hatless, but they bowed slightly. Jordaan said, 'Herr Major . . .'

Von Mansdorff looked hard at them both. 'Why do you think this man killed himself? Was it the result of treatment he received at our hands when I was away?'

'No,' Jordaan said. 'He was depressed.'

Del Renzio couldn't resist it. He said, 'We all are.'

'Show me where he died.'

They took him to look at the lavatory where Purdie had been found. Von Mansdorff stood looking at the place while they stood behind him; at the toilet bowl and the pipe leading up to the cistern. 'A man must have thought little of himself to kill himself here,' he said.

'Or too much,' Del Renzio suggested.

'Hah . . . You could be right.' Von Mansdorff turned to Jordaan before he made his exit. 'Come to my place this evening, Jordaan, if you would care for a drink. I'll tell you about my holiday . . . That is if your friends don't force you to commit suicide in a lavatory before you get there.'

Jordaan shrugged. 'I'll try to resist the temptation.'

10

It had been raining, so that the lights of early evening glistened amidst the eagerly moving crowds of the Unter den Linden, and again it occurred to Von Mansdorff as he sat in the back of the cab which was taking him from the station that as long as these people could behave with such an apparent lack of concern, the war was firmly in German hands.

And at the Adlon the rhythm of the place was as constant as it had ever been. At the desk he was received with something like fuss, and he smiled with the thought that Ilse could have telephoned to announce his arrival. He thought of her again when he was established in his room and sitting on the bed sipping slowly at the drink he had poured himself. Ilse was so very much of his past that had been good. When he had loosened his tunic and walked across to a mirror in which he could see himself full length he thought of the evening a couple of days before and of the way in which she had offered herself as though to soothe him. His head sank a little without allowing his eye to move. Was it possible that more than his flesh was wounded; that when they had cut him, something of his spirit had escaped and that he was standing there looking at a man with no known passion?

Von Mansdorff stirred himself to remove the tunic. If he was to achieve anything there must be a lifting of his mood, so he went again to his drink and smiled with the thought that perhaps the dry Martini was the only decent contribution the Americans had so far made to civilization.

That evening he would dine well, and he would not think of Paul. Paul was for tomorrow. It would be better if he approached this brother of his with as much detachment as the man he would be facing. That way his mind would move faster.

With a shower, and a change of uniform and another drink, Von Mansdorff was refreshed. It pleased him when his appearance in the restaurant caused the usual stir of curiosity. Luigi, who had come from Lugano almost thirty years before to grow wise in the running of that place, hurried towards him with hands held high and fingers extended as though Von Mansdorff was the rose and he about to pluck it as something very special.

'Signor . . .' Luigi cleared his throat. '. . . Herr Major. What an honour. How good it is to see you again. You are well, sir?'

'Exceedingly well, Luigi.' Von Mansdorff smiled before uttering a syllable of laughter. 'It's good to see you.'

'The usual, sir . . .'

'Indeed, yes.'

A waiter was summoned who was already on his way with three neat glasses of schnapps, for the man was also old in the ways of that place. Von Mansdorff was left alone to await the arrival of lobster and champagne. His eye, from where he was sitting in the farthest corner from the little orchestra, could survey the uniforms and the rich expressions of pleasure with which that place was swaying against the music.

When he was sipping the first of his champagne a waiter arrived at his table to say that he was required on the telephone.

It would be Ilse. He was sure of that as he followed the man to the telephone. Perhaps she had followed him to Berlin. She had said she would come with him to help.

'Hello . . .' The voice at the other end was a man's, and as he heard it Von Mansdorff's uncovered eyebrow raised itself instinctively. 'Who's that?'

'It's your brother, you idiot.'

'Paul . . . Paul, how did you know I was in Berlin?'

'It is my business to know who is in Berlin. I want to know *why* you are in Berlin.'

Von Mansdorff smiled as he gathered together his equilibrium.

'Rudi . . .'

'Paul, I am here to see you. That's all.'

'Tonight?'

'No, Paul. I'm a little tired . . . But I would like to see you tomorrow morning, if that is possible.'

There was a pause as the other man seemed to be thinking, and then Paul said with some impatience. 'I have an important meeting at eleven. Can you be here at nine?'

'Yes, you busy man you, of course . . . Nine.'

'At my office here then. Nine.'

'Of course, Paul. Nine at your office. Good-night, Paul.'

'Good-night.'

Von Mansdorff stood there by the telephone for some moments, wondering if his brother was really as pompous as he sounded when you couldn't see his face: or was it simply that the manner he had adopted in his office had become a habit? He had always adapted himself as accurately as he could to whatever role he thought might be appropriate at a given time. The elder brother, Paul seemed to think, had to be serious, even when they had been children. When he had been in Spain he had chosen to fly the lumbering Junkers, and he had come home raving about the theories of Marshall Balbo on air warfare. No, no doubt, as a member of Jeschonnek's staff at Luftwaffe Headquarters with the rank of Colonel he saw himself in the image of the man their father had been. All that was missing was the monocle; but no doubt that would come with time.

In the morning it was somehow easier. Von Mansdorff dressed himself with a special concern. It would be a pleasure to meet his brother, even if nothing happened which would be to his advantage. Perhaps it was something to do with the weather, which was behaving splendidly. He was light and alive; and his mood, too, was helped as he looked down at the building which had once been the British Embassy. The Adlon, he seemed to remember, had been on what had once been the Embassy's garden. He smiled at the thought of the British actually selling all that magnificence, but then, how could he know of the ways of the British Treasury, or indeed of the pressure that had been brought to bear by Kaiser Wilhelm II in order that Berlin could have its most splendid hotel on such a site?

There were at that time three headquarters of the Luftwaffe which could almost have been described as being separate, those of Milch, Udet and Jeschonnek – apart from Karinhall, Goering's place, where the organization's ultimate destiny was determined.

Jeschonnek was Paul's man, and it was there, near that crossing where the Wilhelmstrasse intersects the Unter den Linden, that Von Mansdorff to take him.

It was a short journey: he could in fact have walked, but that hadn't struck him as being an appropriate method of arrival, so when his cab pulled up, he paid the man, and then as though to contradict his appearance, he literally bounded up those shallow steps at the building's main entrance.

The man saluted as Von Mansdorff was halted.

'Major Von Mansdorff for Colonel Von Mansdorff.'

At reception, in the entrance hall of the building, he was asked again for his identity, but only verbally. The shattering aspect of his appearance seemed to overwhelm most people, and it certainly did the Corporal at that desk. Without hesitation he called Paul's office, and within seconds Von Mansdorff was being escorted to the elevator and the office on the third floor.

Paul stood from his desk as his brother entered. Von Mansdorff saluted instinctively. The place was more spacious than he had remembered it.

'Come in, Rudi . . . Come in. How good to see you.' Paul gestured towards a chair which was in front of his desk. 'Please sit down.'

Paul Von Mansdorff's features were refined, carefully modulated. He could have been described as handsome. But there was determination in his expression when he stopped smiling. He said to his brother, 'It's too early for a drink. Would you care for a coffee?'

'No thanks.'

'Tell me, Rudi, why are you here?' Paul sank into the chair behind his desk.

'I want a transfer to the Luftwaffe.'

'You *what*?'

'As I say . . . I want you to help me obtain a transfer to your Luftwaffe.'

Paul, covering his confusion, stuttered something about it not being *his* Luftwaffe.

'I mean it.'

Paul stood and turned his back on his brother to look vacantly at a map which was on the wall there. Then he turned again. 'Rudi, what the hell would you do in the Luftwaffe? I had enough trouble keeping you in the

Wehrmacht . . . What would you do, eh? . . . Fly a Messerschmidt with one arm, and one – one eye.'

'Not exactly . . . But I have a plan.'

'A plan! What plan!'

'Sit down, Paul. It would be better if you sit down.'

His brother, who was two years younger than he was, had always had a certain authority over Paul. It was irritating. It was then, but he sat down.

Paul looked at his watch. 'I have a meeting at eleven.'

'There is enough time.'

'Rudi, my God . . . You're alive when you might well have been dead. Your health is improving. You're still in uniform. Why can't you be content? If you knew the trouble I had to get you where you are . . .'

'Yes. I can imagine . . . But can you imagine where I am?' Von Mansdorff smashed a fist on his brother's desk. 'I am in a prison – that's where I am!'

'Rudi, my dear Rudolph . . . my brother. Why do you say such things to me? I only want to help.'

'Then help!'

'Tell me of your plan.'

Von Mansdorff had gone a long way in the explanation of his intentions. He had talked at some length of Jordaan and the character of the man – he had told of the Italian, Del Renzio, when in his enthusiasm he realized, too late, that he had made a mistake in revealing the Italian's connection with the Republican Air Force.

'Wait . . . wait!' Colonel Paul grabbed at the gaffe with relief. 'Are you seriously suggesting that we should recruit a man into the Luftwaffe who flew against me in Spain? Are you mad, Rudi? Do you think *we* are mad?'

'No, no. Listen, Paul. The scheme doesn't have to include Del Renzio . . . In any case you're forgetting that he was an officer in the Italian cavalry . . .'

'Who deserted.'

'Well, yes . . . I suppose so . . . But he's a member of an important Italian family. He's not a Communist or anything like that. He's an adventurer. Everyone I would choose would be an adventurer, someone who'd rather fly and fight than spend this war in a lousy camp like Leinefelde.'

Paul cupped his face in linked fingers as he leant closer to his brother. '*Rudi*,' he said, 'they sound like a collection of mercenaries to me – riff-raff!'

'What about the French, the Belgians, the Dutch, the British who are already with us on the Russian front – are they riff-raff?'

Paul Von Mansdorff's eyes looked steadily at his brother before he said, 'In my opinion – yes.'

'You'll speak to Jeschonnek, yes?'

With considerable irritation Paul swung his chair to the right, to the left. 'The Chief of Staff is a serious man – a serious soldier. He'd never buy such a scheme. God knows what he'd say if I were to suggest it to him. I'd . . . I'd probably find myself as a movements officer at some out-of-the-way railway station.'

'But you'll speak to him.'

'Rudi . . .'

'I have a letter of introduction.'

'It will make no difference.'

'It's not to Jeschonnek.'

The telephone rang.

'What?' Paul was on his feet, confusion on his face. Quickly, with a hand over the mouthpiece, he cleared his throat. Then standing with his eyes somewhere in the direction of the ceiling at the far end of the room, he managed to say, 'Herr Reichsmarshal . . .'

His brother could hear him saying things like, 'Yes, he

is here . . . He is in my office now . . . Today . . . Certainly. But of course . . . Thank you . . . Thank you, Herr Reichsmarshal.'

When he had replaced the telephone, Paul breathed deeply for some moments. Then he sat to stare with a relentless disbelief at his brother.

'Goering?'

'Yes.'

'What does he want?'

'You, for lunch at his place on the Potsdamer Platz – today. Damn you, Rudi – you'll ruin us both.'

The Reichsmarshal's place on the Potsdamer Platz was in fact a palace. The two sentries in pale blue uniforms had no doubt been briefed as to Von Mansdorff's arrival: they ignored him. Inside, a somewhat elderly servant received him and proceeded to lead him across the chilling serenity of the entrance hall, and into a reception room which was surprising in its informality. The first sound Von Mansdorff heard was that of a child's voice.

When Goering entered he was holding the hand of his little girl, Edda. 'Ha ha.' The man was not as Von Mansdorff had imagined him. He was large, but there was no evidence of flab. The face, when he smiled, had been a battleground. 'This is my girl,' he said. 'This is my Edda . . .'

The little girl almost curtsied. She was dark and delightful. 'Heh!' Goering swung an arm. 'Someone take her.'

His wife, a large lady of striking appearance, was suddenly present to take the child's hand. She smiled at Von Mansdorff. 'Excuse me,' she said. And she took the child away. But Emmy re-appeared to say, 'How good it is to have you here in our house, Major.'

He couldn't help it. He said, 'My name is Rudi.'

'Good.'

There was a very pale sherry served with ice, which amused Von Mansdorff. At the dining table, Goering carved a salmon. 'This is Scotch salmon. Ask me how I got it,' he said.

Von Mansdorff smiled. 'I would not dare, sir.'

Goering had that whimsicality which is only known by those who have seen the face of God in their lifetime. He chuckled. 'I want you to tell me about your war. But before you do that, tell me about Ilse. How is that lovely woman?'

Von Mansdorff considered the glass he held. 'There is so much thought in the woman. In some ways she is above the world.'

Goering looked at his wife. 'Emmy,' he said to her, 'I agree with the man.'

'I know.'

Emmy Goering had a calm assurance. She knew her man, and she accepted everything he was and had been.

Von Mansdorff went on to talk of being with the Army of the Centre. He talked of his people, the men he had loved. He talked of their torture in death without being aware of who he was with. He talked of the dryness of Russia's space, and he was allowed to go on as the other two ate their salmon. When he realized that perhaps he was being impolite, he turned to Frau Goering, who was on his left. 'Madame,' he said, 'I must apologize. I am talking shop at your table. It is unforgivable.'

'My dear Major, not at all . . . All I know of this war is the terrible gin we have to drink.'

Goering laughed, and his guest raised his glass to the lady. Her's was an elegant evaluation of war he considered.

Now when they had finished the wine and were about

his own glass. 'Von Mansdorff, which of my commanders could sleep at night if they knew they had an entire squadron of the Royal Air Force on one of their own airfields – who could shoot down their own men at any given time? No. It wouldn't work. I'd look like a fool.' At that Goering stood, and again he smiled. 'Shall we have coffee with my wife?'

Back at the Adlon, Von Mansdorff lay on his bed, waiting for the call which he knew, inevitably, would come from his brother, Paul. He had allowed the car which they had provided at Goering's place to take him to his hotel, but there was a nervousness within him which wouldn't allow him to rest. After a few drinks he decided to take a walk in the Tiergarten where he could look at the fish in that beautiful aquarium.

But no. He could smile at the fish and admire the easy grace with which they moved; but that day there seemed to be a restlessness in them which matched his own – and he was right: there was.

Amidst the people with their smiles and their perambulators he walked. Von Mansdorff was always aware of loneliness when he was in the midst of people without a purpose. For him it had always been so in places like parks and golf courses or beaches where the sea had drawn them as though they had no will of their own, and where in the evening light there was only the occasional cry of their empty voices and the threatening whisper of water which would always be there: as they gathered together the remnants of their boredom to hurry back to their own worlds, which would not. There was pity in such thoughts. Perhaps that was why he had hurried back to his hotel, and the bed on which he was lying.

Goering had not been unreasonable. He could understand the man. There could have been some sense in scattering a collection of experienced pilots throughout the Luftwaffe as opposed to forming an entire unit comprised of ex-prisoners.

But such an idea was useless to the plan Von Mansdorff had for himself. He had conceived the whole idea in order to get himself out of the damnable position in which he found himself at Leinefelde. That meant having himself posted with the squadron as its adjutant, its watchdog; its gauleiter.

Von Mansdorff had swung his legs to the floor to pour himself a rather despairing drink when the telephone rang by his bedside. It was Paul, and all he said was, 'We'd better have an early dinner – early. You're leaving tonight for Leinefelde.'

'Tonight!'

'If you don't, I think there's a strong possibility that Jeschonnek will have you shot. I am your brother, Rudi. It is my duty to protect you from yourself. I will be with you in an hour.'

Von Mansdorff cursed as he replaced the receiver.

11

Until he had appeared at the funeral, Jordaan did not know for certain whether or not the Commandant was back. But he had the feeling that the Commandant had returned. There was something in the attitude of the German personnel which betrayed apprehension.

In their hut, at the far end of which they had constructed an enclave which gave them a semblance of privacy, Del Renzio was at work on a mural which depicted a rather pretty girl, drunk, sitting spread-eagled on a bar-room floor with a broken glass between her legs and large blue eyes which were trying to focus on a cherry rolling away from the glass.

'You like?' the Italian asked.

'Brilliant.'

Without removing his eyes the Italian said, 'Our boy didn't look too happy. Was it the funeral?'

'I don't think so . . . But then I'm not too happy,' Jordaan added.

The Italian laughed lightly with a shrug of resignation. 'You think our wings are clipped forever?'

Jordaan turned away. 'Before mine are, I'll try a running jump at that fucking wire.'

He lay on his bunk throughout the remainder of the afternoon, dragging through his mind again and again the suggestion Von Mansdorff had made before he had gone on leave; and as the minutes wore on, the possibilities became more and more desirable as the chance of their success became more and more remote. No German of any authority would in his right mind agree to such a scheme. And yet they were a strange lot. Maybe Von Mansdorff had the kind of influence he thought he had. Who could tell?

Fahy, the black-haired Irishman from Mayo, had acquired some extra potatoes and three enormous sausages from a Russian prisoner who drove a swill cart into the village. He was chef for the day, and it was the smell of the stuff cooking on the stove they had rigged up that finally brought Jordaan back into the present.

As they ate, Fahy regaled them with a tale of how they were in fact, in a way – more or less, mind you – eating a pair of the socks his old mother had knitted for him back in Ireland. It was these he had swopped with the Russian for the potatoes and the sausages. And from that Fahy yet again went on to remind them of how civilized the Irish were in allowing Luftwaffe prisoners who were incarcerated in Ireland what he called 'time to go off to the races'.

Someone – Van Reine it was – reminded the Irishman that his country was not at war.

Fahy knew exactly what the Dutchman meant, but it amused him to let the big man think that he didn't. 'Not at war! Who the fuck's not at war, you daft Dutchman? What the hell do you think I'm doin' here?' Paddy had in fact seen a great deal of the war – until his Spitfire had hit the water a shade too near the French coast.

That evening when they'd had a few beers in the bar which Von Mansdorff had installed in the dining hall, Jordaan suggested that the three others should drift with him towards the Commandant's quarters. They were almost there when Fahy said, 'Flash, you realize that this isn't doing us any good with the others – especially the English.'

Jordaan didn't look at him. All he said was, 'What good have they done us?'

Lieutenant Muller was there when they arrived at headquarters, and it was apparent that he didn't at all approve of what he assumed to be fraternization.

'Evening, Muller.' It was Jordaan who spoke.

Muller rose heavily from the desk at which he had been sitting. Poor Muller who had never looked much other than a postman waiting for his pension, had, since the death of his wife and grandchildren during a British air raid, been left with a spirit which seemed to have atrophied. He looked at the prisoners who were in his daily charge with a total apathy. When Jordaan told him the Major was expecting him the man fumbled his way towards the door of the Commandant's quarters in a way which suggested he had been drinking. But in fact he hadn't: the man was sickening.

Von Mansdorff was resting his feet on the desk behind which he was sitting. His tunic was opened at the neck, and as they entered he made the slightest gesture with the glass he was holding before saying, 'Ah, Jordaan . . . Give your friends a drink. Sit down, gentlemen.'

Each of them looked at him with care, as though trying to anticipate his mood. He sensed this, so to reassure them he swung his feet to the floor and smiled dryly. 'Jordaan, touch up this glass, will you . . .' Jordaan always had the feeling that Von Mansdorff was trying to introduce an element of a master-servant relationship when he made such requests. But the drink was more important than his pride right then. 'How was your leave?' he asked, when he had given Von Mansdorff his drink.

'Well . . . I went to the Black Forest . . . which was more than very beautiful.' He was silent then, and they waited. The German seemed to be turning over his thoughts as though he were running a good brandy around his mouth. 'Then I went to Berlin,' he said abruptly. '. . . On your behalf.'

He said nothing until Jordaan asked, 'What happened?'

'Hm . . .' There was again the dry smile. 'They kicked my arse.'

On the faces of those sitting opposite him there was confusion. It would have been difficult to tell whether they were displaying disappointment or relief.

'I did have lunch with Goering,' Von Mansdorff said by way of alleviation.

Del Renzio couldn't resist laughing quietly. 'Was it a good lunch?' he asked.

'Shut up, Tony.' Jordaan turned on his friend. 'What did he say?' he asked Von Mansdorff.

'He . . .' The German emptied his glass. 'He was polite. He's a remarkable man. He was non-committal. I think he thought I was mad . . . Jeschonnek and my brother – they killed it.'

So they drank on for some hours until, when they were leaving and full of drink, Von Mansdorff held Jordaan back when the others were leaving. 'Flash . . .' He was standing now with his back to the fireplace. Behind him now on the mantelpiece was the photograph of Ilse, taken a long time before. 'Flash, I lied to you a little . . . I think Goering would have bought the idea of individual pilots like yourself going to different squadrons . . . But that would have been no good to me.'

'Why?'

'Because I want out, damn you! I want to go with you as adjutant or whatever. That's the reason I dreamt this whole thing up. Don't you understand?'

* * *

Dr Paul Joseph Goebbels had already refused the call twice: this time there could be no escape. 'Yes . . .'

'Frau Goebbels, sir.'

'Hold . . . Er, put her through.'

Searching for something like sustenance, Goebbel's eyes fixed themselves on the huge portrait of the Fuhrer which was on the wall opposite his desk. 'Magda, darling . . .'

'Where were you?'

'Magda, you know very well that it is not always possible to say where I was.'

'I *know* where you were.'

'Listen liebschen . . .'

'Don't you "liebschen" me. Unless you have that bitch out of town by lunchtime, I leave . . . with the children. You understand?'

'I . . . Yes, of course.'

'Do you know what that will mean?'

Fritz Heller, the most reliable and trusted of his assistants, had come into the room, but not even in front of Fritz could he reveal the weakness of his position. All he could say was, 'Of course, my dear.'

'He's coming here on Sunday. You know that. If that woman is still in Berlin, I'll tell him. I promise you, I will.'

Women were so illogical. In one breath she's leaving immediately, and in the next she's receiving Hitler on Sunday at the Palais de Königlich, the town house on which he had spent 3,500,000 m in alterations. God almighty! All he could say was, 'Of course, Magda. I fully understand.' But before he had finished it, she had hung up on him. He looked to his friend. 'Yes, Fritzie. What is it?'

'I have something important.'

'So do I . . . Before you tell me yours, let me tell you mine . . . You know the lady from Paris . . .'

Heller smiled. 'Of course.'

'Get her back to where she comes from . . . today – on the mid-day train.'

'I see.'

'No you don't. Just get her back.'

Paul Joseph Goebbels was undoubtedly a remarkable man. All his life he had been the little cripple who had had to stretch himself. Within the confines of his body there was a ferocious lust which reached for the lost half of his physical being. Since puberty and the consciousness of personal awareness, this need had been there – never satiated. He could love no woman. But the deepness of their flesh brought its own oblivion.

One of the reasons he had married Magda, the Nordic beauty, had been because he had known of Hitler's desire for her; not in the way that he himself had ever wanted a woman, but perhaps as someone who personified a reassurance which had its mystical element, a compensation for the loss of his niece Geli, the great love whose death by suicide had left him stricken.

It was Hitler who had forbidden their divorce: for his own purposes it was necessary that Magda should be married – to someone else, and it was Goebbels' good fortune that he was that other person. Hitler knew the value of Goebbels as a professional propagandist, but Magda was the personal link that bound him to the Fuhrer, and in many ways the reason for his primacy amidst the others who hovered around the flame. Joseph Goebbels had very unpleasant memories of having slipped into disfavour as a result of the behaviour he had offered to his wife in the past: it couldn't happen again.

The note which Fritz Heller had placed on the desk simply said, 'Von Mansdorff'.

Goebbels stared at the message, thinking. Then he looked up at Heller. 'You mean the man who works with Jeschonnek – the flier?'

'His brother. He had lunch with Goering yesterday. He outlined a plan which I think could be of great interest to us.'

'Tell me . . .' When Heller had outlined what he knew of the plan which their undercover man in Goering's headquarters had reported to him, Goebbels stood up from behind his desk to walk awkwardly as he always did, towards the other end of the office. Heller knew he should wait, and he did so until Goebbels said, 'This Von Mansdorff, this brother – do I know him?'

'Perhaps not . . . Distinguished himself on the Eastern Front . . . Was badly wounded . . . Lost an arm and an eye I think.'

'Wait . . . I remember him – the playboy. He once came to me for a job on "Der Angriff" as travel correspondent . . . when no one could travel!'

Goebbels, as he often did, fell into laughter. 'That one,' he eventually said, 'he's a hero. He has to be. All heroes are fools.'

'Joe . . .'

'No, I know . . . That's not true. I'm sorry.'

'Let me think . . .' Goebbels looked at his friend, Heller. In so far as it was possible, there was complete understanding between these two men.

In military terms Von Mansdorff's suggestion was of little importance, if any. But it could have been something for Sunday, and there always had to be something. Goebbels was after all a journalist by nature; and he had the journalist's instinct to know that if on a humid July evening there is no story, you invent one. 'You mean this Von Mansdorff wants us to equip a squadron of shot-down RAF pilots to fight for us?'

'Think of the neutrals, Joe.'

Goebbels was thinking aloud. 'We have Armenians, Azerbaijanis, Georgians, North Caucasians, Turkestanis, and Volga Tartars – Cossacks even. Within a few months we will have half a million Russians fighting against Russians. What are a few RAF pilots against that lot?'

Heller said, 'I agree.'

Goebbels stood. His face was very firm. 'Don't forget what I said. Get that French bitch out of here by lunch time!'

As one offers pre-prandial niblets to one's guests, so did Joseph Goebbels in the world of affairs. There was a flutter in the household. But that was understandable. He was about to entertain the man who, arguably, was the most powerful individual in the world in that summer of nineteen forty-two.

So Goebbels fussed around the man when he had been delivered. Things had changed, but there was still the need, indeed even more so, to maintain the power-structure of the party. He was convinced of that, and in spite of his own relative unimportance in the scheme of things, he knew that he had to go on following the course of action he had chosen.

When they were alone he said, 'How are you, Adolph?'

Hitler looked at him steadily, 'I'll go on.'

'I know, mein Fuhrer.'

'You said that a long time ago.'

'I know . . . and I still believe it.'

Hitler was ill at ease, but when Magda appeared with the children fluttering around her, he seemed to relax.

There were the usual greetings. These children did please the man they called 'Uncle Adolph'. They had been used of course by their father's machine in countless photographs with the Fuhrer, to demonstrate the man's humanity . . . Children and dogs: Goebbels had often laughed to himself when he had thought of what the American comedian W. C. Fields might have said of his idea . . . But it remained true that Hitler did revel in the company of these children.

They had eaten lunch and were in the garden with Magda and the children when Hitler suddenly went into a silence which the adults knew they should not interrupt. He turned to Goebbels and said, 'This idea of yours amuses me.' Goebbels had told him of what he knew of Von Mansdorff's plan at the luncheon table.

'It could place me in conflict with Goering and Jeschonnek. What is Goering's attitude?'

'He's not entirely against the idea.'

Hitler's head went back quickly. 'He's not entirely against anything these days . . . Joseph, do understand that the attitude of these people doesn't concern me. No one can be in conflict with *me*.'

'Of course, sir. I merely . . .'

'You think that having a squadron of experienced Royal Air Force pilots flying with us would be of value to your department.'

'As propaganda, it would be a major coup . . . Especially with the satellites and the neutrals.'

Hitler laughed, to be joined with hesitation by his Minister. 'What neutrals?' he said. '. . . The Irish.'

Goebbels laughed. 'Very good . . . very good, my Fuhrer.'

Hitler stood abruptly. Then he turned to look down at the still-seated Goebbels. 'Investigate this thing fully.

Check on this Von Mansdorff and the man whom he proposes to lead the squadron. I will clear it with the Luftwaffe.'

When Muller had rushed in to say that Berlin was on the line, there was an excitement on the man's face that Von Mansdorff had not seen in the man's expression before. The latter had at first assumed that the caller would be his brother, or better still, Ilse. But when the voice at the other end of the line said that he was being connected with Dr Heller of the Ministry of Propaganda, Von Mansdorff's own excitement came close to causing his heart to stop.

It took almost as long as it took to be in touch with Jordaan and have brought to the office before Von Mansdorff had fully composed himself. And as it was he was even then staring into the fire with an unsipped glass of brandy in his hand when Muller announced the arrival of the South African. That telephone call had raised the white clouds of his imagination upwards towards possibilities of a freedom he had begun to think had gone forever.

Jordaan saluted as he entered.

'I would stand, my friend. But take a drink and look into this fire with me as I talk. There is a chair.'

Jordaan's eyes narrowed as he looked at the back of the German's head. But he helped himself to a drink and sat without speaking.

'Listen . . .'

'Cheers . . .'

'Listen . . .' Von Mansdorff spoke in a way that detached him from the other man. 'I've had a call from Berlin – from someone called Heller at the Ministry of Propaganda. I have to report at his office in two days.'

For the first time, Von Mansdorff turned to look at his guest. 'And they want you to be with me.'

'Me! Bloody hell!'

'You know what this means?'

'They want *me* in Berlin . . .'

'Yes, idiot . . . They want to have a look at you.' Von Mansdorff slapped his thigh when he had emptied his glass. 'This means that we're on, as you people say . . . That is if you don't play the fool or something.'

'Oh, Christ . . . You mean I'm getting out of here . . . I'm getting off this place!'

'And if you do, I am. Let's have another drink.' Von Mansdorff was laughing. They both were.

It was difficult for Flash Jordaan to disentangle his thoughts as he lay on his bunk that night. He tried, lying there with the smell of the block in his nostrils. It had become a fixture of his life, with its mixture of their breath, sweat and the faint mustiness of the damp wood; familiar as to be almost necessary to his composure. Lying there, he was trying to arrange in some kind of order those months which had become more than a year.

Tomorrow he would vomit blood for their benefit. The capsule which he would bite was with him, under his pillow. Then it would be sick-quarters and consignment to the hospital in Halle. He would be on his way to Berlin.

There was a twinge in him with the thought that it would be necessary to leave Del Renzio and the Dutchman out of his confidence for the moment. There was Fahy, the Irishman, too, and the Frenchman, as well as Hugo Dalgleish, the strange young Scotsman who hovered on the edge of their group.

Looking back over the time of his imprisonment, he had to admit to himself that in some ways he had been lucky. His generation of prisoner seemed somehow to have contained a greater proportion of men than were now arriving. Now they were more or less a bunch of confused youngsters from Bomber Command. Poor little bastards, they were the PBI of the Air Force. Most of them had been collected in late forty or forty-one, dragged through a condensed course in whatever they had been doing – as navigators, bomb-aimers, wireless operators, gunners (although few of these latter two categories were at that time commissioned). Then they'd been thrown to a wolf of such ferocity as they could not have guessed. There had been no time for them to develop an attitude to air-fighting.

As prisoners most of them were like schoolboys who were missing their mothers – which in no way detracted from the degree of their suffering.

But they were no match for this kind of slow death. Divided as they were to what they themselves called sheep and goats, the goats if anything came off better. The sheep attempted to rationalize their lives by organizing their lives into some kind of study programme. Some of them wrote long copious diaries or bits of novels; and every so often they would sink into pits of despair which was bad to look at. The pilots and the navigators seemed to be stronger, probably because they were in the main more intelligent, but the others – and thank God there were fewer of them – had to be ignored.

The goats were the hearties, or they pretended to be. They were the little bastards who spent their days goading their guards and calling out in chant such utterances as 'Goon in the block, goon in the block,' when one of the German guards came near. It was a bravado born out of a need to conform which schoolboys can display.

And, God almighty, Flash thought as he lay there that night, it was going to get worse. But he smiled to himself as he lay there. He had been trouble. He knew that. But at least the trouble he had caused had been for real. There had been the awful scufflings when they had pulled him out from the coal waggon where he had lain for three days soaked in his excretions. Then there had been the tunnel fiasco when the man detailed to fuse the camp's lighting had fucked the whole thing up.

Undoubtedly, but for the appearance of Von Mansdorff, he'd have been sent to a camp which would have been much more rigorous than Leinefelde. He smiled again.

It would be over, though, if all went well in Berlin. And it was with that thought that a nervous tingling ran through his body. He'd known it before. He turned. He sat up, grabbling his knees, and pulling at them. But the nerves were inside him like an itch.

There were the doubts now, the uncertainties centred on Von Mansdorff. Could he be trusted? Was there some devious scheme in the man's mind, so weird in its concept that it could be imagined lying there on that bunk? But, Christ, what could he do? He had to go along with the man. He had to, even if his head was being offered on some sacrificial block.

Sleep did come after thoughts of the old man and the Transvaal, and Bobby, and the good days of the squadron. Consciousness fell away behind a memory of Quigley's screaming and everything else which weltered for a time and then faded away in his mind.

12

To find himself in civilian clothes had been a strange experience. They fitted; they were even smart. But Von Mansdorff had laughed at him and apologized when he saw that Flash was not thinking it all that funny. 'All right . . . all right, Flash. You look very smart – you really do. It's a pity we couldn't forget all about wars and just go into business. You could sell anything, looking like that.'

'You're right.' Flash laughed then. 'Why don't we? You get one, and we'll be in business. Let's think up something on the way to Berlin.'

They were on the point of leaving the hospital in Halle, waiting until it was time to leave for the train, when Jordaan said, 'I suppose you realize you've equipped me with a complete escape kit.'

'Of course.' Von Mansdorff chuckled. 'I suppose you realize we won't be travelling alone.'

'Oh . . .'

'And I suppose you realize that if I have to, I myself will shoot to kill. There are limits to friendship, Flash – especially in wars . . . Flash, this is not the way to think – even if you're joking. You must think of this whole thing as though we're partners, collaborators if you like. But you have to believe in what we're doing – otherwise it's no good. We may as well go back to Leinefelde right now. In Berlin, Flash, they are not fools . . . As I see it someone has seen the value of this plan of mine – maybe the man himself has seen its propaganda value. But there must be others who are sceptical. They'll be looking for any suggestion of duplicity in you – and in the others for that matter. But for God's sake you must by now have decided that you're going the whole way with this thing. Otherwise, forget about it . . . You're ideal for this job, Flash. You're South African in the first place, and there must be many South Africans now who look upon you as a traitor because you're fighting for the British. You know very well they've only got one foot in this war – and that's on the African continent. Where is the South African Air Force? Do you think they can't afford one?'

'All right . . . all right. The point is taken.'

'Are you sure, Flash?'

'I'm sure.'

'Flash . . .' Von Mansdorff expelled the breath he had been holding. 'Of course there will be an escort on the way to Berlin. I still have to treat you as a prisoner of war until this whole business is finalized. You must understand that.'

Jordaan held up a hand in silent disagreement.

But it was their arrival in Berlin that for Flash was the truly shattering experience. He had known of course of Von Mansdorff's connections, but the ease with which the German assumed his reception had been beyond Jordaan's imagining. At Propaganda the man, Heller, had been impressive enough; but when suddenly, and without prior warning, they had found themselves confronting the Minister, Goebbels, Flash felt rather as Marco Polo must have done when he found himself in the presence of Kublai Khan.

At first he was unsettled, but something of Von Mansdorff's confidence trickled through to him, and that, with the gradual realization that the man they were confronting was aware of his unease, strengthened him until he was able to stand as four-square as he had done when his grandfather had first thumped him into manhood.

Goebbels' questions were direct, and, to Flash's surprise, not one of them related to the details of his career in the Royal Air Force. In the end in fact it amused Flash to sense Heller's restlessness as the interview went on. The man seemed to be unsettled by the amount of time these two were being granted by Goebbels.

It was obvious that Goebbels had checked on Von Mansdorff, and that he was accepting him at his face value. He even mentioned at one point – when he allowed himself to smile – the occasion when Von Mansdorff had approached him for a job on 'Der Angriff' as travel correspondent. Von Mansdorff himself had forgotten that.

South Africa, it seemed, was Goebbels' preoccupation as far as Flash was concerned. He asked endless questions about his growing up there, and when he asked about his reason for leaving and coming to Europe, he stopped Flash.

'You what?' he said. '. . . In Northern Rhodesia you what?'

'We worked as gangers in the copper mines to gather enough money to get over here.'

Goebbels looked down at his empty desk. Then he looked up, and there was that dark gleam in his eyes. 'I know you, Jordaan,' he said. 'I know you. We are alike.'

The huge room seemed to circulate as Flash was dismissed. There was a longish wait in the ante-room for Von Mansdorff, and then they were off.

He remembered all that as he was sitting in the day-room in the place outside Frankfurt. He was still dressed in his civilian clothes and feeling very much alone with an empty coffee cup before him, but in spite of the fact that he knew he was allowed to go out he had to admit to himself that he didn't yet feel quite strong enough to face the world outside.

So he sat there alone, and feeling more than a little foolish as he tried to take the place in. It was almost twenty-four hours since Von Mansdorff had parked him there, not a long time, he thought, in which to absorb the fact that he was going to be in the bloody Luftwaffe.

Well now. It wasn't quite time for a drink. But he'd read the three day old copy of the London 'Times' which had no doubt been placed there for his benefit, and several times he had walked to the tall windows to look out at the richly tended garden. There was something in this place and its atmosphere which reminded him of one or two of the better houses he'd been in back home. The overall impression was of a heavy cleanness. The room he was in couldn't have been described as elegant. There had obviously been some thought of France in its planning, but that had been overwhelmed by the Germanic weight of the place and its atmosphere created by the portraits of their military, a collection of rather serious looking elderly gentlemen who looked as though they had been born in uniform: people like Hindenburg, Lludendorff, Von Mackensen who thundered from the white walls.

There was still something like disbelief in Jordaan as he thought of the dinner he had shared with Von Mansdorff before the latter had left to get back to Leinefelde. There was to be a squadron, Von Mansdorff had told him, and he, Von Mansdorff was to be attached to it as an officer of the Luftwaffe. There would be formalities of course, but the selected RAF men would be assembled in this house which had been placed at their disposal.

It would be necessary for them to spend some time in the place to help them get rid of any complexes they had developed as prisoners. Afterwards there would be refamiliarization with training aircraft before they could become operational. A couple of experienced Luftwaffe pilots would be joining them more or less in a social capacity to gauge their attitudes as individuals. 'Flash,' Von Mansdorff had said eagerly, 'you have to accept these things.'

Flash had nodded in agreement.

The dinner had been splendid. There had been no need for too much drink, but that morning when the man had come in bearing a tray which he placed over his knees when Flash was fully awake: that had been unbelievable. When he heard the bath running, Flash had to remove the tray so that he could get up to empty his bladder, and then, back in the bed between those much-blessed sheets, he had settled and smiled. Sure as God, life could serve up a marvellous hors d'oeuvres.

The hell with it. He would ring for the man to bring a drink. The house, Von Mansdorff had said, was his. And he was about to do so when the servant in a white jacket arrived with something on a tray. 'This is for you, sir.'

It was a large envelope, and when he had torn it open there was a note inside which said, 'Good news, I hope'. It was a letter from home. The note was from Von Mansdorff.

Since he had been taken prisoner he had heard only once from the old man, for his grandfather held the view that if he couldn't see a man's face there wasn't much he could say to him. Now Flash's eyes swept over the battered notepaper he had taken from its envelope. 'Karl . . .' Flash always believed in establishing contact with a servant by name. '. . . Karl, bring me ein schnapps, ein bier . . . OK?'

The man smiled and bowed. 'OK.'

There was still a firmness in the old man's writing, and as he read, Flash smiled, for there was no expression of concern at his grandson's situation in the old man's words. The only allusion to Flash's difficulty lay in his observations that the letter might never arrive. But that was all. The tone of the letter was in the voice of a man who had reared his boy with the sure rhythym of his words. His woman had died, but maybe he would find another one. A younger one. A man was better with a woman about the place. And the roof of the barn had collapsed, so that he and Mawli, the Bantu boy – Flash smiled, for Mawli must have been seventy years old – they'd fix it, and then they'd paint it.

The man arrived with Flash's drink, which he acknowledged. Then, with the schnapps inside him, he went back to the beginning of the letter again, savouring it. Some bastard had stolen a three year old which had a bit of Arab spirit in it, but by God, the old man insisted, he'd find the bastard and give him the best of both barrels if he had to. But all in all it was being a good year apart from the woman and the barn and the horse. The place was looking good. It had what the old man called 'that old chirpy smell about it'. Flash hadn't to worry about anything. And there was no need to worry about the bitch who'd caused all his trouble in the first place. She'd sold up and gone when her old man had died.

The letter ended with the greeting the old man had always used, 'It's your grandfather, son. Don't forget who you are.' Scrawled across the bottom was something from Mawli which looked like, 'Good luck, Flash'.

Flash sipped at the beer which had come with his schnapps. His mind for some moments was filled with a heaviness which told him that it was unlikely that he would ever see the old man again. He could see himself though, long ago, running laughing with Mawli, but he couldn't see what they were running towards. There seemed only to be all that sky and the long mountains lying hunched on the horizon. He stood suddenly, restless as a young leopard.

In the garden he walked around aimlessly until it was time for another drink and lunch. Von Mansdorff had said that there would be no objection to his going out of the place, but he couldn't quite accept that. When Von Mansdorff or someone arrived at the house, he'd go out. But not until then. His German wasn't good enough.

13

Van Reine and Del Renzio arrived like an eruption. Flash could hear the fuss from upstairs in his room where he'd been asleep that afternoon with the best part of half a bottle of cognac inside him. It took some time for the fuss to get through to him. Then he swung himself from the bed, shook himself and ran some cold water over his head and face. What the hell could be going on?

But there they were, laughing in great gusts somewhere on the ground floor. 'Jordaan . . . Jordaan. Flash, my boy!' The big Dutchman's embrace was breathtaking as he took Flash in his arms. 'We're out . . . We're out. God damn you, we're out!'

Del Renzio was smiling in the background. Then he clicked his heels and saluted in the exaggerated fashion of his old regiment. His teeth were gleaming when he said to Flash, 'We *are*, Flash . . . Thanks to you, we *are*.'

'Thanks to Von Mansdorff.'

'Look . . .' Del Renzio was laughing. 'Look at this stupid bastard in that ridiculous suit.'

'What do you mean? . . . What do you mean?' Van Reine strutted up and down to display the suit, fully aware of how strange he must have looked to them both, for it would have been difficult to cover that bulk of his without the services of the best tailor in Berlin – and that he didn't have.

There was much slapping of backs and laughter before they settled to look around the place and its heavy magnificence. Flash tried to calm them by making them sit down, but it was difficult. They both sat on the edges of their chairs, leaning towards him. 'What are we here for? What's going on?'

To Del Renzio, Flash said, 'Press the bell.'

The man Karl appeared and champagne was brought. That silenced them – to the extent that when Jordaan had filled their glasses, having waved the servant away, he had to say to them both as they stared incredulously at the drink, 'What have they told you?'

'Nothing. We're just here, dressed like this.'

'Well no.' Van Reine had gulped down his drink and was refilling his glass when he said, 'There was something. There was a riot in the library and about six of us were arrested and shoved into solitary. In the middle of the night we were whipped out to the hospital at Halle, I think it was. This morning we were dressed in these clothes – and here we are.'

'You mean Von Mansdorff has said nothing?'

'. . . Apart from telling us to start the riot. It was a helluva punch-up. We wrecked the joint. I think the boys loved it . . . Things only quietened down when the goons started firing . . . But I don't think they hit anyone.'

'Of course not, you fool.' Del Renzio smiled at his glass. 'They weren't supposed to. It was laid on by Mansdorff, wasn't it . . .'

'Of course, yes . . . Of course.' Van Reine puckered his face.

'Tell us. What's the score, Flash?' Del Renzio was suddenly serious.

'Well . . .' Flash went on to tell them of what he knew, emphasizing before he started that it wasn't all that much, but enough for him. He told them why the house had been put at their disposal, and he mentioned the possibility of some tough interrogation. They would also, he said, be having visitors from the Luftwaffe, and he told them why. 'But, really, fellows, you'll have to wait for Von Mansdorff – and if you want to go ahead with this thing, you'll have to trust him. If you don't, and if you *don't* really want to go ahead, you may as well have a few drinks and get back to where you came from . . . It's too late for schoolboy heroics now. You're either in this thing or you aren't. I am. I'm going with it all the way . . . As far as I'm concerned being a prisoner is for some other guy.'

Del Renzio chuckled. 'We're with you, Flash. We're birds that fly away.'

Jordaan looked at him, and he was serious. 'Well, this bird's taking to the air – one way or another.'

In the early evening of the following day Von Mansdorff arrived, and with him he brought the Irishman, Fahy, a Pole called Dilewski, the young sad-faced Frenchman, Oberlin, and Hugo Dalgleish, the somewhat aristocratic Scotsman who had such strange ideas.

Von Mansdorff was in sparkling form. The activity of the past few days had brought back to him a confidence which it had looked as though he had lost. He moved differently, and when he announced to them that he would like them to be gathered in the drawing-room before dinner, his voice had an edge of command which he obviously enjoyed using.

There was such luxury in the thought of bathing and changing before dinner that all of them took advantage of the situation. Del Renzio was lolling in his bath with a large gin and mineral water of some kind in his left hand when Flash entered his room.

'Heh!'

'Here . . . In the bath.'

Flash moved on into the bathroom to sit on the edge of the bath. 'Well, what do you think?'

Del Renzio smiled at his glass. 'If they had some tonic water this would be perfect.'

'But *really* . . .'

Del Renzio looked at his glass again. 'I bet they have some tonic water somewhere in Frankfurt.'

'Shut up, you Italian bastard . . . Of course they have. What do you feel about all this?'

'Right now, great. Where do you think they'll send us, Flash – that's if they'll have us all, and when they've dug out some more?'

'What's your view?'

'Russia . . . It's got to be Russia. They'll sell us as crusaders against the Communist hordes from the east. That's what they'll do.'

'Do you mind?'

'No. I hate that mob . . . Saw them in Spain. They're bastards.'

Del Renzio wanted to know about Goebbels and Berlin, so as the Italian – who still looked remarkably fit – dried himself, Jordaan poured himself a drink from the bottle Del Renzio had already acquired for his room.

'Is he the nut-case they say he is?' Del Renzio called.

'I think so . . . Little guy, big head, narrow shoulders, crippled – not to be trusted. He has eyes that look as though they've never wept . . . Decent enough to me, though – polite even. But I still wouldn't want to fall asleep if he was the only other guy in the lifeboat.'

Del Renzio laughed as he emerged from the bathroom. 'What do you think it's really all about, Flash?'

'Right now it's about what it looks like being about – propaganda. The Luftwaffe turned down the idea . . . But Goebbels liked it. I can see why . . . We'll be OK as long as we've got Von Mansdorff. My impression in Berlin was that the guy's got a helluva lot of clout. They're great snobs these Germans.'

. . . When they were assembled, Von Mansdorff, as the only man in uniform, was effortlessly in command of the scene. He was aware as he entered, last, that they were still looking upon him as the Commandant, and it was in response to their attitude that he opened with: 'Well, chaps, it looks as though we're on our way.'

It wasn't only Von Mansdorff's command of English which allowed him to speak to them as he did. There was in the man a warmth towards them which only he knew to be gratitude. It was that which made his words ring with conviction.

At first there was a murmur of greeting from them, but as they settled there was complete silence before the steadiness of his voice.

It had been decided, he told them, that a squadron of former RAF fighter pilots would fly with the Luftwaffe. They were there, he said, to rid themselves as best they could in the time available of the stink and the stigma which any man worth a damn begins to gather when he's been a prisoner for a long time – no matter of what nationality. His sense of balance, his equilibrium was bound to be affected. They were there to relax.

There would be others, but they still had to be selected from other camps. The first of those already chosen would move, as soon as it was thought appropriate, to familiarization on training aircraft. When all was ready they would be equipped with Messerschmidts – which as they knew were not a bad aircraft, and at that he smiled.

Of one thing they were to be clear: he would not be the Commanding Officer. He hoped to be their adjutant, the 'dogsbody' he thought they called it. And he would be proud to be that. The CO would be chosen from their own number.

Then he said it. He said, 'You will not be flying against your own people. Russians will be your enemy.'

He paused at that, waiting for their reactions; and there was a flurry of muted voices until someone chirped up with, 'Couldn't we fly somewhere where it's nice and warm – like the desert or someplace . . .'

Von Mansdorff waited until they had subsided. Then looking to Del Renzio, he said, 'You wouldn't like it. The Italians are there. They fly well.'

His voice raised itself then as though he was intent on regaining control of the situation before he went on to tell them that for now he would be in administrative control. But he also told them that they were no longer to look on him as they had done. He was no longer their Commandant. They were not in a prison camp. As a matter of fact they could go out of the house whenever they wished, provided they felt comfortable. But it would be better he thought if they were in the company of a German even though they were in civilian clothes. Very shortly he'd arrange an evening for them in Frankfurt where they could remind themselves of what it was like to get drunk in public.

It was when he had completed his briefing that a note of real seriousness came into Von Mansdorff's voice. And that was when he spoke of 'intelligence'. He knew them all, he reminded them; some better than others. But they had to understand that the decision to launch this operation had not been entirely unanimous as far as Berlin was concerned. Concessions had had to be made – and a rigid intelligence had been one. As far as he knew, the whole business would be a formality. But there were other points of view to that of his own, and after all, each one of them was an individual and had to be assessed as such. It was only common sense. He looked at them for a moment, standing there before him and looking at him as though he was being examined. Then he said, 'Now, gentlemen – let's have a drink and some dinner.'

They hadn't travelled far into that evening before any apprehension they had been feeling was forgotten. Perhaps Von Mansdorff himself had set the key, for there was such a sense of relief in the man. They had eaten well on a handsome suckling pig, and the warmth of the wine had brought a richness to the blood which was in tune with the slow excitement which had been gathering in them with the thought of their freedom, albeit qualified for the moment.

But gradually the gathering seemed to slacken as their interest narrowed towards the man on their right or their left. Flash found himself talking to the man on his right, Hugo Dalgleish, the tall dark-haired Scotsman whose quiet reserve had never allowed them to be particularly close at Leinefelde. 'It's strange, Dalgleish,' Jordaan had said without thinking. 'You're the only real Englishman here.'

Dalgleish smiled slowly before sipping at the brandy he was holding. 'I'm no more English than you are,' he said.

'No. But more or less. You've got the same King and all that.'

'As I understand it, Flash, so do you – and more or less for the same reason.'

'What's that?'

'Conquest.'

'Well, now . . . Yes, I suppose so.'

'I did a lot of thinking before I ended up sitting at this table,' Dalgleish said. 'I had intended to be an historian before all this started. Maybe I still do. I was reading history at Oxford . . . Took up flying there.'

Flash laughed lightly. 'Is that where you discovered you weren't an Englishman?'

'No. I always knew that. All my family did. There are still some Scotsmen left you know. I don't mean fat Glaswegian merchants or Edinburgh bankers who began lining their pockets in the seventeenth and eighteenth centuries. People like mine who had to scatter . . . and still do. My ancestors fought for the Swedes, the Austrians. One of them from my mother's side was largely responsible for sending Napoleon reeling from Moscow. He was a Barclay. One of them fought for the French at Waterloo. That's not all that long ago.'

'You're a what-do-you-call-it? . . . A Jacobite, then?'

Dalgleish smiled. 'Not much point now. But I can remember my grandfather passing his glass across the water as he drank to the King 'over the water'.

'So that's your reason for being one of us?'

'Not entirely. I suppose getting out is in my blood. I'm like you. I like flying. I like fighting when I'm not thinking about it.'

'You're right!' Flash laughed and raised a glass. 'Cheers. When you're not thinking about it. I like that . . . It's true.'

The remark had to be retailed to the others as the evening soldiered on towards its conclusion. The laughter became louder as all doubt became shattered with the crashing of Von Mansdorff's glass in the wide fireplace when he unavailingly tried to compose a toast and ended up by saying, 'Gentlemen, here's to us' before making the gesture which was followed by each one of them with great gusts of cheering.

Flash Jordaan was alone eventually with the table's

remnants and Del Renzio. 'Well, Tony my friend, what do you think of it all?'

'I think it's good, Flash. I like it.' Then he laughed. 'Russia will be different.'

'I . . . I should imagine so. But we're not there yet. They haven't finished with us yet. They've still got to stretch us on the rack or whatever little novelty they have in mind. They haven't finished with us yet, Tony . . .'

And they hadn't. As the days succeeded each other, more people arrived until there was assembled a very creditable looking bunch of fellows, eighteen in all. Three Luftwaffe pilots joined them, easy chaps. In a couple of days only their uniforms made them recognizably different from the others.

It was Flash who was the first to be interrogated. Von Mansdorff came with him on a morning after they had spent the previous evening in Frankfurt with Del Renzio and Van Reine, looking, Flash had thought, a shade apprehensive. He had asked him. He said, 'What's the matter?'

'Nothing . . . Nothing much.'

'Go *on*.'

'They want you in Frankfurt.'

'Me. What for?'

'There's some kind of board meeting there.'

Flash smiled. 'A selection board?'

'Well, not exactly . . . Something like that. There's nothing to worry about, Flash . . . Just . . . Just be yourself.'

'What the hell's that?'

'You know . . .'

In truth there wasn't that much to worry about. Von Mansdorff had driven him into town to deposit him at the entrance to a rather nondescript building more or less opposite the Frankfurterhof where they'd had dinner on the previous evening. It was the sight of the hotel which made Flash say, in an attempt to ease his tension, 'Maybe they'll give me a good lunch over there.'

But Von Mansdorff made no reaction. He was worried. His own plans were at stake. All he said was, 'Good luck.'

It was obvious to Flash almost from the start that the men he was facing were conscious of the difficulty in their situation. Their attitude was certainly firm; but it was polite.

Half a dozen Luftwaffe officers of apparently somewhat senior ranks, the grading of which Flash could not decipher, began to tell him things about himself that he had more or less forgotten. Then when they had established their authority their questions seemed to fall into the category of the rhetorical. There was an embarrassment in these men, for they must have known that whatever decision they were supposed to arrive at had already been decided for them. The gamble had been taken, and they seemed to know it. It had been taken away above their level by Dr Goebbels against the weakness of those cards still held by a discredited Goering. As Luftwaffe officers they were going through the motions, but that was all. After perhaps an hour and a half the whole charade frittered into a kind of emptiness. The most senior of them looked at those who were sitting impassively on either side of him. He smiled at Flash before saying, 'That will be all, Squadron Leader Jordaan. Thank you.'

Flash couldn't believe it. Whatever hurdle he had been supposed to cross seemed to have been left behind. He stood, made a slight gesture of farewell, and he was gone. He had been joking when he mentioned the possibility of having lunch at the Frankfurterhof, but it was there, when he left the building, that he headed. He was still laughing at the whole business when he met Von Mansdorff back at the villa.

'I told you . . . I told you,' Von Mansdorff insisted when Flash described his performance with 'the board'.

'No you didn't, Rudi boy. You were just as worried on the way there as I was.' And Von Mansdorff had to admit that he had been.

But it was good. Flash's enthusiasm was heightened when he had gone on to tell the others who crowded around him of how it had gone. 'It's only a once-over operation,' he had said. 'They wanted to look at me. That was all. God knows what they'll think when they see some of you bastards.'

Weeks, two or three, passed, until in the end they were a cohesive group. They liked each other, probably because they had to. But for none of them was it difficult. It all happened. Women – and they had to thank their hosts for that – but women, flashy tarts from Frankfurt though they may have been had been brought to them.

Flash and Van Reine and Del Renzio were in Van Reine's room when the servant whom Flash had made his own, Karl, brought eight of them, of various dimensions and complexions into the room for selection. The men were overwhelmed by embarrassment and – if they admitted it – confused by the man Karl's directness. 'Which of them would you like, gentlemen?' he had asked.

They couldn't decide.

There were these girls, moving with the unconscious embarrassment slave girls on a Louisiana platform must have felt as they waited to be selected; until in the end the most dominant, a dark lady of about thirty, took over the situation. 'You,' she said to one of the others, 'and you,' to another. 'You stay.' The others were dismissed.

Flash Jordaan was laughing with the redhead to whom

he had been assigned. He was drunk. There was no way in which he could have the girl, and she laughed at that. All six of them became friendly, to the extent that when the women discovered who they were they refused to accept any money.

But they arrived on the following day, and they asked for Flash, to his mild confusion when he met them at the door of the villa. When their laughter had subsided they announced that they wished to take him and his friends to lunch in the rather smart Mercedes they were driving. So when Flash had rounded up Van Reine and Del Renzio they were off, to Wiesbaden.

All of them laughed through the meal, for there was no sultry innuendo in the women's behaviour. They were fun. By the time they arrived back at the villa, the six were in great form. Von Mansdorff was there when Jordaan and his friends appeared. He laughed when he saw them, and without waiting to be introduced he said, 'Where have you lot been then?'

'Lunch, old boy, lunch.' Flash executed a kind of mock salute. He was enjoying himself. 'These ladies took us to lunch in Wiesbaden. They've been improving our German.'

'I'm sure.'

Flash was aware that the sight of Von Mansdorff in uniform was unsettling the women. But the appearance of champagne seemed to rectify that, and when he saw that Von Mansdorff was relaxing in the company of the woman who was educating her brother he removed himself to the other end of the table as graciously as he could.

Since he had been cut to pieces, women had been difficult for Mansdorff. But this one, this whore, he felt he could understand. The party had splintered and he was in the garden with this one who called herself Heidi, when he said to her, 'We are very alike.'

'Mein Herr . . .' Her eyes were fixed on the cross around his neck.

'We are very alike. I have the feeling that you have found yourself in conflict.'

'Ah ha.' She laughed. 'My life has had to be lived in conflict. But if you mean that I have spent my life trying to win, you are right . . . But I try to forgive myself.'

He laughed. 'I think I do. I'm *sure* I do.'

'We are both whores, yes?'

He smiled. 'Yes.'

Another week had passed when Von Mansdorff had them assemble in the villa's drawing room. There was the feeling that something out of the ordinary was about to take place. The clue was in the erectness of Von Mansdorff's bearing which seemed to be holding an unusual nervousness. He showed it even more as he spoke. 'Gentlemen' – and by this time he had assembled them around the bottom of the stairway – 'I would like you to meet your new commanding officer.' As he said it Flash appeared on the stairs in the uniform of an Oberleutnant of the Luftwaffe.

There was a roar of cheering and laughter, which was not perhaps what Von Mansdorff had intended. But he and Flash had to join them. There was no mockery in their ribaldry. The German, though, was slower to understand their attitude than was Flash. But suddenly his eyes were alight when he saw the jostling sense of camaraderie that was in them. This was the way of their kind. No individual who took himself too seriously could command the respect of the others. Flash Jordaan knew that: Von Mansdorff was about to learn it as he followed them and their laughter towards this latest excuse for celebration.

These men were different from those he had known. And the faint feeling of separateness he knew served to reinforce the discovery that the ways of their war were different. He would try to remember that in the months ahead.

14

The smell of warm grass was good as they lay there, lounging. Some were fully outstretched with their eyes closed against the sun which was still high above while they thought and dreamt against the steady droning of the old FW 44s as the trainers made their way around the circuit in what seemed to be an endless procession.

They had arrived at Werneuchen which was about twenty miles to the west of Leipzig, and at that time the base of Number One Fighter School which was normally used for the conversion of fledgling pilots on to the somewhat tricky Messerschmidt. But in the case of Flash's lot, they were being given re-familiarization flights on these ancient trainers before being converted to more advanced aircraft. They, all of them, had after all been operational pilots.

But in spite of this there was not a lot of confidence in their midst. It had been a long time since most of them had flown, and the conditions in which they had been living had not exactly been conducive to the building of confidence. It would come though. Van Reine knew that, for, including Flash, he was the most experienced pilot they had. Perhaps not the most successful, but in terms of hours flown he had completed more than anyone else.

On that afternoon as he approached those lying in the sun as he walked away from the aircraft he had been flying with an NCO instructor, the big Dutchman laughed at them. 'You don't look like saviours of European civilization to me.'

Someone told him to fuck off, which of course he didn't. He went on. 'What's the matter with you all? You're only getting the feel of flying back into your arses again. That's all. Don't take it all so seriously.'

One or two of them sat up, and some one said, 'How did you feel, Dutch, when you took that old thing up for the first time yourself?'

'Scared . . . I was scared at first.'

More of them sat up to pay attention, and he knew from their expressions that his confession had surprised them. He knew too that all of them had been scared and that each one of them had been thinking that he was the only one. It was why he had spoken as he had in the first place. He went on. 'Once I had the feel of the thing I was OK. I tell you – don't pay any attention to what these buggers say. Don't take off and then come straight in for a landing. Fly the thing around. Be easy with it. You chaps all know. Aeroplanes are like women. Stroke them gently and they'll do what they're told. Relax.'

'God, Dutch . . .' It was the Irishman, Fahy, who spoke. 'You're right. My guts were doing cartwheels. I thought it was only me.' And suddenly they were all laughing as they talked of their uncertainties. Their voices rose to such a pitch that Van Reine knew they were feeling better. 'Here comes our CO,' he said as he was about to move on, 'with the Count. How do you spell Count, chaps?'

Flash was indeed approaching them with the Station Commander, Count Horowitz. He was a Colonel. Raggedly they stood to present themselves.

Each of them offered the flat-handed salute of the Luftwaffe to the Colonel, who, right from their arrival, had shown himself to be affable enough. He was an intelligent man, most of whose air-fighting had taken place during the latter part of the First World War; and the appearance of this collection of ex-prisoners had seemed to amuse him. Flash he liked. That had been apparent from their first meeting when he had greeted the South African with, 'Well now, Jordaan, I have heard a great deal about you. You are certainly a unique collection. I don't suppose you have realized that you and your people are the only officers of the Luftwaffe who are not German citizens, who in fact have not sworn an officer's oath to the Fuhrer . . . No one seems to have thought of that, eh?'

'No, I'm afraid not, sir. I'm afraid they haven't.'

'Well, I'm not going to raise the matter. Let those who have thought of the whole idea worry about it. I think it adds to what you might call the piquancy of the situation.'

'There's Von Mansdorff, sir. He's the real thing.'

The Colonel smiled. 'Yes, he is. He certainly is.'

Flash introduced the older man to those of his people who were there, and as Horowitz looked at each one of them he did so with something of a quizzical smile on his face. The war for each one of them had been over, but for some reason their youth wouldn't let them have it that way. He said as much to Flash as they were standing a little apart from the group watching aircraft landing and taking off. 'Your people are not really committed to fighting the Russians, are they, Jordaan? They're not politically orientated.'

'No, I don't think they are, sir.'

'Are you?'

'Not really. I think, like myself, they'd rather fight than be half dead in that damned camp. But they'll fight . . . Believe me.'

'I do.'

Still the aircraft droned around the circuit as the two men watched. 'You must realize,' the Colonel eventually said, 'that it is possible you'll meet some opposition on the way along. The Luftwaffe is like any other large organization. It's composed of many different types of people. They'll not all be sympathetic to your point of view. You'll meet the Army when you leave this place, here and there. You'll meet the SS . . . You should be aware of that.'

'Or beware.'

'Hah, yes.'

'We have Von Mansdorff to protect us.'

'Yes. Of course. Tell me, how is your German coming along?'

'I have a splendid "achtung".'

Colonel Horowitz laughed. He had a cryptic version of English, very definitive. 'Shall we,' he said, 'call on Von Mansdorff and see how he is equipping himself as an adjutant?'

They were about to turn away as they heard the agonized spurts of someone gunning an engine on his approach. 'Who's that?' Horowitz barked.

'Not one of mine,' Flash said as his eyes narrowed on the approaching aircraft. 'Must be one of your cadets.'

The aircraft did look as though it was being controlled with uncertainty. The man flying it was levelling out too high. There was no way in which he was going to make a decent landing in that attitude. But the chap seemed to know his degree of error. He opened his throttle to the full gate, pushed his nose down and headed along the runway. But it was evident, as he tried again, that the man's nerve was unsettled. And Flash, watching, could understand the boy. Once, at that stage of the game, you have lost your certainty, that's it, it's gone. And this boy's had. He went around again. He tried again. It was no good. When he came in again with that sinking of the heart which Flash could remember on one occasion, there was no hope. The boy levelled out at about thirty feet. He stalled, and went in with the sickening noise of broken metal, which until he's heard it, a pilot can never be said to have grown up.

Jordaan ran. The Messerschmidt had been too fast for its pilot. He had simply run out of runway. Colonel Horowitz was following. The boy had been thrown clear. He was lying several yards away from the burning wreck. Flash was first to be there, to find the youngster screaming like a pig-stuck creature, covered in blood. Both legs were crumpled beneath the body as Flash held the screaming head. There was blood everywhere. Finally the screaming stopped as Horowitz arrived to stand there, dazed. The boy, whose name Flash would never bother to know, was dead.

That evening in the Mess there was Flash and Von Mansdorff drinking quietly with Count Horowitz when the Chief Flying Instructor, one Kirnowski, joined them. Not exactly a friendly fellow, Kirnowski stayed silent for a long time, in contrast to the mood of the others. Flash knew from the man's disposure that if he could he would find an argument. Eventually Kirnowski said, 'Captain Jordaan, it would not appear that your experience of this afternoon has particularly upset you.'

'Did it you?' Flash asked.

Kirnowski was a well-built man, quite heavy in the shoulder, square-jawed with eyes which were remarkably luminous beneath a pair of heavy black eyebrows. There was just a fleck of grey at his temples. Now, as he looked across the table at Flash, the brows seemed to lower themselves across the narrowing eyes. Flash could feel an instinct of dislike, perhaps mistrust, reaching him from the man. But he didn't exactly help matters when he went on to say, 'I've been trained to accept death. Well, not exactly trained, but I've grown accustomed to it being around.'

'So have I,' Kirnowski said. 'But it still saddens me to see one of my own boys die.' There was a certain emphasis on the 'own'.

Von Mansdorff, who was sitting alongside Flash, said, 'What was that song they sang in the First War . . . "Here's to the next man to die . . ." Something like that.'

But Kirnowski pressed on. 'That was an English song. We sang about life and glory.'

'Oh, was it?' Von Mansdorff chuckled. 'Have some wine, Major.'

Recovering himself, the Chief Instructor took the wine which Von Mansdorff proffered under the latter's insistent smile. But the man's message had been received by Flash and by Von Mansdorff: he wasn't sympathetic to the presence of Flash's men in the Luftwaffe.

'So what?' Flash had said to Von Mansdorff when they were alone. 'So . . . He doesn't like us. I don't think he likes anyone. He objects to anything which isn't in the book. I don't think he even likes you.'

'I know . . . I know, Flash.' Von Mansdorff was beginning to really understand the nature of this man whom he had created as a potential squadron commander. 'But watch him. Watch them all. You realize that when we eventually get there you'll be under the command of a wing leader. Be careful. You can't wear a couple of DFCs on that uniform you know. All of us will have to prove ourselves before we can throw our weight about to any extent – except me. To counteract Kirnowski, I'm going to start throwing my weight around now. I may have dropped a rank to get here, but I'm still me – and they know it.'

'Good.'

'Understand, Flash?'

'Of course.' And Flash slapped the other's knee to reassure him. 'Don't worry, Rudi . . . I'll be a good boy.'

Flash himself had known the initial apprehension of the others when he had first taken to the air in the old FW. But that had soon passed. And when they gave him an Arado 68 which was fully aerobatic, he really found himself. Gradually he was mastering the old skills, for it was important that he show his own people that he was the best – as it was important that he show the Germans that he could really handle an aircraft.

He eased himself in with the Chirrondelle, the stall turn, the slow roll, the barrel roll, successive loops from an altitude which became lower and lower each day until he was making himself gasp. It was the day he broke the flagstaff which held the swastika over the crew-room that finally caused Kirnowski to express his disapproval. Flash had come across the field very low at full throttle, straight at the crew-room until he pulled up and over the wooden structure and its flag so that all who were there had to duck as the flagstaff juddered, cracked and crumbled ignominiously as he went into an upward roll from about thirty feet.

Kirnowski was obviously furious when Flash had landed and walked back to the crew-room. 'Captain . . .' The man was trying very hard to conceal his anger. 'Captain, that is not the kind of flying of which I approve.'

'I'm sorry about the flag. Was that my fault?'

'It was dangerous flying. You were putting one of my aircraft at hazard.'

'Ah, well, Major . . . Aren't we all at hazard in this business?'

'Business? This is war, Captain . . . And in war there has to be discipline.'

'You're right, Major. Of course you're right. When do I get hold of a Messerschmidt?'

'Tomorrow.' There was only silence then from Kirnowski for a moment. The man was angry. 'Everyone starts conversion tomorrow.'

For some weeks now their refamiliarization with flying had been interspersed with lectures on law and administration of the Luftwaffe, the command structure of the organization, as well as lessons in elementary German. It was all great stuff, even, when they had been flying in the morning, it was such a struggle to stay awake in the afternoon.

But now it was to be the Messerschmidt – admittedly the somewhat obsolete E type, but an up-to-date operational aircraft nevertheless. That evening in the Mess Flash said to Von Mansdorff, who'd been groaning over the boring business of learning the rudiments of being an adjutant in the Luftwaffe, 'They must really trust you in Berlin, Rudi . . . If any one of us escapes now we could take back an awful lot of information on the Luftwaffe.'

'Nonsense, Flash. They trust themselves. They know that every intelligence officer in the Royal Air Force knows more about the Luftwaffe than you do now or perhaps ever will.'

Flash turned to him and smiled. 'I suppose you're right. I hadn't thought of that . . . of course. How stupid of me.'

Von Mansdorff was with Flash on the following morning in the small office they had allotted him when Flash told Kirnowski that his intention was to be the first to take up a Messerschmidt and then spend some time explaining to his men what he had learned of the aircraft's characteristics. But it was all too obvious that Kirnowski was not happy about the South African's assumption of such authority. It was in his voice when he said, 'I would remind you, Captain Jordaan, that I am in charge of flying training on this station.'

'My lot are not training . . .'

'Your what?'

'My men,' Flash said coldly, 'are operational pilots who are refamiliarizing themselves.'

'Kirnowski . . .' Von Mansdorff threw the words at him. 'He's *right*.'

'I'd remind you, too, that I am your senior officer.'

'A necessary formality. Jordaan is right . . . You may not agree with the decision to have these men in the Luftwaffe, but I would suggest that it is none of your business. Fundamentally, it is Jordaan's job to bring himself and these men up to a level of fighting readiness. I'd suggest that outside whatever help you may have to offer, you confine yourself to the training of your pupils . . . Let that be understood, Kirnowski.'

They had both spoken to each other in somewhat irate German, but though only getting the gist of their language, there was no difficulty in understanding their tone. It was strange, but in spite of the man's attitude Flash could understand Kirnowski's difficulty. In the RAF, he had been familiar with the introduction of Poles and Czechs; Frenchmen and Belgians. The Luftwaffe was a much more indigenous force. They had allies – particularly the Italians, who they were generally known to despise, wrongly. And, too, they had Austrians, Hungarians, Rumanians, Spaniards. But they were of different air forces. There had so far been no attempt to integrate them as Germans.

Kirnowski was of the generation to which Count Horowitz, the Station Commander, belonged; that which had been involved towards the end of the First World War. His inter-war training had first taken place in Russia. Then he had joined Lufthansa, and it had only been in the mid-nineteen thirties, when Germany had admitted to the Luftwaffe's existence that he had transferred to the military arm, to fly in Spain, Poland and, eventually, France. But, already, he was ageing. Flash could see that. The man was fit, but showing the early signs of settling physically, which, for someone like himself, must have brought its own frustration.

For some moments Kirnowski looked hard at Von Mansdorff, as though weighing the man and considering whatever threat might be in him. With his decision, he said, 'Right.' Then he turned to Flash. 'Your aircraft will be ready when you are. I'll have Sergeant Kuhl show you the cockpit.'

Kuhl was obviously amused by Flash. A Saxon, neatly built with a full black moustache, he had the air of solid practicality which is usually evidenced by someone who knows his own worth, and perhaps his own limitations. His attitude towards officers who were in fact doing the same job as he was himself was four-square.

The Sergeant knew exactly who Flash was, as indeed did every man on the station. In Kuhl's eyes someone who'd survived, been taken prisoner, and had then decided to do it all again was amusingly mad.

Jordaan smiled a greeting, and the Sergeant's response was equally warm. Their comradeship was that of airmen, and it interested Flash to see how similar in type was this man to the experienced NCO pilots he had known in the

RAF. Kuhl reminded him of a very great pilot, a Polish Warrant Officer called Marion Niepiekello. Niepiekello had been a Silesian before the Treaty of Versailles had made him a Pole. In the first war he had flown with the Imperial German Air Force – it was said in the Staffel commanded by the great Von Richthofen. When Flash knew him he was fifty-three years old, and not only a great pilot, but a great man. It was he who had shown Flash Jordaan the finer points of handling an aircraft.

Sergeant Kuhl didn't speak a word of English. But in that situation an oral understanding seemed to be unnecessary. In the cockpit with the Sergeant standing on the wing-root by his side, Flash pointed to the instruments one by one, muttering – more out of politeness to the German than for any other reason – in his fractured German, his identification of each dial there. In minutes he had the feel of the cockpit, for in essence the fundamentals of all aircraft are similar. He checked the trim control, felt gently for the undercarriage, translated kilometres into mph. The rev counter, fuel gauge, oil pressure gauge, altimeter were all recognizable. He laughed. 'OK,' he said to the Sergeant, who was grateful for recognizing something Flash had said. The man showed his pleasure when he replied, 'OK.'

Like the Spitfire, the Messerschmidt was tricky on the ground, owing to the narrowness of its undercarriage; but Flash was aware of that before he started taxi-ing to the edge of the field. He turned into the wind carefully, revved up on the brakes, and then released them before opening the throttle gradually to the gate. Her tail was up, and when he felt her lifting he allowed her to come off until with the wheels up she surged forward towards a thousand feet.

Jordaan had no intention of making an immediate

landing. He had always thought it foolish to do so with an unfamiliar aircraft, so now in a gentler turn to port than was usual for him he flew around the airfield and then away and out of the circuit, 'feeling' the aircraft all the way, until after about fifteen minutes he decided to make a landing, modelling his approach – although with the ME it was not strictly necessary – on that he had used with the Spitfire. Immediately he took off again, this time to handle the aircraft more positively. He flew the thing for a little over half an hour until he knew it. Its characteristics, apart from a tendency to be nose-heavy in the turn, were not so dissimilar from that of the Spitfire.

In days they had all converted. The whole atmosphere of the group had lifted. Von Mansdorff was delighted. He was saying it in the Mess where they were dining at a long table, apart from the rest. 'Gentlemen,' he said with great pleasure in his voice, '. . . to our squadron!'

There was much laughter as they reiterated his toast. But Flash was merely smiling when he said, 'Rudi, it will be some time yet before we are a squadron, or at any rate something I would call a squadron.'

'Ach, Flash, relax.'

'No. Now we can't relax. I've spoken to the Colonel . . . We are going to fly our pants off in the next week or two. Your people are obviously in a hurry. They have a right to be. This is not going to be just a squadron . . . It's going to be a bloody good squadron.'

'Some of our people have done some very outstanding things on the eastern front, Flash.'

'I know . . . I've heard . . . Maybe they're cooking the books.'

Von Mansdorff laughed. 'We'll find out . . . You know, Flash, I should learn to fly . . . You had that man Bader who had no legs at all. I could get something for this arm.'

'Of course you could. I knew a Scotsman called McLauchlan who had a marvellous hook arrangement which he used for a left hand. But how do you get another eye? . . . Rudi, even if you could, it would take a year it would take at least a year before you could fight a Messerschmidt. Flying's one thing . . . Flying as though you're part of the aeroplane is another.'

Von Mansdorff swallowed his drink and gasped as the brandy fired his throat. 'Of course you're right. I'll fly my desk. Maybe I can organize something like airfield defence when we get there.' And having said that he was suddenly on his feet. Colonel Count Horowitz was approaching their table. They all stood.

'Good evening, gentlemen.' It had been the Colonel who had arranged that they dine apart from the pupils. At Von Mansdorff's suggestion he had agreed that it would help to bring them a sense of cohesion. There was a garbled response to his greeting, and then, without fuss, the Colonel pulled across a chair which he planted between Flash and Von Mansdorff. 'So, Jordaan, you are making progress.'

'Some, sir.'

'It is good. Can you have them ready in three weeks?'

'If you give me unlimited flying time.'

'You have it.'

Von Mansdorff chuckled. 'You mean we're going, sir?'

'Yes.'

'Where? Do you know where.'

'Yes.' But that was all.

'I see.'

'Chaps . . .' Flash took over. He stood. Their conversations dribbled to an end. 'The Colonel has just told me that we'll be going in three weeks. Will we be ready?'

Their laughter, mixed with the odd cheer, raised the

hearts of everyone there – even the young Germans at the other tables who didn't know what had been said. Colonel Horowitz, appreciating their enthusiasm, restored a degree of calm. He took over from Flash, and he said, 'Gentlemen, I would like you to understand that I know the difficulty, the sensitivity of your situation. I think you have done very well. I hope that you will all go on to do better in the future.'

They all, for it was getting deep into the evening, responded in a somewhat disorderly fashion. But the CO knew their mood. He slapped Flash on the shoulder. Then he said, smiling, 'With an adjutant like you have, there is no alternative.' They all cheered at that as he left them, quietly.

Sharply, and very early on the following morning, Flash took off with Van Reine and Del Renzio in formation. They did well, and he told them on the RT, 'At least you didn't hit me,' he called.

'Not yet!'

'You'd better not, you bastards. Let's go! When we get to fifteen thousand, you're both trying to get a deflection shot on me.'

In that clear, early morning air, all three were alive again. Away to the east there were some high-banked clouds, and as they climbed, they did so through a thin layer of alto-cirrus until they were in the blue again. Then when they were around the height Flash had mentioned, he abruptly cut his throttle to fall away from them without warning. When he was free he opened the throttle fully and turned away into a steep bank to port. 'Right, you bastards, I'm after you!'

But there was no need to tell them: they were after him. It was fun to play there at that height with friends. Van Reine was first after him, and as Flash glimpsed him in the mirror above, he closed the throttle again and turned into a steep bank to port. 'Right! Hit me, you bastards . . .'

But there was no need to tell them: they were after him. He pulled the stick right over until he was inverted and letting it fall away in a vertical dive. The ME was very fast in a dive, faster, Flash felt, than the Spitfire had been.

Down he went for about three thousand feet until he began easing it out, leaving Van Reine still diving. But Del Renzio was also there with more time to anticipate his move. Easing it out, it controlled well. Back now on the stick with full throttle, he took it up and over until at the top of his climb and back he turned it over in a half roll, the classic Immelmann. Around to starboard he could see Del Renzio climbing vertically, but it was impossible to get his own machine around tightly enough for what could have been a shot. Somewhere below in the fuzz that was half blinding him as a result of the G he'd been enforcing on himself he could see Van Reine climbing fast towards them.

Flash laughed, which he wouldn't have done if there had been ammunition in their guns. But blood was dragging from his brain until his senses were reeling. The pressure had to be relaxed so that he could keep control.

That morning their 'dogfight' lasted perhaps fifteen minutes before he called to them, laughing, 'All right . . . all right, I won.'

The whole sky was their playground then, and the feeling of exhilaration they knew then made them boys again, obliterating all those months of captivity. 'Right, chaps . . . form up on me. Dutch, you're number two. Tony, you're number one, OK.'

He heard their voices, slightly distanced, 'OK . . . OK.'

When they were in position in the Vic and losing height fast he had them manoeuvre to starboard echelon, watching carefully how they moved, and then as they lost height fast, into line astern. They manoeuvred again with apparent ease, Flash leading, then Van Reine followed by Del Renzio. Down and around steeply, first to port, then to starboard he took them. They were really travelling now, stepped down to the rear, with all the time Flash changing direction.

They were around three thousand feet when Flash inverted with a half roll. They followed. But when he began to pull out towards the earth he was giving Van Reine less air-space than he had himself – and Del Renzio even less. Van Reine did follow, and he did come out in the wake of Flash at the bottom of the half roll. But Del Renzio made no attempt to follow. On his RT he called, 'Fuck off, Flash. Are you trying to kill me?'

'Good thinking . . . Good thinking, Tony. You're right. You might not have made it . . .'

Del Renzio was furious when they landed. 'You bastard,' he said to Flash when he had walked across from his aircraft. 'I could never have pulled out from that height.'

'Forget it . . . Forget it, Tony. It shows you were paying attention. That's what we do on this squadron . . . pay attention.' Flash was laughing.

But Del Renzio suspected he had uncovered something in the man, a raw ruthlessness; something more savage than was in ordinary men.

Through the days Flash drove them. They polished their formation flying. There was battle practice in Flights of four. Battle practice with the whole squadron was stepped up. And each day he took two of them, as he had Van Reine and Del Renzio, on a dog-fighting exercise. It was on one of those that they suffered their first casualty.

Dilewski and Jean-Jacques Oberlin, the young Frenchman, were flying with him, and as he did each day he was battling it out with them at around fifteen thousand feet when it happened. The Pole had something of a devil in him. He was a coarse flyer, but very quick, obsessive. Flash had already decided that if he didn't kill himself he'd become a first-rate fighter pilot, which, in a way, he had been when operating out of England. But there was an undisciplined quality in the man which it would have been a mistake to have curbed altogether.

The Frenchman had been assigned by Flash to take evasive action as the other two bore in on him, and he was doing this as Flash tried to get inside his steep turn to port before falling away in a long dive. Oberlin must have flipped to starboard as Flash fell away, without realizing that Dilewski was coming in from that side – and Dilewski really did come in at him. He tried; he really did try to pull up at the last moment, but such was the determination of his dummy attack that he must have shattered the Frenchman's port wing as the latter flipped over.

Flash saw it all from three thousand feet below. He cursed as the fear he felt for them seemed for a moment to grip his whole body. 'Out . . . out,' was all Flash could say to himself as he looked up at them. The Pole was now diving in an inverted attitude, while the Frenchman, poor, gentle Oberlin was spinning crazily towards the earth.

When he pulled over, Flash went down with them in a wide, turning circle to port. He felt an utter helplessness; and there was fear in him, a sudden sadness. He could have been looking at himself.

Most men share the weaknesses, the vagaries, the strengths of their fellows to some degree. Their differences are decided by the order in which their passions, frailties, incisiveness of the mind, predominate. Flash cursed again as he saw these two fall, until he saw something tumble like rubbish from a high window, then flutter and settle in descent. It was Dilewski. The bastard was out.

But there was nothing of Oberlin.

That evening Von Mansdorff drank a little more than had lately been his custom. Most of them had left the table, so that only a few; Flash himself, Fahy, the Irishman, Van Reine and Dalgleish, the tall dark-haired young Scotsman were still huddled over their glasses.

It was Flash who said, 'Where's everyone gone?'

'Bed, I think,' Dalgleish said.

'Bed . . .' Flash looked at his watch. 'It's bloody early.'

'They start bloody early.' Van Reine reached for some more wine. 'Maybe today upset them . . . Have you noticed that when something how do you say is available, you don't want nearly as much as when it's not there? . . . Look at Tony and all that gin he used to spend his time making. Now he hardly drinks at all.'

'Where's he gone?'

'Bed.'

'Jesus . . .' Flash seemed to be thinking, and then he said, 'What's come over everyone?'

Von Mansdorff fingered his glass. 'Maybe it's like Dutch says. Maybe he's tired. They're all tired. I can tell that.'

Flash was on the point of slamming the table, but he held himself to merely slap it firmly. 'Rudi, that's balls! They're upset by what happened today. That's all. Are you suggesting that I'm pushing them too hard?'

'How you push them is your business.' Von Mansdorff turned to Flash and smiled. 'I'm only the adjutant here.'

'Oh, shut up, Rudi. You know that's not true. Look

. . . All of us, every man in this unit, has to be operational. Most of us have been cooped up like budgies for a year or more, more or less. In a couple of weeks we'll be heading for the Russian front. Everyone has to know what that *means* . . . I have an awful feeling that it's going to be a bloody sight tougher than anything we've seen so far. If you feel I'm driving them too hard now, Christ knows how you'll feel when they start driving us out there.'

Van Reine, with that slightly Americanized overtone to his Dutch accent said very soberly, 'You're right, Flash. I know that. I think they all do. Today was just bad luck.'

'Today has nothing to do with it. People get killed when they're flying aeroplanes. Once they are, there's nothing you can do about it except shut up.'

'You're right.' Van Reine was smiling, for he knew that Flash was to some extent feeling responsible for the death of young Oberlin that day. 'Let's have a drink. We are very lucky people.'

Von Mansdorff stood to refill their glasses. 'Cheers,' he said when he had done . . . 'Any day now they'll be giving our unit an identity. Then we can drink to that. But for now, cheers.'

'There's one thing.' There was a thoughtful look on Dalgleish's face as he spoke. 'There's one thing . . . I've been thinking . . . If we get the chop here, what do they do with our personal effects?'

There was laughter at that. Von Mansdorff suggested that he would be in charge of such things. Maybe he could sell them as souvenirs. Van Reine suggested a raffle and a bloody good drink afterwards.

But later, when he was alone with Jordaan in his room, Von Mansdorff, speaking in measured, controlled cadences said to Flash, 'I wasn't so much thinking of how you were driving them when I spoke at the table; I was thinking of how you were driving yourself.'

'You know the deadline, Rudi.'

'Hah, deadline's an unfortunate word. Let's say startline.'

'Good point . . . But deadline, startline – whatever you want to call it we're going in a couple of weeks and I don't want some bastard who'll probably object to our arrival in any case, suggesting that my lads aren't up to the standard of his Geschwader or whatever.'

'Flash, you forget why I'm here. You should know that I have a direct line of authority. It's not something that I want to over-use, but when I have to, if I have to – I'll use that authority.'

Flash, standing, turned his eyes to his friend across the room. 'Drink?' he asked.

'Of course.'

Flash had poured them both a drink when he said, 'Do you know something?'

'What's that?'

'I've never, since I've first known you . . . I've never asked you what it was like to be out there. So far I've fought my war from the basis of a dry bed and three square meals a day. What's it like out there, Rudi?'

'Hm . . .' Von Mansdorff emptied his glass and held it out again.

'What is it you people call your soldiers?'

'Brown jobs.'

'Good. That is of course what I was. I saw it all from that vantage point. Maybe it will be different for you. But Flash . . .' Von Mansdorff stared into his glass with an expression on his face that Jordaan had not seen there before. Ruminative, perhaps a little troubled, he was quite still for some moments before he looked steadily at the other man. Then he smiled. 'It's pretty bloody awful, Flash. It is.'

'I can imagine. But you were out of it, and now you're going back.'

'There are all kinds of reasons for that. I had a battalion of tanks, Flash. There is a beautiful power in a situation like that. Something reaches out of you which would otherwise be locked up forever. You feel that all of your life has been driving you towards a certain point. You've staggered into the middle of the forest and all of your mind and your body is involved in the business of trying to hack your way through. You feel that maybe there's nothing on the other side which is worth reaching. It's – how would you say? – the apotheosis of all that you are.'

'The what?'

'Never mind. It's something to do with that and the sharing of the fear. Have you ever noticed how little boys laugh when they're all afraid together?'

'Pretend to laugh.'

'Yes. I suppose. Flash, I can't see why they couldn't have given me an infantry battalion if they didn't want me in tanks any more.'

'You still drinking?'

Von Mansdorff nodded and Flash poured another drink. 'Rudi, when they had you on that slab or whatever, they probably thought you were going to die. Their attitude to you, medically I mean, has been based on whatever was written down then. That's how the system works in any army . . . Who knows, maybe you'll get back into your own uniform one of these days. But I don't want you to. I want you with us. We need a soldier around. We really do. It's good for the lads.'

'Normally the Luftwaffe doesn't much like us.'

'My friend, haven't you noticed? This is a different kind of Luftwaffe.'

Von Mansdorff laughed. 'I must go to bed. So must you . . . You're doing your Geschwader formation thing tomorrow morning, aren't you?'

'Yep . . . We'll show them.'

Flash had been half sitting against the table in the centre of his room as Von Mansdorff stood and moved to the door behind him. 'Rudi,' he said as the German was about to leave, 'tell me . . .' He turned to face his visitor, and when Von Mansdorff turned back, great-coat hanging from his shoulders, his eyes fell on the bottle on Flash's table. It was almost empty, so he moved to pour its remains into his glass.

'Tell you what.'

'Are you going to win this war?'

Von Mansdorff sipped at his glass and looked keenly with his one eye at the other man. Then, as though blowing the word across his glass, he said, 'No.'

'But you're going on . . .'

'Yes, and so are you . . . Flash, we won't win this war because of our Fuhrer – and it's nonsense to make him carry all the blame. No one individual can control the destinies of eighty million people, but he, they, have decided to go for the belly of Russia: they should have gone for the heart, in spite of all the difficulties. Maybe they have no choice. Maybe they think they need the grain of the Ukraine and its minerals; the oil of the Caucasus. Maybe they lost it before it was started. Attacking Russia is like punching a bag of potatoes. But the first rounds have been fired, and we have missed. There are still the variables. Who knows? Goodnight.'

* * *

Next day Flash's squadron took off in Flights of four to fly on the port wing of twenty-four other aircraft under the command of Major Kirnowski. It was an exhilarating experience, flying again in that weaving cluster of aircraft in full wing formation. Kirnowski came up on the RT occasionally, in German, brusquely, controlling them as he led them around the three points of a triangle which covered around two hundred kilometres or thereabouts. It all went off splendidly. To such an extent that when they landed and Kirnowski came across to make his comments to Flash, the first thing he said was 'Good . . . Your people did very well. I'd like you to fly with me, Jordaan, on my wing.'

'Really . . . when?'

'Why not now?'

Flash smiled. 'Why not?'

In fifteen minutes the two MEs were taking off with Flash to the starboard and slightly behind when at around five hundred feet Kirnowski banked steeply to port. Flash followed, more tightly than possibly the other had expected, for it was well after the war had started that the RAF had adopted the German tactic of flying in a loose 'finger four' formation. Prior to that, all Flash's training, particularly pre-war, had been concentrated in developing a close formation technique. But that had been more suitable for flying displays than for fighting.

Around the airfield once, with Flash tightly tucked in, and then Kirnowski took them straight up to ten thousand feet. Beneath they had quite an audience, for every pilot, every fitter, rigger, all of them, had the feeling that some kind of conflict was taking place above them. Flash himself certainly was: he was sticking to his man like a leech.

From the height they had reached Kirnowski took them

straight down to about five thousand. Flash stayed with him. Then up into the vertical and over, still in a tight formation, and then around in what appeared to be a perfect loop. There were mutterings on the ground, especially when Kirnowski really pushed his luck and went up into a half roll with Flash still there – before turning over and into straight and level flight.

Kirnowski had never seen anyone fly as Flash was then. They went on, with the Major at one point even turning into Flash who had to throttle back fiercely to stay in position. It was then around and down with Flash on the inside, before flipping smartly over to port in an attempt to lose his man. But Flash stayed there as Kirnowski dived towards the field before breaking at about fifty feet and waggling his wings. He'd had enough. He was away.

But Flash stayed at his height and started into a long turning arc around the field to make an approach perhaps three miles from the perimeter. It was then he turned his machine on its back, and, completely inverted with throttle fully open, he dropped his nose a shade until he was flying at less than thirty feet, straight across the field. Nose up and over, a turn to port, up to about three hundred feet, throttle back, wheels down, a little flap – fifteen degrees; full flap: around and down.

When he taxied back to his dispersal Kirnowski was waiting for him, smiling. 'Excellent, Jordaan . . . truly excellent. I congratulate you.'

Flash had been expecting something of a rocket for that last rather extravagant gesture. But Kirnowski laughed as he shook the South African's hand. 'Now I know why they call you Flash,' he said.

There was a difference in all of them, and it was apparent when they were gathered, jostling, enjoying their laughter in the bar that night. Their confidence had reached that pitch where they could flaunt their experience. Their difference had nothing to do with nationality. Their strengths had been regained, and Flash's performance with Kirnowski that day had stroked the t's and dotted the i's. They were in great form when Von Mansdorff came into the bar. 'Gentlemen . . . gentlemen, I have an announcement.'

Gradually they quietened. He looked up at them and smiled. Then he glanced at Flash before he spoke. 'You are now officially Jagstaffel 70, attached to Geschwader 55.' Von Mansdorff nodded to Flash. 'Oberleutnant, they are all yours.'

Flash took over. 'Tomorrow you will receive uniform, additional flying kit and the daggers of an officer. You are appointed Leutnants of the Luftwaffe, even Dilewski. It is to be hoped that in three days from now we will leave for Russia – if someone can find a JU 52 which will carry our equipment.'

His words were piercing. They made no reaction whatever until someone broke their confusion – big Dutch it was – by saying, 'Let's drink to it.'

And they did, far into the night; long enough for those still containing a trickle of doubt to feel that they were hardening into a kind of certitude.

15

As Flash Jordaan walked back to his place from that of the commander of the Jagdgeschwader there was a strange misty light which seemed to rise from the squelch of the grass beneath his feet right up to the tips of the young trees which were trying to grow behind the wooden frame of his HQ. The feeling of it being all so alien was seeping into his brain.

This was Gretorsk, fifty miles to the north west of Sebastopol. Six weeks before Jordaan and his people had joined the Gruppe it had been decided that the main German thrust in that summer of 1942 should take place in the south.

Flash was troubled. The man he had just left had seemed to be a decent enough chap, but distinctly sceptical. Oberst Dietrich, Flash had judged to be about twenty-eight years of age; a firm, thick-set man with a smile which seemed to come easily. The whole idea of Flash being one of his squadron commanders appeared to amuse him. In fact it wasn't difficult to imagine that the situation in which Dietrich found himself then was affecting him with a wry resignation. He had said to Flash that morning, 'You're lucky, Jordaan. You've missed the winter up north where we've come from. In a week or so the mud here should become dust. Dust is better than mud. This is a bloody awful country. If I were a Russian, I'd give the place away.'

Flash had smiled.

'Sit down, Jordaan. Tell me about yourself.'

So Flash had told him as much as seemed appropriate.

'I've just come from headquarters. Have you met Kommandeur Lenze?'

'Yes.' Flash's expression betrayed nothing, but the other man smiled.

'Ah, well . . . You mustn't expect everyone here to welcome you with, as they say, open arms. He's, down here, had to cope with Rumanians, Bulgarians, Italians, everything . . . And don't forget, many of them have fought the Royal Air Force. Many of them have lost friends. Some of them don't have too much imagination . . . Even I think you're crazy.'

'Herr Oberst, there are people who'd rather be dead than be a prisoner.'

'I know . . . I know . . . I think I can understand. But, Jordaan, lots of these people have read of you in the German press, you and your people. They presented you as though you were heroes of the Third Reich. My people here are survivors, most of them. They've been through a great deal. Understand that. It will take time.'

Flash winced at the thought of those damned press men on the day before they had left for Russia. 'We'll try to live that down,' he said.

'I'm sure . . . But, Jordaan, do you realize that as far as Berlin is concerned, you have served your purpose. They could have taken you out, taken those pictures, and sent you back to where you came from. I'm surprised you trusted those bastards in Berlin.'

'I trusted Von Mansdorff.'

'Yes, I suppose so. I know about him.' The Oberst's voice deepened as he mentioned Von Mansdorff's name. 'He's quite a distinguished man.'

'We think so.'

'I must make a point of knowing him better. But look,

the idea of your continuing as a Staffel comprised entirely of ex-RAF pilots simply won't stand up. Any day now our aircraft will be ready to take part in this offensive. There will be losses. These Russians are beginning to learn their business as far as we are concerned. The Ivans are not all fools. I ask you, Jordaan, where are your replacements coming from?'

Flash looked straight at this man. For some strange reason – perhaps because of his pre-occupation with getting the whole thing going – he hadn't thought of such a necessity. But he revealed nothing of his thinking when he said, 'It's of no consequence, Herr Oberst, we'll take yours. Whatever we can get . . .'

'Or we'll take yours.' The Gruppen Commander stood, as did Flash. 'Berlin used you. Your propaganda has expired, in terms of value. In a few days we'll see the value of your fighting.'

All this was in his mind when Flash entered his office and called to Von Mansdorff.

'How was he?' Von Mansdorff asked.

'He's fine . . . fine. I like him.'

'Not like Lenze.'

'Different type.'

'What's wrong?'

'Nothing, really . . . Sit down, Rudi.'

Slowly, with his eye never leaving Flash's face, Von Mansdorff sat, and when he had Flash repeated what the Gruppen Commander had said about replacements.

'Flash, I'd thought of that. But does it matter? You have the Staffel. I'm back at the front. That's what we really wanted. We're here.'

'I told him it wouldn't matter.'

'. . . But it won't be the same.'

'No. No, I don't suppose it will.'

'Ach, Flash . . . Let's have a drink . . . When do we strike?'

'Three or four days I think.'

'Then you can show that bastard Lenze.'

'We can try. But we can try. We won't on the first two or three. The lads will be scared shitless.'

'Prost!'

'Prost . . .' When he had tasted the warmth of the drink, Flash laughed before saying, '. . . And so will I.'

The Jagdgeschwader to which Flash and his men had been posted was part of VII Air Corps, of the Fourth Air Fleet, and under the overall command of Frieherr Wolfram Von Richthofen, a nephew of the man who had made such a reputation for himself in the First World War. Just weeks before the new squadron had joined them the whole Air Fleet had been brought south to assist Von Manstein in his struggle for the Caucasus and eventually the Crimea. These objectives were the basis of Germany's operational plans in the east for the summer of nineteen forty-two.

Flash had chosen Van Reine and Del Renzio as his Flight Commanders – not only because, of them all, they were his friends, but because, on balance, they were possibly the most experienced of his pilots. It was Del Renzio who said, 'This 109F is a good aeroplane, Flash.'

'We could do with some more of them. We've only got twelve.' Flash had another thought. 'Don't break one for God's sake.'

Del Renzio ignored him. 'They're better than those bloody old Ratas and Kittyhawks the Russians have got.' His longish legs were outstretched on a second chair, as Flash's were on the desk before him.

'What I'm waiting for,' Jordaan said quietly, 'is to get alongside those bastards. They're all so bloody operational. They look at us as though we're a bunch of boy scouts who're thrilled at having their pictures in the paper.'

It was at that moment that Von Mansdorff came into the office. 'Well, gentlemen, we brief this evening. I think you'll find that the Geschwader takes off before five in the morning.'

Feet hit the floor. 'Good!' Flash stood up.

Von Mansdorff was excited. 'You're being unleashed.'

Del Renzio laughed and rose to prod Van Reine's stomach. 'All right, Dutch: you happy? Now we'll separate the men from the boys . . .'

The Dutchman's shoulders shook and he made something of a wry face. 'I think I need a drink . . . I'm one of the boys.'

Flash asked when they briefed, and Von Mansdorff told him with the eagerness of a young boy bringing good news to his father. 'This evening. Twenty hundred hours.'

'All right, we'll have a drink. This is something worth drinking to. Christ, we've had a few together, but this time, this time it's different.'

'Next door, gentlemen. My stuff is better than anything Flash has.'

Del Renzio clicked his heels and bowed. 'We know that, you bastard. How do you manage it?'

'I have connections.'

'We know that too.' The three spoke as though in unison.

Each of them, as they sat around Von Mansdorff's desk, smiled over their drinks at no one but themselves. They were silent with their thoughts locked within until Van Reine said, 'We've come a long way since you were making that bloody awful stuff in sick quarters back at Leinefelde, Del.'

Still no one said anything. Outside the sun was high in its afternoon, and there was all the flurrying noise of an airfield in action; men's voices raised in agitation, the quick bursts of an engine breaking into life, the whine of moving vehicles. 'All right then,' Flash eventually said. 'You chaps had better have a word with your flights. Rudi, you and I will have a walk around. I want to have a word with Dalgleish. He'll be flying as my number two.'

There was a distinct curiosity displayed by those men who saw Flash walking with Von Mansdorff towards that corner of the airfield where their aircraft had been dispersed. They had heard of 'the English', but the sight of Von Mansdorff with his eye-patch, his decorations and his sleeve tucked into the pocket of his tunic, that intrigued them.

Now it was May, and the last of the mud was disappearing. Here and there odd flutters of dust were swirling into the air. 'Is this country ever normal?' Flash asked his companion.

'Never. Can't be. There's too much of it.'

The whole airfield was a great beating nerve of activity. Flash had seen something of the same before in England. But here there was more of the atmosphere of a battlefield. From away to the north east came the sound of guns battling for Kharkov. Von Mansdorff said it. Just one word, 'Kharkov'. And as Flash turned to him he added, 'They've been at it all winter.'

Instinctively Flash looked in the direction towards which Von Mansdorff had nodded. Out there was only the long line of trees, freshening now with the early summer, while above them white spurts of careless cloud were hanging in the afternoon's haze. Young Dalgleish was at their dispersal, apparently fascinated by the efforts of the fitters attaching bomb racks beneath a Messerschmidt's wings.

'All right, Hugo?'

The tall, dark-haired Scotsman seemed cheerful enough. 'Fine, Flash.'

The fitters working there paid no attention to the three officers. Flash followed their movements for a moment or two before saying, 'It looks like we're being fighter bombers tomorrow. What are we carrying?'

'Little things . . . lethal . . . anti-personnel fragmentation bombs. Better than looking for Russians up there who probably won't show.'

Von Mansdorff spoke with authority when he said, 'Don't underestimate them. They fight hard, those Ivans . . . And their equipment's getting better all the time.'

'See you at briefing.' Flash turned to go, after he had tried with little success to show some encouragement to the man working there.

'Flash . . .' Dalgleish had raised his right arm in a gesture of friendship. 'We didn't have briefings in Fighter Command.'

'Yes we did, when we had time. This is a different kind of war. Out here we're flying artillery. After we've done our stuff we'll be protecting those Stukas.'

With Von Mansdorff, Flash walked around the other two flights. Most of his people were there, apprehensive. Flash could feel it. Von Mansdorff did. He was smiling as they walked towards their Mess for a drink and a meal before appearing at the twenty hundred hours briefing.

They were billeted in the battered remains of what had once been a modest villa in Tzarist times. Now the place had the bedraggled look of some discarded old woman. Grass, the ancient shrubbery, the few trees left standing, everything in that afternoon heat gave the impression of having been left behind by nature itself. The laughter which came from inside the place as they approached was almost startling.

'A little different from the Rhineland,' Flash said.

'Or France.'

'Indeed. The Luftwaffe were living there in great style when they gave me lunch at our first meeting – on the ground.'

'Ach, no matter. We won't be here long.'

'You think not?'

'I'm sure of it.' Von Mansdorff chuckled. 'This is a war of movement.'

'Eastwards . . .'

'Not at the moment. Southwards, I would say.'

They ate rabbit with some Russian wine. It was drinkable. When they had eaten Flash went to his room to stretch on the bed his man had arranged for him. He had thought of some sleep. But that was impossible.

The anger he had known as a prisoner had more or less gone. Something else was replacing it. The men here were different from those he had met when training in Germany. He wanted to be like them. In England, from the first day, he had been operational. His kind of men had always been so different from those others in the Air Force. There were so many who had flown but never grown. Here, these Germans were of his own kind.

More and more since he had come to Russia he had known a creeping sense of deficiency. He had thought it all out back at Leinefelde. He had been right – he was now sure of that – when he had made the decision to follow Von Mansdorff. But out here, as you looked at it, the earth seemed to have no ending. All this vast movement of men and machines seemed almost to be beyond imagining. One individual's rightness or wrongness was of little consequence, But there was still a faint itching sense of shame in thinking of what he was doing and where he was. Now, whether or not he was rotting in that damned camp seemed to be of no consequence. To that extent, he had released himself.

The briefing was tense, but lucid; and to his surprise Flash understood enough of what was important. Von Mansdorff was there to make sure that he and the others had, and he was delighted with their understanding.

At 04.45, just before the sun would rise above them, they would take off. The whole Gruppe, or the best part of it, four squadrons of Stukas escorted by a fighter Geschwader under the command of Dietrich would be attacking the Russian salient at Kersh. The Staffel led by Oberleutnant Jordaan would attack a Russian tank battalion said to be advancing strongly. This attack to be followed by three squadrons of Stuka dive-bombers. All fighters, including Jordaan's, would act as an escort to the Stukas when they had completed their attack.

Flash was lying on the rather rough blanket which covered his bed when Von Mansdorff pushed open the creaking door of the peeling room which he had occupied since his arrival. An oil lamp was on the table beside the bed.

'All right?' Von Mansdorff asked.

'Fine.' Flash moved his body and Von Mansdorff sat on the bed.

'He's given you a tough one for starters.' Flash could see the German's shoulders shrug in resignation.

'He's a bastard.'

'No. I like Dietrich. I like the man. Mind you, I think he could have let us fly as high-level escort to let us have a look at the place. But I understand him.'

'You've got map references. The Stukas know where they're going . . . Don't worry. You'll see those tanks.

There'll be infantry with them. That's what your bombs are for.'

'We'll hit them, Rudi. Don't worry, we'll hit them.'

'My friend . . .' Von Mansdorff struggled with a pocket. 'Maybe Dietrich's not big enough to be a real bastard. But I have the feeling he wants rid of you. Here . . .' A smallish bottle of brandy was extracted from the pocket. 'No glasses?'

'Use these coffee cups.' Flash swung his legs to the floor as the other man stood.

'Prost.' Flash took the extended brandy as the other man added, 'Wish I were coming with you.'

'You know . . .' Flash flexed his knees before saying, 'I had a Station Commander in England who always said that, but he never did.'

'I would, if I could.'

'I think you would.'

When Von Mansdorff had emptied his cup and replaced its contents he said, 'We're moving further south.'

'When?'

'Two, three days . . . Within the week.'

'Where's the party?'

'Sebastopol.'

Jordaan raised an eyebrow. 'The British had a go at that during the Crimean War.'

'You're right. It's the key to the Crimea . . . Say nothing of what I've said, Flash.'

Flash nodded as he received another drink from the German. Then Von Mansdorff turned towards the door. 'Sleep,' he said. 'I'll see you at take-off.'

But Flash didn't sleep much. He lay there listening to the occasional sound of a man's voice, and the humming life that surrounded him in all that wildness.

* * *

And neither did the others. Van Reine's mind was not troubled. There was a relief in thinking of the following morning, but there seemed to be no defence against all the signposts that rose up in his memory. There were thoughts of being a Boy Scout in Haarlem, where he had grown, and a girl in school whose name he could not remember. Once she had giggled and tickled the palm of his hand when he had been about thirteen. She had frightened him a little, for the gesture for him had no meaning.

There was America, where they had sent him to learn his airmanship. There had been the Darr School of Aeronautics in Oklahoma and Mr Taylor and Mr Clutter and Mr Hill. What men they had been, talking always as they had done with that deep Southern sureness while they swaggered so easily in those high-heeled cowboy boots they all wore.

Van Reine was working at his memories now. They brought him comfort. There was Red Lewis the cab driver and there were his fellow pupils, Nelson and Pope. There was Tex Ryan, the huge Texan instructor who'd been so effortlessly friendly and who'd been killed, in spite of his strength, when a fledgling pupil had frozen on the controls and taken them both into the ground.

There had been the thrill of achievement when he had joined Braniff, those great days of making it as a Captain on the Chicago, New Orleans route.

And there had been those months on the Trans-Atlantic ferry when he had made all that money flying Hudsons via Gander and Iceland to Prestwick in Scotland; and the long sailings back to Halifax when they had played endless poker and been more frightened in those convoys than they had ever been in the air.

There had been Samantha, she to whom he'd always

been afraid to declare himself because he stood in such awe of the chief flying instructor. There was a memory of her running alongside the train when he was leaving Ponca City forever. Now she was a misted figure in a flurry of blonde hair with a tentative hand raised to her lips. Jesus, it had been a shiftless life; very different from anything his father had ever known. But maybe it was bloody impossible to break through to the meaning of your father.

Eventually the big man, accepting that he was unable to beat sleep into subjection, cursed and swung his legs to the floor of the room he was sharing with Fahy, the Irishman.

'What's the matter?' came from the Irishman's bunk.

'I can't fucking sleep.'

'Have a drop of the Jamieson's and give me a fag.'

'Can you sleep?'

'No.'

Van Reine poured them both a brandy before lighting two cigarettes.

'I'll tell you one thing, though . . .' Paddy got into a sitting position and carelessly scratched his head.

'What's that?'

'We'll sleep the morra.'

'Cheers, Paddy.'

'I'll tell you one thing, though, Dutch. I wish . . . I wish it was time to get up. That's a fact.'

Dalgleish was at his aircraft when Flash Jordaan arrived at Flight dispersal at around four in the morning. He was a rather silent, remarkably self-contained man for one who after all was still in his early twenties. 'Morning, Flash,' was all he said.

Flash said almost nothing before he drifted off to have

a word with the other two flights. Von Mansdorff was with Del Renzio when he reached the Italian's flight.

The three chattered, but there was nothing very much that had to be said. Flash walked around the other pilots offering words of encouragement which he knew to be rather pointless. But they had to be spoken.

The whole field was starting into life. First there was the sharp bark of the Stukas. They would be first to take off. There was the first sign of an encouraging light in the east, and as it spread across the lower ridges of the sky there gathered in Flash a slight suggestion of restlessness as he thought of the shield that sun would provide for the enemy. No matter. He bantered in broken German with the crew who were there, and when Von Mansdorff approached out of the noisy confusion which was gathering all around them, he smiled and slapped the German on the shoulder. 'This is better,' he said, 'in . . .' He looked quickly at his watch. 'In eight minutes we're off.'

A white Verey-type light had burst over the far end of the field. There was a strong surging of engine noise as the Stukas started to taxi. The first of them was off, followed in threes by the rest of their force. Flash climbed aboard his aircraft. Outside and below, standing feet apart with that trenchant look which never seemed quite to leave him, Von Mansdorff was smiling. He raised his hand in a gesture which was not quite a salute, more a salutation. Jordaan felt a goodness within himself as he looked at the man standing there. There was a sharp burst of throttle to move the machine from where it had settled. Then he was moving towards take-off with the other three machines following closely.

The Stukas were ahead and above at four thousand feet. Flash, Dalgleish, the Pole, Dilewski and his other fellow were hugging the earth at about three hundred feet. In fifteen minutes or thereabouts they should be seeing their enemy.

Quick bursts of convection hit them now and then as the earth melted from the chill of the night. It was fun. Flash waved to Dalgleish on his starboard. To his port, the Pole, Dilewski, was a little further behind. What, he wondered, was Dilewski thinking at that moment?

Throttled well back so that their airspeed was not much more than two hundred kilometres an hour, the Messerschmidt, with those damned bombs under the fuselage, was heavy on the stick. It didn't feel at all like the machine he'd been throwing all around the sky in previous weeks. But at that height the speed was enough to exhilarate.

When Flash saw the black tanks crawling towards him, the others in the flight had done so at the same moment. They moved up alongside until all four were flying more or less in line abreast. Flash opened his throttle, forcing them to follow. Now it was to hell with everyone. Ahead those crawling, insect-like outlines began to assume the aspect of brutes. At full throttle, Jordaan had his nose down. He sat balanced, square, moving alive, tensed. Everything was sweeping past, and in his veins there was the lovely, surging expression of the blood rising, drenching all fear. Quickly he looked from side to side. They were there and there was a kind of pride in having them there. His gun-sights were switched on. He fingered the bomb-release gear. Now he could see the infantry moving amidst the tanks. There must have been more than a hundred there. There it was, the Russian tide.

Down and on, and very fast. They were firing at *him*. Now he switched on his RT. 'Go lads . . . go, go, go! Fuck them . . . Yaah!'

Up and at them came the long lines of tracer. Tanks too were firing their heavier stuff, but that was probably meant for the Stukas above and behind. That was it. His bombs were away, and he could feel the machine lightening, as though taken between the fingers of a giant hand. All around and below their bombs were bursting, sprinkled amidst the slow-moving tanks. Now it was cannon and machine guns and there was the gutsy relish of feeling the kick of the guns. When he pulled back, Flash was almost touching the aerials of the tanks, his target.

But Dalgleish was gone. Up, straight up with the black splurging smoke from his machine as it tired to a stall, and then staggering to a fall as Flash watched while he pulled back until it disappeared behind his starboard wing and he turned with the other two following through the heavy machine-gun fire that was coming at them from the Russians below.

Down there amidst all the confusion Jordaan could see the burning remains of what had been Dalgleish and his aeroplane. There was momentarily a clear image of Dalgleish; tall, stooping as though always in a gesture of politeness, with the long dark hair and the face which seldom revealed more than the suggestion of a smile which he seemed to use as a cover for his family's Highland glories of the past. Now he was down there, burnt on Russia; but not the first of his family. Some of them had died at Borodino. Even then Flash remembered Barclay de Touche, the Prince. Dalgleish had been fond of recalling that.

Flash took them around to starboard for another burst before skipping over them to clear the way for the Stukas. It was then up to be escort, tagging in behind Dietrich's Geschwader.

Some had seen Russian aircraft, but on that occasion

not Flash or any of his flight had seen one. They landed on the wide, uncharted grass which was their airfield, and as Flash climbed down from his aircraft Von Mansdorff was there. 'All right . . . All right, Flash?'

'All right . . . We lost Dalgleish.'

In an hour they were off again. But this time Flash's flight was carrying no bombs. Their job would be to escort the Stukas, for it was assumed that by now all element of surprise would be missing. The Russians would be bound to be covering those tanks attempting to advance.

Flash, on this second sortie, was to have Dilewski act as his number two. He talked to all of them, or rather, he listened to them, for each one of them was filled with the excitement of their first run. Only Del Renzio mentioned Dalgleish. And as he did so he seemed to speak out of a mood that Flash had not known in the man before.

Everywhere men were hurrying to re-arm and re-fuel while Flash, with the sound of their alien voices all around him, studied the instructions that had been brought to him by Von Mansdorff. This time the centre-piece of thirty plus Stukas would be escorted by a fresh wing of Messerschmidts. That, with Flash's Staffel, would provide high cover at fifteen thousand feet.

It was almost exactly an hour after they had landed that take-off took place.

Thin dust was whirled up as aircraft taxied towards take-off point. Then it was into the wind and through it in formations of four. Action had now dampened all thought. Each of them in his way could feel that resolute tension which once had been an everyday part of their lives, and strangely, with only one operational sortie behind them here on this front, the intervention of their captivity was now obliterated; maybe for ever to only re-appear in tiny corners of their minds.

The sun was now very much on the side of the enemy. White puffs of early cirrus at eight thousand feet was partially helpful, but through that and above they were in open sky. Dietrich's Staffel was leading, while the others, almost fifty aircraft, followed, banked in fours. Flash felt the awesomeness of seeing the guns below, the irritation of their flashes. To the south there were glimpses of the mountains, but away to the east and north was only the long sweeping earth with its massive indifference to the men struggling below.

'Achtung!' It was probably Flash who saw them first. Over and down he went, with his immediate flight on his tail. And at that they did. He threw a quick glance to his starboard to see that Dilewski was following, and then, having cut his throttle, opened gradually until it was close to the gate. Something like a dozen Russians were heading down for the Stukas. Their aircraft had a remarkable resemblance to the Germans' FW 190; but for the action of the others he would have had doubts as to its nationality. It was in fact the Lavochkin LA5, a very fast radial engined brute of a thing which he had been told was something to be reckoned with.

The Messerschmidts below and around the dive-bombers had obviously been taken by surprise. But the Russians cut through them to go straight for the Stukas who broke, scattering. But they were late. Flash saw three of them wobbling, hit, while others seemed to be dropping their bombs at random in their anxiety to get away.

It was a long way down, and when he had reached the height at which the Russians had struck, Flash went straight on down, heading on to the nearest Lavochkin he could get his sights on. On the point of firing a Messerschmidt crossed his line and he cursed. Then it was out and after them to the east to which they had run. Somewhere on the way down he seemed to have lost Dilewski, and he couldn't catch those LA5s. Flash turned steeply to port and stayed there as he sped back across the front and through the fire that was coming at him from both sides on the ground.

They hit him, clipping the wing-tip on his starboard. All he could do was to go on down through the hail of tracer until he could remember to breathe. He was out and over. When he could, he swung his neck up and behind, but there was nothing he could see that made any semblance of a formation.

Those aircraft that were serviceable made another two sorties that day, and one on the following day. But for then it was over. Von Mansdorff announced on the evening of the second day that they would be preparing to move south to begin the assault on Sebastopol. They could relax, and they did with the thought that they'd taken rather more of a battering than they'd expected.

16

The Irishman, Fahy, had gone on the second day. Someone had said they'd seen him bail out, but he'd gone. He'd been a strange big fellow, Fahy. It had always been difficult to know if there had been much inside. He'd made a lot of noise with his Irish jokes and his songs, but it was difficult to remember him ever *saying* anything. It had almost been as though he'd been embarrassed by being in the RAF, and when Flash thought back to him he wondered if perhaps he had taken his Irishness more seriously than he had ever revealed.

Dietrich had come to talk with Flash on the evening of the day Von Mansdorff had said they were moving south. There was a certain hunger on his face which hardened at the chin. 'So, Jordaan . . . you were hit, I hear.'

'Nothing too serious.' Flash offered him a drink which he didn't refuse, but only accepted with a silence which suggested that his mind was on other things. When he had the drink he looked hard at it for a moment, as though examining its glow and its warmth. Then quite suddenly his lips parted, and he said, 'Prost . . . You did well, Jordaan. You lost two of your people.'

'Yes. I'm sorry. Thank you.'

'You have a state of readiness?'

Flash turned to Von Mansdorff who was standing there. He had heard, so he said, 'Yes, sir. It will be on your desk first thing in the morning.'

Dietrich's eyebrows flickered, as though such an answer was not quite satisfactory, but all he did was to take a step backwards before saying, 'Well, gentlemen, we move further south. It will be really warm down there. We'll get our shirts off at last.' Then he told them of the time of the Gruppe briefing on the following day before looking around the room in which most of Flash's people were standing in small groups. 'This is a terrible place. In the south we can live under the sky if we want to. It will be better. Goodnight.'

When he left he seemed to leave behind something of the embarrassment he had obviously been feeling in the presence of Jordaan. 'A strange fellow,' Flash suggested. 'I was right about him. He's strong.'

Von Mansdorff chuckled. 'The last two days have rattled the blood around his veins. That's all.'

They ate and drank in the villa which had been assigned to them when they arrived. Truly, it was a dreadful place, but nothing else around was much better, so it was easier to be in the place where they slept.

'Chaps!' Flash's voice ran around the room, and gradually they were silenced.

'Speech!' someone called.

'No, no . . . No speech. But listen . . . Dietrich was pleased with you. He thought you did rather well.'

'So did I,' added Von Mansdorff.

'So did we,' someone shouted. 'Yes!' They all took it up. 'So did *we*.'

The whole room seemed to crumple in laughter, and then there was a great bustling of drinks and glasses. It was a party. Eventually Del Renzio and Van Reine gravitated from the lads in their flights to join Flash and Von Mansdorff. It was he, Von Mansdorff, who saw the differences in their attitudes. Already there was a heaviness in Van Reine which was not physical. In Del Renzio, too, there was something different, a sobriety, which he had never revealed when everything had been so hopeless for him.

It wasn't that they appeared to be unwilling to join with the mood of the group: perhaps they were reflecting the attitude of the gathering there which in itself had changed. Von Mansdorff looked at them and knew. He had seen it in the men of his tanks when each one of them seemed, almost imperceptibly, to have drawn back from his comrades in self-defence.

By now Von Mansdorff had almost forgotten his reason for being there. But he had surrendered to the inevitability of his situation. Even to himself, he had to admit that his thinking back at Leinefelde, the prison camp, had been more or less infantile. But for whatever reason, they were there; and with that thought Von Mansdorff himself withdrew. The others understood: they left him alone with his remembrance of the young Scotsman, Dalgleish, and all his pride and innate gentility which was now dead, as was Fahy's Irishness and Oberlin's quiet arrogance, he who was the descendant of the Marquis de Montcalm, the protagonist of Wolffe at the Heights of Abraham – and who had been a late addition to their group: it was all dead, as was young Oberlin's life. Had he been wrong? To satisfy his own need to be free, had he killed them?

It was something he could not discuss with Jordaan. Flash, his friend, had to go through with the ritual of apparent unconcern. It was their only shield. But he knew, and he knew about himself. They would all have to go on. Von Mansdorff looked at his drink as it receded in his outstretched arm. And as he examined the glass his fingers tightened; and he knew that he, and all of them would have to go; perhaps go. He turned to them. 'Gentlemen, let us drink to this Staffel.'

There was a kind of riot of loose laughter which

descended into ribaldry. Tunics were undone, hair was much ruffled. Eventually they were joined by some Germans from the neighbouring Staffel who had been attracted by the noise they were creating. It was a gathering which never achieved a conclusive ending. It just died. But for Flash it died slowly in his room with the Dutchman, the Italian, Von Mansdorff and himself, odd bottles and the remains of a dead chicken from which fingers had plucked most of its flesh.

Flash had become more than a little drunk. He asked, 'Fellows, what the hell are we doing?'

Von Mansdorff, at that, placed his good arm around Flash's shoulders. 'We are fighting a war, Flash. That's what we are doing.'

Jordaan sat down and shut up. But his mind was still invigorated; so that he could still remember all the space and freedom which had been of his life, the smell of that coarse grass. And when he had thought long enough of the old man and Mawli, who had taught him to accept the responsibility of being a man, he said quietly to Von Mansdorff, 'I want a woman.'

'In the village there are some. I will send for one.'

When she came, there were the thick thighs and the lumpy breasts and the belly. 'What is your name?' he said.

'Victoria.'

'Victoria, Victoria, Victoria.' For some long moments he looked at the poor soul, and then he lay back and was asleep. And in the morning, when his eyes had opened once or twice, it took some time to realize that there was someone else in the room. There, huddled, against the corner at the bottom of his bed, she was, wrapped in a blanket she had taken from him.

'Who? . . . What?' Flash raised himself to a sitting

position. He was utterly confused and then silent when he really could see the woman and realized that she was much afraid. He tried a little German, but that seemed to mean nothing, and when he stumbled into English a look of terror crept across the woman's face. Flash swung his legs out of the bed and grabbed his breeches. 'Rudi . . .!' he called in the direction of Von Mansdorff's room. And when a flustered Von Mansdorff appeared, minus his eye-patch and half shaved, Jordaan could only splutter, 'What the hell? . . . What the hell's going on? Who's this woman?'

As the two re-entered Flash's room the woman cringed in terror at the sight of this one-eyed man with a face covered in shaving soap who was trying to utter a few Russian words which to her were apparently incomprehensible. 'Smile . . . smile at her for God's sake,' Von Mansdorff growled.

'Who is she?'

'She's yours . . . You fell in love with her last night.'

'Christ!'

'Give her some money. Pay her . . . Let her get dressed and out of here.' Von Mansdorff was laughing now as he staggered from the room while Flash threw the woman some money before following him.

In Von Mansdorff's place he tried to extract some kind of explanation, but the German could only laugh at him. 'I promise . . . I promise,' Von Mansdorff said eventually, 'to tell no one. No one will ever know, Flash, that our good leader fell asleep before take-off. Honestly, I promise.'

'Shut up. Tell me about the arrangements for today.'

Von Mansdorff was quiet as he finished with his shaving. Flash realized that the man had switched into seriousness, so he said nothing as the German went on dressing with a determined independence. Eventually, with the suggestion in his tone that he had decided that he was ready, Von Mansdorff spoke. 'What do you mean? Are you asking what our little Staffel is doing or are you asking what we are all trying to do, the millions of us?'

'I don't know. But I'd like to know something of what the hell's going on.'

'I can only surmise – based on certain knowledge which is occasionally available to me.' This was a man seldom seen by Flash or anyone else. The tone of his voice had a weight, a seriousness. 'Flash, have you heard of Manstein?'

'I think so. Yes.'

'He's our Army Commander. In my opinion the finest General in the German Army . . . Probably, right now, the finest General in any Army.'

'You think so . . .'

'I do . . . Look at it this way: he needs to take Sebastopol. It's the key to the Crimea, and the Crimea, my friend, is the key to the Caucasus and all that lovely oil . . .'

'I suppose so.'

'You suppose so. I tell you so. Colonel-General Halder, Chief of Staff, prepared the plan for this summer's offensive. He had wanted to go for Moscow, but Hitler wouldn't have it. Hitler, in all fairness, is no military fool, but he seems to be haunted by Napoleon's embarrassment. Or maybe, to be serious, his reasons are economic. You understand, Flash?'

'Of course.'

'Well, anyway, as I understand it Halder's plan was finally approved by Hitler a couple of months ago at Supreme Headquarters in the Mauer Forest . . .'

'Where's that?'

'Near Rastenburg in East Prussia. Would you like to pay a visit?'

'No thanks.'

'So meanwhile while Von Manstein is tied down in the south, there's still the problem of clearing the residue of last winter's set-backs in the centre and the south. In January the Russians recaptured the Kerch Peninsula. Things are even worse at Kharkov. The Russians are trying to cut off the place with a massive pincer operation. We must avoid this at all costs.'

'It sounds, shall we say, daunting,' Flash suggested with a smile.

'To say the least . . . At Belgorod and Volchansk we're holding their effort, but in the south they've broken our front on both sides of Izyium on a stretch of fifty miles. They're threatening Dnepropetrovsk, and that's the supply centre for the whole of Army Group South. To avoid a major breakthrough we have to hold Blakleya and Slavyansk . . . So there it is.'

'How the hell do you know all this?'

'Never mind.'

'Doesn't sound good.'

'No it doesn't.' Von Mansdorff, finally dressed, lit a cigarette. It was one of the Russian variety with a long cardboard holder which he had found somewhere. He drew long on the thing, and then he looked at a rather confused Jordaan and smiled. 'I like their cigarettes,' he said.

In fact Colonel-General Halder was worried about the overall state of the German Army at that time. More than a million men had died since 'Operation Barbarossa' had first rolled east in the previous June. With most of his fellow professionals he felt that a re-grouping was necessary in order to establish a more stable front before heading yet again for Moscow which in his opinion was the nerve centre of all the Russias.

But there was to be no holding Hitler. The Fuhrer's plan when it finally emerged, was that two Army Groups in the form of a massive pair of pincers were to advance from the Kursk-Kharkov area and head down the middle Don to the south-east. The right arm of the pincer movement would drive eastward from the Taganrog area where the two armies would meet west of Stalingrad. The Russian forces between the Donets and the Don would be annihilated.

The advance into the Caucasus mountains would continue, heading between the Black Sea and the Caspian. The oilfields of the Caucasus would be Germany's.

The ground-plan for the Battle of Stalingrad had been laid.

17

God, to have a bath, thought Van Reine. But there was as little time as there was water. And in any case, what the hell? Only he could be close enough to notice the difference.

The big Dutchman lumbered himself from his bed and looked across at the other bed in the room. It was empty. It had been Fahy's bed, and for a moment the image of the Irishman was there, so that in the shirt which was all he wore, Van Reine stood there staring at the emptiness which seemed to have a physical existence. Then he shook himself and cursed before throwing some cold water over his face and head. Briefing was in half an hour. Christ, his head felt as though it was filled with gunge.

The trouble with mornings now, Van Reine considered as he looked at himself in the broken mirror streaked with soap, was that his being in this place seemed to have nothing to do with a decision he had made for himself. America had been his own decision. Transferring to Ferry Command and then to Fighter Command with the Royal Dutch Air Force, these had been decisions he had made for himself. And of course he hadn't been forced to follow Flash and Del Renzio or Von Mansdorff; but somehow there seemed to have been little choice in the whole business. If anything, being here in all this strangeness was better than the slow death of a prison camp when you didn't know whether you'd be there for months or years or forever. It was better. He dressed and decided to regret the previous night's drinking.

Outside, in the rising clearness of the morning's air, there was Del Renzio.

There was such a chasm, in spite of their easy familiarity, between these two. They could laugh together, when laughter was the only release; but Van Reine knew that they were very different people, bound together by the brute necessity of survival. Del Renzio, in terms of any man, was personable. But there was a casualness, a willingness to throw it all away, which Van Reine didn't have.

Their arrival in Russia had changed Del Renzio. He seemed to be a harder man than he had been when he had been concocting that gin back at Leinefelde. That morning as the big Dutchman emerged into the new day and Del Renzio was standing there in the uniform of the Luftwaffe, there was a difference in the man which had nothing to do with the uniform.

'All right?' Van Reine had said.

'Yes. I think so . . . All right.'

'Hungover?'

'A little.'

Van Reine smiled. 'Today we go south to the sun.'

'That's where I grew, my friend . . . in the sun.'

'Of course.' They started to walk towards the briefing-room which in fact was little more than a large wooden shack, and as they did so there were other groups converging on the place.

The two, the Dutchman and the Italian, were silent for a time, thinking and wondering of the place to which they were going, until Van Reine said, 'It was different for me in Holland.'

'Never been there.' And Del Renzio laughed. 'Good place for riding horses I hear.'

'Ah, it's not so bad.'

Del Renzio chuckled again. 'From what you've told me, you got out as fast as possible.'

'KLM sent me to England for the language and to the States for Flight Training, and then I absconded for the broad horizons. Do you know my first memory of England?'

'Guten Morgen . . .' Del Renzio waved a greeting to some Germans who were walking in their direction. 'What was your first memory of England?'

'It must have been in the very early thirties I suppose. I can see him now. It was a guy driving a coal cart, and it was raining. Not just raining, pissing down. His cart was laden with bags of coal, and he was wet and filthy with the stuff. His soaking old horse was labouring up a slope, pulling all this coal, and he had an empty bag over his head trying to keep off the rain . . . D'you know he was wearing an old khaki tunic which he must have worn in the first war, and as I looked at the poor bastard, I thought to myself that maybe his war was better than his peace. I've never forgotten that man. Funny how some things stick in your memory.'

'You're right. Funny is subjective. But I know that you didn't mean funny. Even I know that.' He laughed in a peculiar Italianate way. 'I know what you mean, and we all drag it with us. Maybe that's why we're here.'

'I suppose . . .' The big Dutchman slapped his friend on the shoulder as they walked now in rhythm. All around them was the early stirring of the base.

'Do you know what I'm thinking?' Del Renzio waved again to some German Jagdflieger. He was a friendly fellow. That was unquestionable.

'What are you thinking of – breakfast served by a man in a white coat?'

'In a way, yes. I'm thinking that I might abscond again.'

The Dutchman's eyes flicked quickly to his friend's face. 'Who to? . . . The Russians?'

'Those bastards . . . never. There are two hundred million of them. There's only one of me.'

'There's me.'

By now they could hear the loud hum of voices inside the place in which they were to assemble. Instinctively they kicked their feet against the primitive steps to remove the mud from their boots before entering, and when they did they made their way to those of their own Geschwader who were already there. In ten minutes there was the crash of their feet on the primitive flooring as, en masse, they were at attention.

The Kommandeur gave no strategic briefing. Three Geschwader would be flying south at intervals of thirty minutes, including one each of Stukas, Heinkel 111s and Messerschmidts of F and G development. Senior ground-staff NCOs and as many men as could be accommodated, would fly in the available JU 52s; the remainder would make their way south by road transport to be at the bases prepared for them in no longer than three days. That was virtually all. The situation on the Sebastopol front would be examined when they were battle-ready.

Within three hours Flash Jordaan and his Staffel were airborne. At that time of day they were flying into the sun obscured by high alto cirrus, but in that great strange flatness of a country which must, had it been left alone, be so enrichening, there could be no certainty about its sky. With Del Renzio and his three on one side and Van Reine and his on the other, the Staffel flew high on the port, guarding Dietrich's flank. Tingling through Flash was a feeling of goodness at being there in his own sky with the earth and its furies a world away.

In little more than two hours they were circling the

marked field which was their destination. From three, two, a thousand feet the place looked as though it was little more than an enormous meadow, which, in the circumstances, it presumably was. In Flash, as he slid back his canopy and pulled down his goggles, there was a sudden surging of respect for these Germans. That there was something in them which was a warrior's true essence, there was no doubt.

Touchdown; and then there was some confusion as they were being shepherded to their dispersal bays, and as he swung his aircraft around at the man's bidding and switched off Flash laughed to the crew on the ground who were there to serve him. When he used his fractured German to greet them, they were obviously confused until one, the ever-present German-American, explained to them that he was the Englishman. They had all heard of the Englishman.

Within an hour they were installed in tents which had already been erected, and around Flash there was the usual cluster of tension as he tried to get the cabin of a half-dismantled truck which he intended using as a headquarters into some kind of order. Van Reine turned up much later than the others. He it appeared had become confused during the let-down and had taken his flight into the wrong field. There was much cursing from the Dutchman as he was explaining to Flash the details of his mistake, until in the end Flash had to silence him by rasping, 'Shut up, Dutchy, for Christ's sake! Thank God it was you. If I'd gone in there, my German would never have got me out of the damned place.'

'OK, OK. I'll shut up.'

The smell of an aircraft – for there was no time to really clean them so that the odour of oil and petrol and glycol was removed – had an effect on a pilot then which stirred the blood. Over the next days Flash and his fellows were drenched in the stuff.

The days whirled in a maze of sunlight and dust. Mud was drying, voices hoarsening. Their job was to help Manstein's eleventh army to batter Sebastopol into submission. Richthofen's VII Air Corps, of which they were part, was flying a thousand, fifteen hundred, sometimes two thousand missions a day. Night and day von Manstein's heavy mortars and artillery were thundering at the city and its defences with greater power than was to be used at Alamein. The bombardment of Sebastopol was the heaviest of the second world war.

Mostly Flash's Staffel were being used as low-level attack fighters, but occasionally there was the relief of getting up as high-level escort. It was on one of those occasions that Jordaan shot down his first Russian.

By that summer the Russian Air Force was being equipped with the new Lavochkin LA5 and Yak 9 fighters; aircraft which had been designed to match the performance of the Messerschmidt. As well as this the Americans and British were shipping them Hurricanes, Kittyhawks and Aerocobras at a time when the total strength of the Luftwaffe was down to about a thousand aircraft of all types. But for the fact that the Russians were holding back their Airforce for an expected attack on Moscow, the Luftwaffe in the south would have been heavily outnumbered.

Flash was at nineteen thousand feet when he saw them. Van Reine's flight was on his left; Del Renzio's on his right. They were well over the Black Sea, to the south of Sebastopol around three thirty in the afternoon, and the sun was over his port quarter, so that he had a slight advantage when the Russians hit. But not much.

It was Van Reine who first saw them. 'Look out, Tony . . . Look out.'

They were the new Yaks. They had been told about them, but none of them had seen one before. The Yaks came in from the starboard very, very fast. Del Renzio slid away down into their direction. That was the last Flash saw of him. Was he dead?

Someone else was hit. Flash looked up and could see the white smoke streaming from one of his own aeroplanes. Christ knows who it was.

There was the feeling of the air around resisting. Every movement of the controls was against a pressure. An aeroplane is always fighting its own element. That was its strength. Take off the power and it's loose. It was like taking off a sweated shirt. Flash felt free as he went down. He was after those Yaks. They were clever. They had struck and were content. Down after them, he felt everything he had ever wanted to be in that sloping descent. All right. He cursed. You've killed my friend or maybc more. He had to have one of them. With his throttle right to the gate Jordaan gradually gained on a Yak which was trailing slightly behind the others. Down he went and down, until he was slightly beneath and behind the Yak at a hundred and fifty, a hundred yards. It was now. He pressed his gun button and felt the machine shudder. Then again. There was smoke, then flame. He'd hit the Russian somewhere behind the root of the port wing. It was a kill. It had to be.

Swinging his neck from side to side, Flash looked up and behind for his own, but there was futility in the gesture as he pulled back and up into a tight spiralling climb which drained the blood from behind his eyes and drew down the flesh around his mouth until his whole body felt as though it was sinking against the aircraft's climb. As he eased the control column, he rolled on to his back. No one was there below him. Back around and up he clawed his way into an empty sky. In minutes, little more than seconds, his own people had scattered. Away below and to the north west was the smoke and flash of Sebastopol's battle. Flash made one circling movement to his port. There was no one, nothing. A glance at his fuel gauge suggested it was time to head for his base at Skadovsk.

In the Ops trailer Von Mansdorff was sitting at one of the two desks as Flash entered. 'Do you know, Flash,' he said, 'I've been thinking . . .'

'Good. I got one, a Yak. One of the new ones. A beautiful kill.'

'Ah ha!' The German struggled to his feet. 'Ah ha, congratulations! You're what do you call it?'

'Blooded. I was blooded a long time ago. Different blood.'

'What of the others?'

Looking through the window, Flash announced that they were coming in, most of them. 'I think they got two of us. Didn't see who they were. But I think they got Del Renzio. He went down as they hit. They hit us fast.'

'*Del Renzio*. Christ, Del Renzio . . . Mmm.' Von Mansdorff looked out at the approaching aircraft but he didn't speak. The smile which crossed his lips was mirthless.

In his tent, Flash poured himself a drink and sat on his canvas chair. His mind went back over the Yak he had destroyed before settling on his memories of Del Renzio. He could hear in his imagination the enthusiasm of the Italian's laughter and see the eagerness of that ruffled smile of his.

His own life seemed to have been stirred in all directions by whichever wind was blowing. So had the Italian's, as to some extent had the lives of all of them who were with him in that place, those who had followed him into the Luftwaffe. He could sense the difference in his men from the regularity of the behaviour displayed by the Germans. They talked of their families, their wives, and some of them, of their children. They wrote endlessly to relatives and friends. The arrival of mail from home was the highlight of their week. His own men lived, divorced from all contact with their past. Now for Del Renzio it was over; his wandering, his dedication to survival.

Flash walked to the blanket-covered table and poured himself another drink, before sitting again to stare thoughtfully at his drink and smile at a fleeting thought of Del Renzio and his gin, when he saw the letter lying on his table. It was from Del Renzio. Flash sat down again, sipping his drink as he began to read.

'Dear Flash,

As you know, I'm not one for getting myself killed – never really found a good enough reason. So it seemed a good idea to wait for a high level one and then use the height towards taking a chance on getting myself to Turkey, now that it's more or less across the way.

I do hope the Turks are nice, although all that I've heard suggests the contrary. But I'm giving them an aeroplane. Let's hope they accept the gift – if I get there – in the spirit in which it is offered.

Flash, I didn't have to say a word, but in all fairness it seemed right that I should do so. You've been a good friend, and I appreciate that but for you I wouldn't have had this opportunity. Try not to be angry with me. I've thought this out, and to me it seems a better idea to sit this nonsense out on a beach in Turkey while I wait for those idiots who are trying to change the world to their own advantage to trip over their own bootlaces. They will. Believe me. I liked a lot of the Germans we have flown with, but I'm sorry for them and for my Italian friends and all the poor buggers who're hanging on to their coat-tails.

If you feel you dare tell him about the nature of my departure, give my best to Von M. He's a good guy. Maybe I'll see you for a drink in the bar of the Excelsior when this is all over and they've cleaned up the streets in Rome.

Good Luck.
Del R'

For a moment there was the blankness of disbelief in Flash's face. Some words spilled from his lips. 'Well I'll be damned. You've done it again, you old bastard.' And then he laughed until only another drink could calm him.

18

For another six weeks Flash Jordaan and his Staffel were engaged in the Crimea. It was air warfare as none of them had ever known it. The summer and its endless churning dust created their difficulties for men and machines. Machines were tiring, as were the men who flew them, and the men who maintained them.

For Jordaan his tiredness was tempered by the four victories he had added to that of his first. There was the satisfaction now of acceptance by Dietrich and by the recognition he received from those who came up from Gruppe. Von Mansdorff was no longer looking on the people he had brought there as some kind of novelty.

They were in the adjutant's tent, Jordaan and Van Reine and a Pole called Kirste who had joined them and was running Del Renzio's flight, when Mansdorff said, 'I think we're moving further north.'

'Surprise us, Rudi,' Van Reine said. 'Why?'

The warm dampness of the night clung to each of their bodies. Von Mansdorff again wiped his brow before pouring himself a drink. When he spoke he didn't do so as though addressing any one person. Instead, he seemed to be balancing the words he was using for his own consideration. 'Manstein has almost reached the Kersh peninsula. That man is brilliant . . . But the bastards at OKW won't leave him alone . . .' They were drinking sweet Crimean champagne. 'One of the things about this place . . . This stuff is good, eh . . . The Ivans can't be all bad.'

Kirste, the Pole, said 'They are all bad. Their champagne is good. That is all.' He was a tall, serious man of about twenty-eight, fair-haired and handsome, whose family had owned large estates in Eastern Poland before the war, and now were scattered. The others looked at him for a moment, knowing the extent of his bitterness.

'I suppose you're right, Kirste. Have some more . . . Help you to sleep.' Von Mansdorff went on thinking aloud. 'The OKW, or should I say the megalomaniac who's running it, is pulling out about half of Manstein's troops, including two of his best divisions. Can you believe it? They're being sent to France for re-fitting. He's heard something about the British and Americans striking from the west. It'll be years before they're ready for that. Meanwhile half of Manstein's army are to help with the push into the Caucasus – after they cross the Don and the Volga . . . We're going up there to help.'

Jordaan said, 'Maybe he's worried about oil.'

'Tscah. We have Rumanian oil.' Von Mansdorff was filled with irritation. 'He's breaking every German military precept of the past hundred and fifty years. Maybe he's mad.'

'Maybe,' Van Reine suggested, 'he wants to hit the Russians before they retreat into the mountains and build themselves defences that are too tough to break. Maybe that's his plan.'

Von Mansdorff stood. 'We'll find out soon. Drink up, chaps. What is it they say? . . . There may be no tomorrow.'

Flash wrestled with the humidity which was denying him sleep as he lay in his tent trying to rid his mind of thoughts which troubled him about the Staffel he was leading. His maintenance Sergeant had said that only half his aircraft would be serviceable in the morning. Del

Renzio had gone, and the other man who'd gone down had been the crazy Pole; but he'd managed to get himself down further west near Dzankoj. But Dietrich had congratulated him on his victory. That was something. He smiled, remembering the man saying as he had entered the Ops Room, 'Ah, Jordaan . . . You have a victory. Congratulations.' Still, the men were showing signs of tiring. Six of his originals had gone. Gradually, as the mists of sleep began to gather, there was the thought that perhaps the move north would be good for all of them.

In the morning there was again the surging of his engine's power, the high climb above Von Manstein's advancing forces, the satisfaction of throbbing through the deep blueness of an arching sky.

But it was later on that same day that Flash Jordaan achieved his sixth victory for the Luftwaffe – against a Hurricane. He was about to return to base as the sun was slowly edging towards the west when he saw it almost six thousand feet below him. There seemed to be something like two flights of them flying at the Hurricane's best operational height of fifteen thousand feet. Flash smiled as he went over and down with his wing men doing their best to follow. The thought that the Russians must have read the book before they flew the aeroplane fled through his brain.

At full throttle he hit them, for he knew that in the hands of someone who knew how to handle it a Hurricane was more manoeuvrable than his Messerschmidt. At a hundred and fifty yards, and obviously before the Russians knew he was there, he hit their lead aircraft and went straight on through. It was a kill. It had to be: and he was right. For as he turned steeply to port and away he saw the Hurricane he had hit falling with black smoke pouring from its engine and cockpit. That was enough.

With his throttle cut and the control column well forward he went into a dive towards base.

'Success, yes?' his laughing fitter called as he jumped from the wing of his aircraft and pulled off his helmet.

'Yes, yes. One more. Good, eh?'

Flash's feet seemed to wave over the ground as he made his way towards the Ops trailer and then paused at its door to watch the others come in.

Dilewski was laughing. He'd got another. But the real victory came when Flash entered the trailer to face a smiling Von Mansdorff, 'Ah, Major . . . Glad to have you back.'

Flash halted. 'Major?'

'It's just come through. You're taking over Dietrich's job when the wing moves north.'

'God.'

'Exactly. You're God . . . well, nearly. I'm to be the Angel Gabriel. They're putting me in charge of Wing Administration, and they've given me my old rank back – no doubt out of sympathy.

The villa was like something out of Chekhov, but crumbling. It had been organized by the newly restored Major von Mansdorff. They were three miles from Michajovka, and much heartened by their move and by this place they had found.

The huge room in which Flash had installed himself was of a peeling white. He loved it. He was laughing to himself when Von Mansdorff entered. 'Rudi, you're a genius. How the hell did you find all this?'

'It's *my* job. I am in charge of administration.' Then Von Mansdorff allowed himself to laugh. 'Ach, my boy – that's the thing about life. It has its ups and downs. This is an *up*. But I have even better news . . . We have been invited to dinner.'

'By whom?' Flash had discarded his tunic and was washing himself. 'By whom?'

'By our next door neighbour. The General commanding the Corps we are supporting – von Stumme.'

Von Stumme was a man with an elastic imagination, and a considerable reputation as a commander. He enjoyed giving dinner parties, and when he had heard that Von Mansdorff was in his vicinity – for they had known each other two or three years before when Von Mansdorff had served under him – he immediately suggested to his aide that Mansdorff, and, if he liked, a friend, should join him. It would be interesting to know those people of the Luftwaffe who were backing him.

To walk into the brightness of the General's house was like living again. Their coats were taken; they were ushered into the presence, and there, splendidly uniformed, were the warrior class. Jordaan matched Von Mansdorff's performance. Heels were clicked, and heads were smartly bowed.

'Rudi!' Stumme was a totally confident man. He seemed to leap from his chair before coming forward to greet Von Mansdorff. There was a warmth in their meeting. 'Hah, my boy!' Stumme turned to face Jordaan. 'You are the new Staffelkapitan. You are English?'

'Not really, sir.'

Stumme laughed. 'We have all kinds of people out here. I don't understand it. They are crazy. Gentlemen . . . a drink. Meet my people. We want to listen to you fliers . . . I know . . . I know, Rudi. You're one of mine. Have a drink.'

'Herr General . . .'

'How is your brother?'

'As always.'

Stumme laughed. 'I like Paul. He's a good man.'

The villa in which General of Panzer Troops, Stumme, had installed himself had formerly been occupied by the commissar in charge of heavy industry in the Kharkov region; and the commissar had done himself proudly. The place was double-storeyed, white, and had its own two or three acres of grounds. There was an air about it which suggested to Jordaan that long before, it had been the home of minor nobility. In spite of its present use it was not difficult to imagine the sound of children's laughter in that house.

But then there was a loud buzzing of conversation as the General led Von Mansdorff and Flash towards a substantial gathering of his own people standing there between walls decorated by the commissar's collection of heavily representational examples of contemporary Russian art. It had been Stumme's sense of humour which had allowed those pictures to stay where they were – to the irritation of his staff.

The senior officers present included three divisional commanders, Major General Von Boineburg-Lengsfeld, Major General Breith and Major General Fremerey. General Angelo Muller, Chief of Corps Artillery, was there, as was Lieutenant Colonels Hesse and Harry Momm, who both Von Mansdorff and Flash recognized as being rather a famous pre-war show jumper throughout Europe.

The arrival of the two Luftwaffe men, and particularly Von Mansdorff's appearance, caused something of a muted stir among the other guests; and it was apparent to Jordaan that something of his origins had been communicated to the Germans. One or two of them were looking at him with a fascination which was not usual in such people.

There was nothing of the ascetic intellectual in General Stumme's appearance. The highly flushed face with its monocle said something about his liking for food and drink. In fact one of his favourite sayings was, 'War is bad enough. Why eat badly as well? No, not me.' He was a rather short, thick-set man who radiated energy: a front-line soldier whose men loved him because of his concern for them which they could see; and perhaps too because of the cavalry man's swagger which he displayed as he moved through their ranks.

Dinner was served. 'Well then, gentlemen, this could be the condemned man's last meal. Enjoy it. In a few more days there will be no leisure. We're off again. This time, let's hope we can bring Stalin to his knees.'

Heavily curtained windows kept the light from the table within the room in which they were dining. There was a flurry of white-coated waiters as caviare was produced and then followed by venison from a young roebuck which one of Stumme's staff had shot some days before. To Jordaan there seemed to be oceans of Crimean champagne. Stumme stood holding up his glass. 'Gentlemen, this is the stuff the Russians drink when they don't want to weep. But, first, a toast . . . To Manstein and his eleventh army and their victory at Sebastopol . . . Two Soviet armies smashed in the Crimea, ninety thousand prisoners taken, as well as over twelve hundred pieces of artillery. Magnificent. Let us hope that with his and his splendid army's help we can emulate that achievement with the Sixth against Stalingrad and the Caucasus.'

Everyone stood. 'Von Manstein!'

Flash was sitting next to Colonel Harry Momm, Corps Adjutant. 'You have known Rudi Mansdorff long?' Momm asked.

'We met in a prison camp for Allied airmen. He was

the Commandant, I was a prisoner.' Flash laughed.

'How strange.' Lieutenant Colonel Momm seemed to be confused. 'I have heard that you led a Staffel of Englishmen, and that you have been successful. You are now a Staffelkapitan leading a Wing which will be supporting me. Your men must be very strange Englishmen. I know England rather well.'

Flash paused. 'There are no Englishmen with me,' he said. 'I am not English.'

'But you are known as the English.'

'I am South African.'

'Know it well . . . You have some good horses in your country.'

As briefly as he could Jordaan explained his presence in the place where they were. Momm smiled. 'I have heard of many things,' he said as though trying to overcome his smile, 'but yours is a very unusual story.'

'It's not a story, sir. It's a fact. Can you tell me anything of our objectives in the coming battle?'

'No.'

Flash looked at his neighbour and smiled as he raised his glass. 'I understand.'

'Please understand me. I am not being intentionally rude, but there is a difficulty. Hitler is obsessed with the strictest security measures. He doesn't, I think, trust anyone.' Momm spoke with a tone in his voice which suggested that he didn't altogether trust Hitler.

They had reached coffee and brandy when Stumme, without undue officiousness, re-arranged his table. He called to Jordaan when he had caused a couple of his people to move, 'Come here, Englishman, I want to talk to you.' He also signalled to Von Mansdorff that he too should move.

'Well, now, Englishman – tell me about yourself.'

Von Mansdorff interjected. 'Herr General, he's not English.'

'I am South African, sir.'

'Ah, yes. When I was young, I spent a brief time in East Africa, which was ours then.'

'I was asking Colonel Momm what our objective might be in this coming offensive.'

'. . . And he wouldn't tell you.'

Flash smiled. 'I'm afraid not.'

General Stumme sipped from his glass. 'He was probably right. We have a rule here which comes from above.' He laughed. 'From the all highest in fact. No one, not even our tank commanders, knows where they're going until they're moving. It creates difficulties. A tank commander must know in which direction he is supposed to be moving, and he must have enough authority to change direction at a given moment. You can't keep tanks on too tight a rein. You understand?'

Flash nodded.

'No orders here are ever committed to paper. Even my divisional commanders had no verbal instructions until two days ago.' Stumme, perhaps rashly, then went on. 'I have been assigned the task, under the first phase of "Operation Blue" to cross the Oskol as part of Sixth Army, and then wheel north in order to encircle the enemy. I have given my divisional commanders their instructions on a half page of a type-written sheet . . . But isn't this, isn't this good – your name is Jordaan – isn't it good to see my officers relaxing after that hellish winter they have all gone through?'

'It is, sir.'

'There is optimism here.'

The General looked to Von Mansdorff, and the latter nodded. And indeed, no doubt as a compliment to the excellent food and drink they had consumed, there was much gaiety at that table. Stumme, at one stage, brought the waiters in and insisted that his guests drink to them when they had filled their glasses. 'Men,' the General said, standing, 'you are soldiers. Thank you for the way in which you have served us.' For Stumme it was an echo of his youth when as a young man it had been obligatory for a platoon commander to eat with his men three nights a week.

There was a toast to Mackensen who with his four mobile and four infantry divisions had destroyed superior Soviet forces dug in along the high ground on the Donets. He had taken twenty-three thousand prisoners. At one stage when the meal was being followed by much brandy there was indeed something electric in that atmosphere.

And then the chief of operations rose from his chair. 'If you'll excuse me, Herr General, it appears they want me on the telephone.'

The General laughed. 'Don't come back with bad news.'

The news was not only bad: it was disastrous. And at that moment Jordaan had to admire Stumme. The General listened to his man's whispered information. He stood, replaced his monocle when he had carefully rubbed it with a silk handkerchief; and then he said to Jordaan and Von Mansdorff, 'You will have to excuse me, gentlemen. I'm afraid this party is over.' There was no apparent fuss.

In the back of their car, when they had extricated themselves as decently as possible, Jordaan said to his friend, 'What the hell went on there?'

'Bad . . . very bad.' Von Mansdorff's voice had hoarsened. 'Some idiot, Chief of Operations at twenty-third Panzer, has gone missing in a Fieseler Storch. He was having another look at the division's redeployment area.

It looks as though the Russians have got him or his body. They will also have the typed operational instructions for the divisional commanders. It could be the end of Stumme. He authorized those instructions to be in writing in spite of Hitler's personal objections. Jesus Christ!'

'It's a funny war,' Jordaan said.

'All wars are funny, but this time no one will be laughing.'

19

It was much as Flash Jordaan had expected it would be. His new-found authority quietened him, as it had Von Mansdorff whose time was now much occupied in organizing ground defences for their airstrips on soldierly lines while von Paulus and his Sixth Army was pushing against the pull of the Russians. The Gruppe which Jordaan had grown to lead was beginning to feel the snarling of Russian air power as its own strength became depleted at the edges. It was so as Von Mansdorff late on an afternoon in mid-August walked into the peeling splendour of Flash's room in the villa which had become their headquarters.

Without pausing the German walked towards the desk, removed a glove with his teeth, threw it down and said, 'How would you like to breathe again?'

'Is everything ready at the new strip? We'll be using it in two days. The bloody place is so close to them we're almost in the range of their mortars.'

'Good. It means we're moving forward. We'll soon be at the Volga, and then it's across for Stalingrad.'

Flash had been reading an intelligence report – his German was by now just sufficiently proficient. He didn't look up, even as he spoke. He said, 'I have the feeling they'll have to swim across . . . What did you say about breathing?'

'We're going for a rest. Rest, man – to Germany. You and me.'

For Flash there was total confusion. He looked at Von Mansdorff for a moment, his incredulity matched only by the other's smile. 'We can't,' he said eventually. 'Not now. It's impossible.'

'Everything's possible – especially if you know the right people. I've convinced them you need a rest; and you do, Flash. Someone else can do your job for ten days. You'll feel better and stronger when we get back. We leave in the morning. I'm your keeper.'

'How do we get out of here?'

'By JU 52 of course. We're important men.'

Flash had to admit to himself on the long flight towards Berlin that he was tired. At first the droning discomfort of the ancient JU 52 transport sent him recurrently to sleep, while Von Mansdorff, by his side, was content to leave him as he comforted himself with the large flask which on such a journey was his constant companion.

For some time before they landed at Pruszkow, south west of Warsaw, Flash was awake and silent. His mind was in that delicate state which precedes total awareness. God, what had he done, and where was he?

Something like complete relaxation allowed his whole body to sink into the bucketed basketware seat in which he slumped. There had been so much of it all. The way back to Leinefelde and beyond had been so long. Of course there had been the crutch of laughter which for so long had been his only personal weapon. But somewhere outside of the animal action there must be something which he had never found.

The cold alien land slid beneath the window as the lumbering Junkers was into its let-down. Which was the alien? The unfolding earth beneath or he? But, Christ, a man can't go on examining himself or what he's been or is. Flash stirred. 'Where are we?'

'I think we're landing to refuel.'

'Rudi . . .' Jordaan stirred himself. 'Rudi, let's hope we can refuel ourselves.'

'We will in Berlin. Be sure of that. Jeschonnek wants to meet you. That's why we're in the bloody aeroplane, you stupid bastard.'

'Oh . . .'

Berlin at that time, when all the world was at its feet, was much alive. Even the rain which fell seemed to approve of the place. It glittered.

The Adlon was as always. They shared a suite and the salutations of the staff; and on the morning following their arrival they were at Jeschonnek's headquarters where brother Paul awaited them. Paul's attitude, if not exactly obsequious, was awfully close to it. 'Jordaan,' he said, smiling, 'we have heard much of you. And you, Rudi . . . how good to see you. You will meet the General in a few minutes.'

Jeschonnek reacted with difficulty where people were concerned. It was Flash's feeling when he and Von Mansdorff entered the long room with all its heaviness that their presence had been stage-managed; perhaps by Rudi's brother, Colonel Paul.

The man himself stood up awkwardly from behind his desk. 'Jordaan' – and he wasn't looking at Flash directly as he spoke – 'you have done well. I think maybe I should apologize for my misunderstanding in the beginning. How are things where you are?'

'There are difficulties, Herr General. Your men are overstretched.'

'Ours, Jordaan . . . Yours.'

Jordaan smiled. 'Sir, they are all yours.'

'Let us say, the Fuhrer's.'

'Morale is still high.'

'Good.'

Around this point of their meeting the tall double doors were opened and a guard marched in; NCOs of the Luftwaffe. Six men were there. When they halted at attention as though automated they turned to their right to face the desk of Jeschonnek who walked slowly around to confront Jordaan who was standing rigidly to attention, as were the others present.

An aide had appeared behind the General, and from him Jeschonnek took the decoration from the outstretched purple cushion. 'I am authorized, Major Christian Jordaan, to appoint you a member of a very distinguished company.' The Knight's Cross with its ribbon was placed around Flash's neck. Jeschonnek smiled. 'I realize that for you this may be somewhat confusing, considering your origins. But you have done well. In your short period with us you have achieved twenty-two confirmed victories, to say nothing of your activities closer to the ground . . . It . . . it is my understanding that the English award their decorations to their allies who have done well for them. We do likewise. My congratulations.'

Flash saluted and turned with some disbelief on his face to Von Mansdorff who was smiling broadly. 'Rudi . . .'

'My friend.' They shook hands, and Von Mansdorff said, 'We are not resting. It was for this reason that we are here.' And he laughed. And at that moment, in his attitude, there was a man looking at a man who was his friend.

Jeschonnek joined them in Paul Von Mansdorff's office for a celebratory drink. Paul was not quite the man he had seemed to be when Flash had first met him. He said to Flash when they had spoken a little, 'Forgive me . . . My brother always refers to you as "Flash". Why this "Flash"?'

'An old African servant first called me that. It stuck.'

'I thought my hearing was at fault when the General addressed you as Christian Jordaan. Shouldn't it have been Christopher?'

'No, Christian.'

'Your name is Christian?'

'Yes.'

Paul Von Mansdorff was an extremely handsome man. Thirty-three years old, his fair hair was already streaked with grey; which played its part in adding to the commanding nature of his appearance. The chin was firm beneath a narrow nose. But it was his eyes which intrigued Jordaan; blue-grey, they were piercing in their intensity, and contrary to anything Flash had expected, richly humorous. 'Christian,' Paul said, 'how very strange.'

'Not at all. There have always been Christians in my family. We were French Huguenots who fled first to England before moving on to South Africa in the seventeenth century.'

'How interesting . . . Tell me, do you have any regrets about falling in with my brother's somewhat extravagant scheme?'

Flash smiled as he looked at Von Mansdorff, who was somewhat taller than he. Then he said, 'Sometimes, but on the whole, no. As I saw it at the time I had little alternative. There will be those who disagree with me.'

Covering the hesitation in the other's voice, Von Mansdorff hurried to say, 'Jeschonnek was right when he said you had done well.'

'Thank you.'

They talked on for quite some time of what Flash had seen of the air effort on the Southern front. Then Rudi joined them, and there was some bantering laughter until Paul said, 'I wonder what happened to that Italian friend of yours, Del Renzio. I know all about him and his past. He wasn't shot down, you know . . . I wonder how far he got.'

The other two looked at each other with some uncertainty. Then together they said, 'So do we.' And at that all three burst into laughter.

Restraining them, Paul managed to say, 'Don't worry, the Turks will get around to telling us when they're ready.'

The evening went on with all three of them wandering towards the Adlon. Paul seemed to be enlivened by the occasion. He insisted they be his guests at dinner, and splendidly did he arrange it.

In that dining room, amidst the uniforms and the comfortable figures of those who were cheering on the warriors these three were an impressive trio. Eyes, particularly those of the elegantly restive women, were constantly flitting in their direction. But the high, brilliantly moulded ceiling, the splendour of the room's appointments with its differing levels, all belonging to a century which had turned a time before, washed over Jordaan's consciousness. In spite of the champagne they drank he couldn't rid himself of the varied thoughts which troubled him.

'Chris . . .' It was Paul who spoke. 'You are curiously restrained. This is an occasion for celebration. I was led to believe that you are a roisterer.'

'I'm sorry. Forgive me. I think I'm a little tired.'

'Ach no . . . Drink, eat.'

Rudi Von Mansdorff reached out to put his arm on Jordaan's back. 'You need fresh air. I know what we'll do. I know where we'll go.' He stood. 'Excuse me. I won't be long.'

When his brother had gone, Paul Von Mansdorff said, 'I love that man.'

Flash looked quickly at the other's face.

'Curiously, he doesn't love me. I could never understand why.'

It was a difficult moment for Flash. There was nothing much he could say, but he did say, 'I think perhaps you're wrong. Maybe he resents you being the elder brother. It often happens. It's something that goes away in people as they get older.'

'Chris . . .' And Paul's voice was very steady when he spoke. 'Chris, I don't think we'll get older. Not much.'

They ate on in some silence until Rudi returned. His face betrayed trouble, and in silence he sat down at their table.

'Something wrong, Rudi?' Paul asked.

'Ilse's husband was killed three months ago. The silly bastard fell off a horse.'

The other two for a moment said nothing, until eventually Paul spoke. 'She's such a charming girl. Can we do anything?'

'I said we'd get there as soon as we can; perhaps by tomorrow evening.'

'We?' Paul said.

'Flash and I . . . Chris I mean.' He turned to Jordaan. 'From now on I'm going to call you Chris.'

'I'm sorry about your cousin . . . Call me what you like.'

There seemed now to be no point in eating, so Paul said, 'Shall we have our coffee and cognac outside?'

Rudi Von Mansdorff, as though to himself, said, 'Do you know, I used to laugh at that Italian, but he was a good chap. He just kept the wrong company. That's all.

The Schloss at Freudenstadt held a glimmer of light against a fading day when they arrived on the following evening. Von Mansdorff had engaged a driver in Stuttgart to get them to the place, and on the way there Jordaan had relished the peace of that countryside as they headed south and into the Black Forest.

'Beautiful country.' They sat in the back of the car, for the most part silently, with Von Mansdorff taking the occasional sip from his flask. 'In all the world this is my favourite place to be,' he said once.

'But this is your cousin's place we're going to.'

'Yes. It's been in her branch of the family for some generations. I spent a great deal of my time here when I was a boy. Her father was a marvellous man. I always felt much more at home here at Freudenstadt. Sometimes Ilse would come to our place, but not often. I think she was afraid of my father a little.'

'Where is your place?'

'About twenty kilometres south of here, near Freiburg.'

At the main entrance, the Spaniard, Augustine, was waiting to greet them. Somehow, to Von Mansdorff the man looked more chastened than usual, even as he greeted them. The smile was tight when he said, 'Herr Major . . .' To Flash he bowed impassively before leading them up the few steps towards the opened doors.

The house was brightly lit, almost dazzling, as they entered the hallway. Augustine was taking their hats and gloves as Ilse appeared. She was wearing a simple grey dress which was topped by a black velvet band around her graceful neck. The ash-blonde hair, swept back, encompassed a streak which appeared in that light to be almost silver. The face was held high, proudly, and when she held out her arms to her cousin as they approached each other, the smile she offered lit up her whole face.

'Rudi, my darling.'

'Ach . . .' He held her tightly with his one arm.

'This is wonderful. It's good that you should come.'

'This . . .' Von Mansdorff released her, and with a sweep of his arm said, 'This is my friend Chris Jordaan.'

Ilse smiled at Flash as he took her hand. 'I've heard about you much from Rudi . . . My goodness, you look very splendid.' There was the gush of a girl in her words, and in response, Flash, not quite knowing how to address her said, 'Your Grace . . .'

'My goodness, no. Call me Ilse.'

Augustine saw them to their rooms, but not for Mansdorff as before, the Duke's room – there would have been an indelicacy in that arrangement – but next door to that assigned to Flash, with a connecting door. They had been installed and had removed their tunics when Flash wandered next door. 'She's a beautiful woman,' he said.

'Very.'

'I don't think I've ever met anyone like that.' Flash sat down.

'I'm sure you haven't. Have a drink.'

As they were sitting there in shirt sleeves, sipping their drinks, Augustine came in to announce that Madame had said that dinner would be served in half an hour. He turned then to leave them when Von Mansdorff halted him. 'Augustine . . .'

'Sir.'

'I'm sorry about your master, Augustine. He was a good man.'

'It is very sad. Will there be anything, sir?'

'No. No, we're fine.'

When the Spaniard had left the room Von Mansdorff thought for a moment and then said, 'That little bastard loved Dino. Dino changed his life.'

'I can imagine. Wasn't he the Republican, the prisoner?'

'He was a peasant. A Republican . . . a Fascist. How the hell would he know the difference? Very few people know what they're fighting for. Now he has an identity. For him, for anyone that's what's important.'

They prepared for dinner and went down to the salon where Ilse was waiting for them. She had changed into a long black gown which accentuated the sombre beauty which she expressed then.

With drinks Von Mansdorff felt able to offer his condolences, as did Flash in a somewhat cursory fashion for he had known nothing of her husband. And in response Ilse smiled wryly before saying when she looked at her cousin, 'I did love him, Rudi . . . in a way that you *could* love him. He was very funny, very kind.'

Throughout dinner it was apparent that Ilse didn't want to talk of herself. She asked them both about Russia, and Flash about the decoration he wore, and at his attempt to reduce his experience to the ordinary she really laughed for the first time.

Ilse seemed to be curious about South Africa, and as Flash talked, at first hesitantly and then as memories of his boyhood came back to him, with much enthusiasm, there was a gradual strengthening of interest between these two which he felt that night as he lay between the luxury of his sheets, until in the end the rustling of the breeze amidst the trees surrounding the house led him slowly towards sleep.

20

In the morning Ilse was ready with the horses, and when Flash saw the stallion she rode she smiled at the admiration he displayed. 'You like him,' she called. 'This is Kaiser. Would you like to ride him?'

Von Mansdorff was there. 'Careful, Chris . . . That's a helluva horse.'

Flash said nothing, and in spite of the obvious reservations of the groom who was there he mounted the beast. 'He's . . . he's a lively fellow. But I . . . I . . .' The horse was indeed restive. Flash laughed. 'I know his type . . . He plays poker.'

With Von Mansdorff waving to them somewhat disconsolately, they rode off down the driveway and into the wood. 'Not the best of riding country.'

Ilse laughed. 'Rudi calls it bad tank country . . . In a little while it opens out for a mile or two . . . a little, towards the lake.'

For Flash the stallion was a delight. The fellow seemed to have an immediate understanding of his rider's knees. The horse felt as though he was enjoying himself. At the lake, after Flash had really opened him out, he pulled Kaiser to a halt with something of a flourish. Ilse arrived, dismounted, and flushed with admiration, said in a voice which was filled with enthusiasm, 'You're the only other person who's ever ridden that horse except myself. Even the groom won't get on him.'

'Maybe Kaiser likes us both.'

Flash patted the stallion as though he had known it for

years, and they stood together, horses and riders, looking at the shimmering lake. He said, 'This is very beautiful.'

'I come here often, nearly every day.'

Away on the far side the sun caught the sails of a dinghy. The only sounds were those of the horses breathing, the lapping water and excitement of birds in the still trees around them. 'Who would be in that boat?' Flash asked.

'It's an old man from the other side who fishes.'

Months before a thousand British bombers had attacked Cologne. Over a million men had already died in Russia. Flash thought back to his own men. Yet this too, this place which had a calmness which was close to the primeval, this too was Germany. Flash looked up to the sky. It was the late summer of nineteen forty-two.

Ilse sensed something of his thoughts. He was still looking across the lake when she said from behind him, 'When they told me my husband was dead, coming here was like going to Church.'

He turned to her. 'I can believe that . . . I mean I understand. You must have been devastated.'

'One of the reasons I came here was that I wanted to feel his loss, but I couldn't. Dino and I were not like that. We laughed at each other instead of . . . I don't know. He was someone who always seemed to be scratching at the surface of life. Dear Dino. So many people are dying in this war. He was hardly even in it, and yet he was killed.'

'What did he do?'

'He was on someone's staff. Most of the time he trained his horses. He was a brilliant performer on a horse . . . But one of them killed him. He gave me Kaiser.' She turned to pat the horse's nose. 'Didn't he, boy?'

'I think I would have liked to have known him.'

'He was fun.' Ilse smiled briskly. 'Shall we go back?'

Over the following days they rode; they tried to fish on the lake, and on one occasion when Rudi insisted that he could handle a gun with one arm they went shooting. The evenings became treasured. They drank and laughed, but yet, with the passing of each day Jordaan began to feel a seriousness settling on him. He said nothing to his friend, but the German was aware of a difference in the man. There were the traces of a communication between his cousin and Flash of which perhaps neither of them was fully aware. But Von Mansdorff saw it and said nothing.

Two days before they were due to leave Freudenstadt to make their way back to the front as airborne hitchhikers, Von Mansdorff did drink too much after dinner. At first he was very funny, but gradually his mood changed until something like anger occasionally snarled into his voice. It was then that Ilse said her smiling goodnights.

Jordaan drank on with his friend, but when they were upstairs and Von Mansdorff allowed him to remove his tunic he knew that the German was out of character. Something like a blackness had descended on the man. After what appeared to be considerable thought, he eventually said, 'In two or three days we'll be back in that abattoir. Christ, what a mess.' He had been looking in a mirror across the room before he turned to Jordaan. 'I envy you, Chris. I envy you the wings they've given you. You can look at it all down there as though we're ants . . . Little bloody ants waiting to be crushed or flipped off the earth by a finger nail. Sometimes I hate it all. I hate the smell of it all.'

Flash stood – they were in Von Mansdorff's room – to reach out for a bottle. It had occurred to him that the sooner he made Von Mansdorff drunk enough for bed, the better. 'Have a drink, Rudi.' The German held out a glass without saying a word. He drank, and as though he had reached out to pull the words into context, he said, 'Soon it will be shadows again.'

Jordaan was momentarily irritated. 'Come on, man – for Christ's sake cheer up. We're on leave and we're in this beautiful place. What more do you want?'

With that exaggeration which only a drunkard can turn into bad acting Von Mansdorff declaimed, 'What more do I want? . . . I want to renounce the lie that is in me. That's what I want.'

'What lie?'

Von Mansdorff's eyes were everywhere. 'No . . . no. There is no lie. There is a truth. I live a lie.'

'What truth?'

'The half of me that is Jew and the half of me that is Gentile.'

'What are you talking about?'

'Fear . . . that's what I'm talking about. And my mother's whoredom, that's what I'm talking about.'

'I don't understand you.'

'Of course you don't understand me. Most of the time I don't understand me. But right now I do. By God I do. I know what I'm fighting . . .' He sat down, perhaps confused.

Quietly, Jordaan said, 'What are you fighting?'

'I'm fighting me.'

'Rudi, why don't you go to bed?'

Von Mansdorff poured himself another drink. His mind seemed to be clearing. 'Flash – Chris – fuck it. I'm telling you . . . You've met my brother who's not my brother. You saw him. He's not what I said. He has the blood . . .'

'Rudi, please . . .'

'No, I'm telling you. But only you . . . My mother's lover for a time was a man called Wolfgang Rosenthal

. . . Wolfgang Rosenthal. I rather like that . . . He was a theatrical impresario, rather an important one – in Vienna.'

'Who told you this.'

'He did. I met him in Vienna when I was about twenty-one. He didn't seem to be a bad chap. It was not long before he was killed.'

'Killed?'

'He fell out of a train when he was drunk on his way back from Salzburg.'

'Does your mother's husband know about this?'

'Of course he does. In families like mine we bury such things.'

Flash looked carefully at his friend, but he said nothing as he poured himself another drink. Then he said, 'You don't hate Jews?'

Von Mansdorff smiled. 'Of course not. There's nothing I can do about them.' And then he said, 'I like me. I'm a Jew. My father was a Jew . . . I think I'll go to bed now.'

'Yes . . . Goodnight.'

By the time the slow-moving JU 52 had dragged itself across Europe they were excited at the thought of their return. Based at Zelski they were not more than twenty-five kilometres to the north west of Stalingrad: Jordaan had not been exaggerating overmuch when he had said they were almost within range of the enemy's guns.

Their arrival was greeted with the shock information that Van Reine had been badly wounded and was awaiting evacuation. Light anti-aircraft had hit his machine when he was making a low bombing run over Stalingrad. When they saw him he looked awful. But the big Dutchman could raise a smile when he saw them standing beside the cot he was lying on. 'They missed my balls,' was all he said.

'You'll be alright. They'll get you out of here.' Flash tried to be reassuring.

A mistiness seemed to be coming over the Dutchman's eyes. He was speaking very slowly when he said, 'Of course I will. I'll dream of Oklahoma and Ponca City and the girl I knew there. She had long blonde hair and she smiled. She smiled.'

Back in his office, Flash immediately busied himself with the details of ascertaining the state of his Gruppe's readiness. His engineering and armaments officers were there with Von Mansdorff. It was not a happy gathering. Replacement aircraft were not coming through and they were running out of spare parts, but there was nothing they could do. Resignedly they agreed that they would have to make do with what was available. When they had parted Flash walked around his dispersal points. He spoke in his halting German to some of the men who were there, and then in shirtsleeves – for the day was hot – he made his way back to the tent they had erected for him under some trees. He would write a letter of thanks to Ilse and rest. That evening he would conduct a briefing when his orders for the following day had come through from Geschwader headquarters.

Stretched out on his bunk Flash thought at first of the letter he had written to Ilse. He knew there was more he could have said. He certainly felt more than he had written, but somehow a revelation of his feelings to a woman like Ilse, especially in her present circumstances would have been inappropriate. His mind drifted to Van Reine and the others who had formed the original selection. The first squadron had been shattered; even its concept. It's raison d'etre no longer existed. And in any case his new job meant that he was responsible for three squadrons. He had been distanced from those who were left.

Flash was washing the tiredness from his face when he heard the first of the firing. At first he thought an armourer was testing guns. Then with the explosion of something which sounded like a grenade and the chattering bursts of more automatic fire, he dashed from his tent. 'You . . . you, what's happening?' The man looked at him and ran on. He grabbed another. 'What's happening?'

The fellow's face was streaked with fear. 'Russians . . . everywhere.'

Flash made his way towards his headquarters to kick open the door of his office. 'Jesus Christ, Horst, what's going on? Where's Major Von Mansdorff?' The clerk muttered something about the Major being out there somewhere. 'We're being attacked, sir. Partisans.'

Jordaan grabbed an automatic rifle and ran outside. A Sergeant shouted to him, 'Take cover, sir. They're using grenades.'

'Where's Major Von Mansdorff?'

'Somewhere over there near the perimeter, I think. I saw him heading there.'

Flash made his way in the direction the man had pointed. He saw the first of them after the first few yards, and he saw too the fire of their guns as they ran, shooting from the hip. He threw himself into the long grass as he waited for their approach. Swinging himself on to an elbow he tried to see if they were coming from other angles, and he did see two other groups. Already some parked aircraft were burning. Flash aimed at the approaching partisans. It was then a quick burst and they dropped. He felt he must have hit two of them, but there had to be a dozen of them right there ahead of him, lying low as he was. Looking behind him for any movement of his own men, he did see a sign of activity. About fifty of them were making an attack which appeared to be orderly. They started to spread out as they approached, and from his vantage point in the grass Flash felt his heart quicken with the thought that Von Mansdorff's training attempts had not been entirely in vain.

A second wave seemed to be following the first, but it was when those in advance were about thirty yards from him that Flash leapt to his feet and began firing in the direction he knew the Russians to be. There were three parties of partisans, but there must have been more in the thinly wooded ramparts of the field looking for aircraft in their dispersal bays; for now some half dozen machines were aflame and exploding. The Russians ahead, in some desperation, leapt to their feet and faced him, firing. His own gun was again in action, as were those of the men now on either side of him. Russians fell and started to run. There were guttural groans on either side and behind as Germans were hit. One man screamed. But still they went after those Russians who were still able to flee towards the trees. Flash came upon a slack-looking body lying on the grass. He turned it over with one foot. It was a woman. He stepped on, but then some instinct made him turn back to look again, and as he did so the creature was reaching for a hand gun. The fire from his own weapon reduced it to a bloody mess of pulpy flesh from which he had to turn with his stomach in a spasm of retching.

He looked around the field, and standing there in that grass with an elongated shadow of his body reaching ahead of the sun behind, he appeared as a man who was utterly alone. Those invaders still standing were running now for cover. His own men now were everywhere. A scattered confusion of noise was all around him, but when he could he grabbed at a man who was nearby and asked him if he had seen anything of Von Mansdorff. The man looked at him, dazed and half afraid. Flash's German seemed to elude him, but he did point vaguely in the direction towards which the Russians had retreated.

Jordaan moved on with the man at his heels. Now there was concern, especially when Kirste, the Pole, joined them and announced that he had seen nothing of Von Mansdorff since the beginning of the action when the Major had been seen running around with a sub-machine gun under his arm as he roused his men to meet the threat which he had been about the first to recognize.

When they found him Von Mansdorff was in a kneeling position, leaning against a young tree. At the sound of Flash's voice he looked up blankly. It was obvious that he had been badly hit. There was blood at the mouth and one side of the head. His good hand was clutching at his belly. Very quietly, as Jordaan knelt beside him, he said, 'Flash.' There was an attempt at a smile, which was only something like a reflex action of his face.

'Rudi . . . Rudi, let me lay you down.'

'No . . . No . . .' His body seemed to relax momentarily against the tree. 'Let me stay.'

Flash turned to Kirste and the airman. 'Get something. Let's get him out of here.'

When they were gone and the two were wrapped in a silence which was only broken by the sound of Von Mansdorff's need for breath and the gurgling noises of his body, the German looked once at his friend with something like a plea in his eye. Then he keeled over and was dead.

21

As they approached October and then on towards its end, Flash's remaining serviceable aircraft were gradually adapted until in the end they were being used exclusively as fighter-bombers. The army had eventually crossed the Don until the battle for Stalingrad had set the city aflame. Daily, the pilots of Eighth Air Fleet, to which Jordaan's Gruppe was now attached, swept over the city in its role of airborne artillery. It was on such a sweep that light flak juddered through Jordaan's aircraft with a sickening punctuation. It was the fight for a thousand feet that stilled the consciousness of pain.

Flash Jordaan never did remember being pulled from that aircraft, nor the later transference to a battered Junkers; nor anything of the flight into Poland. But he did remember controlling that aircraft with only his ailerons when the rudder controls were inoperative. He was rather proud of that and the wheels-up landing he made. The first face of which he was truly conscious was that of a grizzled middle-aged doctor who was smiling down at him when he emerged from deep anaesthesia. His first words were, 'Hello. Where am I?'

'How do you feel, Jordaan?'

'Where am I?'

'Lublin, south east of Warsaw. When you are ready you will go to Berlin for more specialist treatment. Here, we did manage to save your leg. Your thigh and shoulder were badly smashed up. You lost a lot of blood.' The doctor smiled more broadly. 'We gave you some more . . . good German blood.'

Flash sighed as he tried to lever himself up a little. 'Is it different?'

'Not really. I wouldn't try to move if I were you. Lie still.'

And he did for days, until eventually he was wheeled by a nurse into the garden of the place. She was a well-fleshed girl with a breezy smile which seemed to be habitual. It obviously pleased her that a holder of the Knight's Cross had been entrusted to her care.

'Is it too cold, Major?'

'It is Hanna. But I like it.'

The girl stopped to tuck the wrap more tightly around his legs.

The hospital had once been the home of a rich industrialist, and if the grounds were not exactly grand, they gave him pleasure. Flash was content to be wheeled along the gravelled paths. There was no thought in him. Once or twice Von Mansdorff fled across his mind, but the image did not stay. It was enough to lean back in that perambulator and have only the responsibility of a child as he looked at the winter's grass, the flowerless beds, the starkness of trees temporarily bereft of life. The mood of the place at that time was in tune with his own.

'What of Stalingrad, Hanna?'

'Very bad, Major. The Sixth Army seems to be surrounded.'

It was a week before Christmas when they flew him to the military hospital at Potsdam. There were two further operations on his leg and then there the long, dragging weeks of waiting until the time came when they gave him crutches and he could make his way from the room they had given him into the ante-room which had the heavy elegance of a pre-war officers' mess. On his first visit there were perhaps a dozen or so men in the room, and for some time, when he had chosen a chair, Flash surveyed them with a casual scrutiny.

When a youngish Captain with a very pale face beneath loose brown hair came across to speak, Flash had to restrain the flow of the man's German by smiling as he held up one hand and explaining in his own halting version of the language his difficulty.

The man spoke in English, and was obviously much intrigued as Flash sketched as briefly as he could an outline of his origins. They became quite close these two, and as the German Captain transmitted his knowledge of Flash to the others, Flash Jordaan, quite apart from the military distinction he wore, became something of a celebrity in that place.

But it was some weeks later, when a servant announced the arrival of Colonel Von Mansdorff that Flash's status really reached the heights in the hospital. On the walking stick which was now all he needed to propel himself, he hurried out to greet his visitor. 'Paul, my God . . . How good to see you!'

'Chris . . . It is good.' They shook hands.

The commanding figure of Paul Von Mansdorff seemed to enervate the room as they entered. But not until they sat together in the ante-room did Paul say anything of his brother. When they were together and seated in armchairs in a corner, the tall fair-haired Colonel, having acknowledged those who were present, said, 'Rudi . . . Did he die well?'

'Would you imagine otherwise? I was with him.'

'I loved his wildness . . . He did cause a great deal of trouble in our family. My father, for instance, was a good man. But Rudi never accepted my father's understanding of what life should be all about.' As Paul paused there was a question around his lips. '. . . don't think my father ever understood Rudi. But that boy was such a fool. He could have retired honourably from the Army. But he pleaded with me to arrange that he stay in uniform. There was no need for him to die.'

'Paul, maybe he thought there was.'

The Colonel looked straight at Jordaan. His eyes glistened. 'Maybe.'

There was talk of Ilse, and if she knew where Flash was. She didn't. Flash explained that he had found it impossible to write to her since Rudi's death. He had known how close they were. But she did know, Paul told him. Why didn't he go to her place?

'Chris' – for Paul Von Mansdorff refused to call him by the name of 'Flash' – 'when you are fit to leave here I will send you on indefinite leave. When you return, you will return to me in Berlin. That is if I am still here. There is talk of my taking over an appointment as Generalmajor with Richthofen and one of his divisions in Russia.'

Eagerly, Flash said, 'Congratulations.'

'I don't know. We'll see. I will be in touch with Ilse. I think you should go to her place. Rest . . .' He smiled. 'This war is tiring.'

Flash leant his elbows on his knees and looked at his feet. 'Paul, why do you talk to me this way? In your life my arrival on the scene was a kind of joke, and yet you talk to me in the way that you do.'

'You were my brother's friend. Other people, even he, thought we were at odds as you say. Not I.'

There was an early stirring of life in that late winter which was fast becoming the spring of nineteen forty three when Flash Jordaan disembarked at Freudenstadt's elderly railway station. There was the man, presumably the station master, whom he had seen before; but then there was Augustine with the horse of the house and its trap. Presumably Augustine approved of the strange Major – perhaps because he himself in that place was looked upon as being 'strange'.

On the way to the house, Augustine, a thin man, sat hunched in charge of the horse. Nothing was said for quite sometime as Flash looked past the man in front towards the horse's flanks until eventually – and the tone of the man's voice told Jordaan much – the Spaniard said, 'The Major's gone then, sir.'

'Yes, I'm afraid so.'

The driveway, apart from its conifers, was lifeless, but the house on that late afternoon was alive. Ilse was on its steps, waiting as they approached. She stood as a younger sister would stand, awaiting the arrival of a brother who had been gone for a long time. When the horse with its burden slithered to a halt, Ilse dashed towards them as Flash, unsteadily, was disentangling himself from his transport. There was a faint suggestion of the ridiculous in him as his feet touched the ground.

'Chris . . .'

He was gathering his stick as he turned to her. 'Ilse, it's good of you . . .'

'Oh, Chris . . .'

There was a confusion on the part of both of them for some moments. For both of them there were memories of their last meeting when so much had been unsaid. His face assumed a firmness when she said, 'Rudi . . . You were there?'

'With him? Yes.'

Ilse swung away from him towards the house while he followed, leaving the man, Augustine, to gather up his luggage when the groom had taken away the horse. In the entrance hall Ilse turned to him quickly. 'Chris, I'm sorry.' She took his shoulders and leant her head against his right breast. 'All my life he was so like a brother to me. He was a brother; silly, funny, marvellous Rudi.'

He said nothing.

When she was quiet and stood back to look at him, one hand swept the hair away from her face as she tried to smile. 'I'm sorry, Chris. I'm such a fool.'

'No . . . No, Ilse.'

Augustine had arrived with his luggage. 'Please,' Ilse said – and she was attempting to get some animation into her voice – 'take off your things.'

When he had done so and Augustine had taken his greatcoat, his hat and his gloves, he rubbed his hands against his thighs as though trying to stir some life into his body.

'You must be cold.'

'No, no. That carriage of yours is delightfully cool, that's all.'

'Hah . . . Come.'

In the salon he stood leaning on his stick, and as he sat there was an obvious discomfort in his right leg which he held out rigidly before he was gradually able to bend it at the knee.

When she had poured a drink Ilse sat opposite him. 'You've had a bad time, Chris. How is it?'

'On the mend. God, how I hate hospitals . . . But soon I'll be flying again.'

'No.'

He smiled. 'It's the only thing I know how to do . . . And since I don't think my old firm will have me back, I'll have to carry on with this one.'

. . . The sun was shining through his windows when

Augustine brought his breakfast and pulled open the curtains. 'Good morning, sir . . . Sir, the Major used to have some cognac in his coffee. Would you like some?'

Flash thought. 'Yes. Why not?'

When he appeared downstairs Ilse was already back from her early morning gallop. Outside they walked across the crispness of the gravel's frost, and then into the edges of her woodland. His limp was still decidedly marked and after a little while he paused and smiled as she turned to him. Instinctively steadying himself on the mound on which they were standing he reached out to lean with his left hand on her shoulder as in silence his eyes swept towards the richness that clothed the foothills to their east and south. The cool, scented air reached deep into their lungs. There was a separate life in that aroma.

'Are you tired, Chris?'

He flicked away some pine cones with his stick and said, 'I'm not . . . But this leg is complaining.'

'Let's go back, Chris – slowly.'

'It's unfair. You want to walk.'

'Don't be silly. I have all my life to walk . . . Careful. Take my arm . . . Every day your leg will become a little stronger. It will. I promise you.' She turned to him, laughing. 'Didn't they tell you that? Every day . . . You'll see.'

And every day Flash willed himself to use the leg a little more. Everything in that place was there to help; the quietness of the hours they spent together brought a peace which was such that he began to feel as though time itself had fled. At night only the whispering of the wind in the trees around him was there to soothe the thoughts with which he was recurrently disturbed.

The days became weeks, and still there was no word of

recall from Paul Von Mansdorff. Flash began to forget sometimes when he was alone the reason for his being in Germany, but there were still tinges of regret when he thought back to his friends in England. Where would they be now? Dead? Their faces were still there. Were they scattered across the world? He was sitting alone one morning on a chair they had brought to the lawn which spread before the house when in his imagination the whole world at war seemed to have stretched open its petals like some great bursting plant reaching for the insects it would devour.

Occasionally some of Ilse's neighbours would come in for drinks. All of them – except when some fellow was home on leave – tended to be elderly. Flash's appearance obviously disturbed these settled people. He was aware of their whispered comments and amused by the hesitancy with which they spoke to him. On one occasion there was a Colonel present who was something of a caricature. Everything about him: the hairstyle, the moustache, the stiff collar, added up to an expression on his face which could only be described as steadfast determination. Ilse introduced them. 'Chris, this is Colonel Max Born.'

'Colonel Born . . .'

Ilse turned to some other guests as the old boy said, 'You are English then . . .'

Flash looked hard at the man and then turned to Augustine who was standing nearby with a tray of drinks. He signalled and took a fresh glass. There was no humour in his smile when he said, 'Not then. Not now, sir. I am South African.'

'I see . . .'

'I don't think you do, Colonel. There are many people fighting with your forces who are not German. It is very complex.' Flash was in a mood which allowed this character to bore him. He paused for a moment before adding, 'It can also be very uncomfortable.'

'I'm sure . . . I'm sure.' And there was such embarrassment in the man's voice that Flash felt immediately sorry for having spoken as he had done.

'You'll have to excuse me, Colonel. I think I must sit down.' Flash moved to sit on a chair which was placed beneath a large portrait of Ilse's mother. But there was no shaking off the Colonel. For a moment he stood looking at the portrait before sitting alongside Jordaan. He spoke in German before switching to English to say, 'I knew her well. She was a very remarkable woman.'

Flash nodded. 'I can imagine.'

'In the war I was with the artillery.'

'You probably fought against my father. He was on the Western Front.'

'And now . . . What does he say of you?'

'He doesn't say anything, Colonel. He shot himself some years ago.'

'Oh, I'm sorry . . . Ilse.' They both stood at her approach. She was smiling to cover an inner knowledge which told her that Flash was in need of rescue. She made the suggestion that perhaps he was over-tiring himself which allowed them both to leave the gathering with some decorum; but later when they were having dinner alone she apologized for them. 'I know, Chris, I know. They are very different people from any you have known. But they're becoming old. It's difficult for them to understand the world of today. Theirs was a very different Germany.'

'Don't apologize for them, Ilse . . . I just can't help feeling that they're hiding behind Hitler and his dog – hoping that something good will happen for them.'

'Yes. You could be right . . . Don't let's talk about them, Chris.'

'Prost.' He raised his glass. 'Ilse we should be talking about the fact that I can't go on living here forever . . . You have been very kind.'

She laughed quietly. 'No I haven't. You can stay here forever. I am very selfish. I need you . . . if you need me.'

From where he was sitting he could reach out and take her hand. He did. A fountain of words welled up inside him, but all he could say was, 'Ilse . . .'

Flash was strengthening. His mind was beginning to click into its old rhythm. As the weeks wore on and still there was no word from Paul Von Mansdorff – who, presumably, was still in Berlin – he began to wonder if they had forgotten his existence. But it was easy to imagine what things must be like in Berlin. Stalingrad had fallen with the loss of an entire army. In North Africa, Rommel was in retreat after Alamein. The fate of an individual like himself must be of little consequence in the light of such disasters. The words of Rudi Von Mansdorff came back to him, for it had been he who had said that the war was lost when Hitler turned away from Moscow.

As he grew stronger he could go shooting with Ilse: it brought him closer to a way of life which he had always felt was his own kind of reality. Sometimes when he was out in the woods with her he would remember old Gus who had taught him to shoot, and she would be entranced when he talked to her of the old man. The last letter Gus had received had come through Portuguese East Africa, but there had been nothing for a very long time. Maybe the old man was dead.

'It would sadden you, Chris,' she said, when he had mentioned the possibility to her.

'No. It would be natural for him to die about now. He would know that. It was part of his wisdom. He once said to me, when I was too young to understand. He said, "My boy" – and Flash tried to imitate the old man's voice – "every child is born with its hands wide open . . . The trick is to learn how to close them" – and he clenched a fist as he spoke – "so that you're holding on to everything that is life, and then, my boy, you must learn to let go . . . so that you allow it all to slip away so that when you die your hands are as wide open as when you were born." I remember him saying that.'

'He must have been a wonderful man.'

'He was full of magic.'

'You never mention your mother, Chris.'

One of the dogs raised a flurry of birds, and, instinctively, Flash brought up his gun. He aimed as she watched, and then for some reason he lowered the gun without firing.

'Why did you do that?' Ilse asked.

'I was thinking of something else. There'll be other birds.' He laughed lightly. 'Maybe someone will do the same thing for me one day.'

Ilse could have an expression of gravity sometimes which fascinated him. It was there then as he said, 'My mother is a kind of dream as far as I'm concerned. There was a photograph of her sitting in a deckchair in old Gus's garden. She was very young. Her hair was very dark. It shone in the light. She was beautiful. Her shoes were highly polished and there was a little dog at her feet. I remember that.' His eyes narrowed slightly as he went on, 'When I was a kid I used to lie in bed at night and swear to myself that someday I would look for her.' He smiled. 'I used to tell myself that I'd have forgiven her for going away even if I'd found her in a Chinese brothel in Durban. How the hell I knew about Chinese brothels at that age, I've no idea.'

'Do you still have the photograph?'

'. . . My father tore it up one day when he was drunk. But I think I can understand it all now. My father came home from that war a wreck. Maybe he destroyed all her dreams. When she couldn't take any more, she fled. Old Gus never forgave her. His idea was that a woman should stick it out regardless. He did his best, though, to poison me against her – especially after my father killed himself. But we were all right, old Gus and myself. He taught me everything that I think it's important to know.'

When they dined together on the evening of the day the telegraph arrived summoning Flash to headquarters in Berlin, the room in which Augustine served them, perhaps in response to their voices encased within the portraits, the candelabra, the glittering crystal, seemed to reflect an air of finality. They were both aware of the atmosphere.

On that occasion, in recognition of his departure on the following morning, they were being somewhat formal. Ilse was at one end of the table, he at the other. There was a smile which seemed to stay around her lips, sheltered beneath those broadly placed grey eyes and the loose elegance of her hair which could only ever be described as gracious. Her bearing and the acceptance of her quiet laugh told only of her courage.

The whole aura of that room; she, singular, in a strange way alone in spite of his presence, was determined by a woman who was offering his manhood something which would be replete. For Jordaan, perhaps for Ilse, there would be no ending to that evening.

22

Much later in the unwelcome flatness of Holland when it was winter Flash Jordaan remembered that night, and in a way was afraid. He remembered the gleam of her shoulders when they had lain together, and he remembered their talk when they had been by each other's side. And he remembered her hands enclasped in his, their naked thighs touching each other's in peace. He came to know that life is a series of incidents of differing value. It was all a remembrance which came often to his eyes.

In Berlin when he had returned Paul Von Mansdorff had departed for his new command in Russia. He had left instructions for some others as to the proper disposition of Major Jordaan, but someone else had other ideas, and as a result Flash found himself commanding a Staffel of FW 190As based at Soesterburg in Holland with the rank of Hauptmann.

Conditions on the Russian front had meant that someone else had long since taken over his command. And in any case, he was assured, his experience would be most valuable with the fighter defences which were being built up to counter the growing menace of the American Bomber force gathering in England for its daylight offensive against the Reich. Flash did try to insist that it had been agreed in the beginning that his efforts with the Luftwaffe would be confined to the Russian front. But it was hopeless. His protests amused them. He was an officer of the Luftwaffe. No individual could decide where he wanted to fight. No one at Headquarters seemed to know anything of the original reason for the formation of the Staffel he had taken to Russia; and it was impossible to see Jeschonnek. He was a sick man. Only months were to pass before he would blow his brains out as had his old friend, Udet, some eighteen months before.

In a little time Flash began to feel that there were consolations in his new posting. At Soesterburg, apart from the day fighters, there was a Jagdeschwader of night fighters commanded by Major Prince Heinrich Zu Sayn-Wittgenstein who already had many victories, and in time was to prove one of the most successful night fighter pilots of them all. Wittgenstein was a warm-blooded fellow and in time he and Jordaan became close. It was good to be back in Europe.

The Focke Wulf Flash flew was a splendid machine. Faster than an ME, or for that matter a Spitfire, he could remember the awe with which the RAF had regarded it when it first appeared over the Western Front in 1941. By late 1943 the aircraft Flash's Staffel was flying were equipped with four 20m cannon and two 13mm machine guns. A potent weapon, it handled well; and it was strong enough to take something of a battering. Within days of his arrival Flash was loving the new machine which had been designated for his personal use.

But there were doubts, though, as to the role he was filling; occasional questions of conscience. But even if the Americans were the allies of the men with whom he had once flown, the questions with which he was sometimes assailed seemed to bounce off the armour in which by then he was encased. It didn't bother him, not beyond the extent of sometimes wondering what kind of man he had become. Major Wittgenstein raised it one evening when they were having a drink in the Mess before dinner. 'How does it feel,' he asked, 'to be flying against those Americans, Jordaan?' Then he smiled, as though in preparation for Flash's answer.

Flash thought for a moment. In some ways the Major reminded him of Von Mansdorff. He was taller, fair-haired, and perhaps in his demeanour, a shade more relaxed. The title he wore lightly. Flash knew that the easiness with which they communicated had been the result of the curiosity that always surrounded the 'Englishman'. In a way that curiosity was still there when Wittgenstein asked the question.

Jordaan smiled. 'In a way it was curiosity that took me to England . . . I loved it all in the RAF, but that prison camp would have driven me insane. When I joined Mansdorff I didn't give a damn what happened to me. I wanted to fly again . . . Now, I think the war has brutalized me.'

Wittgenstein raised his arm and a white-coated waiter appeared. 'Have some Dutchman's gin . . . Perhaps you're right about being brutalized. Perhaps we all are.'

Flash reached for the moustache which had not been there since he had been in hospital. 'Cheers . . . Have you ever thought how little women care about nationality even in war? I wonder how many men on this camp have been with a Dutch woman. How many Frenchwomen have wrapped their arms around a German who invaded their country in 1940? Women are different.'

Wittgenstein laughed. 'Thank God . . . I must eat and be off. Tonight I attend to your friends of the Royal Air Force.'

'Of course.'

'There's much in which you say, Jordaan. Myself, I only fly for my own Germany – not theirs. Maybe I'm a fool to imagine that it will ever come back. But I go on in the hope that it will; and I love flying.'

'At night? We have a saying, "Only owls and fools fly at night".'

'Ah ha . . . plus la difference.'

A waiter approached and said to Flash, 'There is a gentleman asking for you, sir.'

'Me?' He looked towards the doorway, and standing there with the correctness which was always with him was Kirste, the Pole who had become one of his Flight Commanders in Russia. 'My God – excuse me . . .'

Kirste was excited to the point of near incoherence. He could be like that, but when he was introduced to the officer who was with Flash as being Major Prince Heinrich Zu Sayn-Wittgenstein, he quickly pulled himself together.

'So you two were in the same Staffel in Russia?'

'Kirste was conducting a personal vendetta against Ivan.'

Wittgenstein smiled. 'But now you are here . . .'

'It is a nonsense. I should be there revenging . . .' He looked to Flash. 'Revenging?'

'If you like.'

'Revenging the slaughtered and buried in a mass grave . . . my friends.'

To ease something of the tension Kirste had introduced, Flash said to Wittgenstein, 'Kirste and his friends began their war by charging your tanks with sabres.'

Wittgenstein smiled. 'Brave . . . perhaps foolish.'

Kirste's eyes were alight with the eagerness of a terrier at an old slipper. 'Major, do you think you could do anything . . .'

The tone of the German's voice had kindness. 'I'm afraid there is nothing I can do now. Perhaps in the end you will have another opportunity . . . Gentlemen, I really must go now. We should see much of each other. Good luck, Kirste.' And with that Wittgenstein was gone.

'Come on, you Polish madman. Let's eat. Tell what's happened to the others.' Flash took Kirste by the arm and led him towards the dining room.

Flash had forgotten when he had first met Kirste. He thought at first it had been at Leinefelde. But Kirste hadn't joined them from that camp. They had met at the Operational Training Unit where Flash had been serving when he had taken the day off and had been shot down while flying with his old squadron on that day which had become so fateful.

'Of course . . . It was you I sent to Newcastle to buy that fellow's wife a bottle of gripe water for their baby.'

Kirste laughed. 'It cost a shilling and it cost the taxpayer about a hundred and fifty pounds to get me there and back in that old Spitfire . . . Not only that. You saved me at that court martial when that bloody batman reported me for having a Waaf in my room.' Kirste's laughter became almost uncontrollable. 'You said that it wasn't a Waaf, it was you. You said that when you were naked you probably looked like a woman from the back . . . You said that you'd come in to borrow a cigarette and a light. You saved me.'

'Think nothing of it, old boy.'

'Ah, but do you remember Marion Niepiekelo?'

'Old Marion . . .'

'He was a very great pilot.'

'Very.'

'He was the one who really taught me to fly. Do you know he was forty-seven years old. He'd flown as an NCO with Von Richthofen in the first war when he was a German. For twenty years he flew the night mail from Warsaw to Budapest. He was a kind of miracle.'

'A German?'

'Of course. He was Silesian. In the first war he was a German. After Versailles he was a Pole.'

'It's a funny old world.'

Kirste spun in on his first approach in a FW 190 which had developed a flap fault. The ceremony of his funeral was muted: no one except Jordaan knew who he was.

It was difficult at day's end to lie on a bunk, even one as clean and dry as those at Soesterburg and not allow your mind to wander across the faces you had known. Such thoughts didn't necessarily sadden Jordaan, but they brought a sense of being prised loose from the people with whom he had shared fear and high action; and with whom he had laughed.

Flash had taken to sleeping in his clothes, which confused his Saxon servant, a stalwart man with a dark, waxed moustache and a sense of humour which he tried to conceal without complete success. But in the dampness of Holland – especially when his billet was under dripping trees – it made sense to keep his body's sweat between his shirt and himself. On a Friday afternoon, if it was possible, Flash bathed himself in sick quarters, courtesy of a doctor with whom he was on drinking terms.

The Staffel which he commanded had its sprinkling of veterans, but of these none had been in action before 1941. For the main part they were keen youngsters, few of whom had yet been blooded. Flash worried for them, for from their talk he learned that they were nervous of the B 17's defensive armament. He had led them into action twice and their fear of getting in close had shown. Flash knew he had to do something, so when he decided to put on something of a performance for them in their crew room he selected one of the more senior pilots, Guttmann, to act as interpreter.

Since he had arrived in their midst Jordaan had been aware of the way in which they had distanced themselves from him. It was not because of any antipathy they held towards him. But they knew nothing of the real reason for his being with them, and rumours which had been invented made him laugh when he had heard them; and then of course there were the decorations he wore. They were inhibited by those, for, apart from the Prince Sayn-Wittgenstein, he was the most decorated man on the entire airfield.

But also – and of this perhaps he was unaware – he was beginning to withdraw within himself. The days of roistering bonhomie had gone. He had seen so many and so much. Now he had honed it all down to a control of himself. His flying had become automatic, lucid, brilliant. But his absolute confidence, without his realizing it, erased something of theirs.

'Gentlemen . . .' He had mounted a make-shift dais and had nodded to Guttmann who was beside him as they stood to their feet. 'Please sit down – relax. I am not here to criticize . . . Lads . . .' He paused for Guttmann to get that one right. '. . . In Russia, especially in the early days, shooting down their fighters could be like shaking a fig tree when the fruit was ripe. But the man who could shoot down an Illyushin II – he was something special. Here we are undertaking the job of fighting the most heavily armoured four-engined bomber in the world. But do not forget this . . . Behind each gun is a man, and, believe me, when you are going in at him he is as frightened as you are . . . and I am.' There was a rustling as they moved in their seats and looked at each other.

'I have a suggestion – ' Flash fought to cover the embarrassment of hearing his own voice at that moment. But he went on. '. . . I've decided that we'll invent some

Americans. Two flights in line abreast will attack the third . . . They're Americans. No one attacks until I give the command. Today, if there is no alert, we start. C Flight will be Americans . . . Details later.'

There was a howl of laughter at that. Then Flash turned to Guttmann. 'Did they get that?' The other nodded and smiled.

. . . Always when he climbed into a cockpit Flash Jordaan was invigorated. They were never quite as clean as they could have been – which was the way he liked it. There was something warming in the familiar smells of petrol, oil and the lingering whiff of cordite. That afternoon, when he had checked his controls and gunned his engine into warmth, Flash thrilled as he always did with the feel of the aircraft's life as he led the two flights he would be leading towards take-off point.

When he took off the flight which had been detailed to act as bombers was already airborne and flying on a twenty mile long reciprocal course.

On that day the sky, largely free of cloud, was engulfing. Beneath was the receding flatness of Holland and away to the north west the sea which reached towards England. At ten thousand feet Flash saw C Flight reaching the northern end of the course it was flying, and as he had instructed them at briefing he formed his own people into a loose line-abreast formation on either side of him. It had been impossible in the time available to disarm the aircraft, so he had reminded them again and again not to forget that they were attacking their own people.

It was attack. But no one had to break until he gave the order. He held them on course relentlessly, closer, closer. At a hundred and fifty yards he waggled his wings, indicating that at that point the would have fired. The men on either side did likewise, and then Flash called, 'Break! Break now! Below them . . . Don't go above them!'

As he broke Flash cut his throttle and allowed his aircraft to fall steeply. The others were with him in a ragged line, but it was when he was about to turn to starboard and then thrust himself into a steep climbing turn that he saw them some three or four thousand feet below – twin engined bombers heading in a south easterly direction. God! Tactical bombers. He turned back east and on down, clawing at the sky. His wing men followed him, but the others were confused. They broke off to climb back to their original ten thousand feet.

The blood was draining from Flash's brain, so steep was his dive; but he uncovered his gun button, and gradually eased the angle of his dive to make a long sweeping turn in his descent to end up about two thousand feet above and behind the attacking medium bombers. Were they Marauders, Mitchells. It didn't really matter, but Flash could see as he closed on them that their markings were American. At a speed of something like four hundred miles an hour he bore down on them, oblivious to the fact that there must be an escort somewhere.

Quickly, with an upward flick of the eye he could see Soesterburg. They were about to attack his own airfield, and in minutes the first of their bombs would be dropping. Raggedly aimed light flak was being thrown at the attackers. A smile creased Flash's lips beneath his mask. It would be bloody bad luck if they hit *him*.

When he had closed to about three hundred yards above and behind, the gunners in the light bombers had picked him up and were firing. Long fingers of tracer were reaching out to him. Close in and above he aimed his rockets slightly ahead of the lead aircraft. Momentarily the recoil rocked him, but the quick burst of his 14mm cannon at the aircraft on the port side of his first target, and he was through them and down.

Flash was sure his first rockets had gone home, but now he was swinging his neck from side to side in search of the escort. They were there, obviously taken by surprise. But through their confusion as they closed in fast, Jordaan was through them and away. He had no idea of the whereabouts of the two men who first followed him; but there was only one thing to do – get down. Bombs now were being straddled across Soesterburg. He could see their eruptions from the east into which he had sped close to the ground.

At zero feet he flew for thirty miles before turning back towards Soesterburg.

A quick recce showed that the airfield had been hit, but the main runway had been left undamaged. There was no sign of the intruders, but as he circled the field Flash saw something burning about five miles to the north. Slow, rising smoke and the flicker of a fire was all that remained of the aircraft that had gone down there.

Beneath, he could see from the circuit the confusion of those on the ground. The scene was no different from that which he remembered from 1940 in England. Trucks and fire engines were racing in all directions. Aircraft were taxi-ing slowly around the perimeter – no doubt those he had taken up on the exercise. It wasn't difficult to imagine the confusion down there. Flash cut his throttle. There was the hold-off and the deep rumbling of his engine settling. He touched and was down.

Major Anton Hackler commanded the Geschwader of which Flash's Staffel formed part. He was waiting as Jordaan climbed from his aircraft. Delight replaced the concern which had been on Hackler's face as Flash pulled off his helmet. 'I saw you get him. It was good, Jordaan, very good. How did you know they were coming. They must have sneaked below our coastal radar . . . It was very good. Two of your men claim to have damaged them.'

Flash laughed. 'I was lucky. I was up there teaching my little boys to hold formation when I saw them below me. It was very, very lucky . . .'

'No matter. You did well.'

And Flash knew he had done, for it was something special to be seen to be in action when everyone else was helpless. There had been casualties on the ground, but that evening in the Mess there was something like a celebration, even if they didn't quite produce the spontaneity of the old days.

Later, when he was lying alone in his room, there was a stabbing of something like quick remorse. These men he had attacked had come from the same direction as he had come from on that morning of ages before when he had been shot down.

If there was remorse, though, it wasn't quite regret; perhaps something rather akin to the emotion a man might have known when thinking back to a woman he had once loved and had subjected to a betrayal which could never be erased.

It was a Wednesday, and the whole Geschwader was on full alert. Before fourteen hundred hours bells were ringing and men were running towards their aircraft. A massive formation of American four engined bombers with a heavy escort was approaching the Dutch coast and heading in a south easterly direction. Flash looked at the sky when he reached his aircraft. It was a reasonably bright day with the sun glinting on indeterminate clouds at about four to six thousand feet. Away above there was some alto cirrus at about ten thousand.

Positioned, he checked and had the feel of his aircraft. The other two squadrons would take off first, as they would be making the initial attacks. His would go in last for the coup de grace, attacking the bombers head on. Flash saw the others go off as he warmed up. Then, with a signal to his wing-men, he waved away his chocks and was moving.

There was always a tremor of excitement as he opened his throttle to the gate. It was there then as his left foot reached forward to control the direction of the Focke Wulf against the pull of the engine's torque. At something like a hundred and sixty kph the tail was well up and he was off.

Wheels up, she seemed to lighten, and as he started a long slow climb to port with the Staffel in echelons of three on either side of him, Flash hunched himself tightly over his control column, knees slightly bent, stomach tensed he had the feeling that he was flying for all of them. Maybe with time he would feel more assurance with them, but it wasn't there yet.

Above and ahead the other squadrons were reaching up as they headed towards the coast. That day there seemed to be so much that reminded him of 1940: only the markings on the aircraft were different. And he was different. The feeling in his hands was different. The aircraft was a little harder, heavier.

Through the alto cirrus and on up there was at first the suggestion and then the certainty of the sun glinting on aircraft high above and ahead. Muttered instructions from Major Hackler came over the RT before he clipped off quickly. Flash was beginning to feel the old tingling in the gut as they climbed. Unnecessarily he checked around his cockpit, readying himself. On either side and behind the others were holding well. It was all beginning to look like a proud procession as the rhythm of his engine and its eager drone added aggression to all he saw and felt around him.

Now the sky was clear. They started their long climbing turn into the sun. It was from there and above the attackers they would erupt.

There was a song on the American Forces radio programme to which Flash had taken to listening almost every day. A girl called Lily Anne Carrol sang it: 'I'll Walk Alone'. It had become almost as significant to the Americans as 'Lilly Marlene' had been for the Germans. Then in that aircraft in that sky it kept coming at Flash Jordaan. Flash smiled and turned up his oxygen. Dammit. But the brain is a strange receptacle. Quietly he went on humming into his mask.

They were around now and into the south. Flash checked again on the flights on either side. All was well.

At twenty-six thousand feet they turned on to the reciprocal. And there they were away ahead and coming on with a relentlessness which somehow – no doubt in Jordaan's imagination – gave the impression of being tentative. Flash decided to give himself another thousand feet. Gently, back on the column, he eased them upwards.

'Prepare for attack!'

In minutes the sky ahead was now a tapestry of darting aircraft. Flash's men had loosened well apart, waiting for his lead. To the north, from which the bombers were approaching, Flash could see the first two Staffelen going in for their attack. Lumbering bombers wallowed like startled whales as they panted in desperation against the fury of cannon fire the Germans were unleashing. The scene was marked now by drifting smoke and the odd erupting flame. It was all a massive tinted water colour of melting paint.

Flash's tongue wiped his lips as he dived to the attack. His eyes narrowed. He closed. Poised, his sight was alight. Steadying, he fired his first burst at a lead bomber. Now there was obsession. He was aiming at *things*. Down, down and on with a gathering momentum. His aircraft felt as though it was thrusting, and then, as he broke, he was close enough to see movement in the nearest bomber when something hit his port wing and it dropped.

Both hands grabbed at his stick to restore the angle of his wing. But he was above them, so he pulled away juddering into a half roll. A quick glance at the wing and he saw that he had been holed, but it still felt as though he was functional so he pulled himself out of the dive and almost into the vertical before releasing his rockets at the only aircraft he could get into his sights. The range was a shade extended, but he had a hit. Hard left rudder, and he was turning away from his quarry's belly.

A sweat which he couldn't feel encased his body. One Thunderbolt flashed past; then another. But there were so many. Now Flash was weaving, but the aircraft was not as responsive as it might have been. The throttle danced as something hit him again in the engine nacelle and behind the cockpit. His confusion touched the point of fear. When he raised his goggles to wipe his eyes, he didn't know that he was wiping blood. There was pain in his neck and shoulder when he was hit again, and this time in response to his action on the stick, he climbed in a desperate, unthinking reflex to get away from it all, until wavering, wounded, he held arrested against the pale blueness of that now empty sky with its eternal backdrop. On the point of stall it seemed to hang there, wings extended, as though pleading in its surrender. Then it fell away, the aircraft which had been Flash Jordaan's, to leave behind a trace of smoke which in a little time scattered, until in the end there was nothing.